So Many Misunderstandings . . . Could She Learn to Trust Again?

*"You still don't believe me, do you?"
Nathan asked in frustration.*

*Suddenly, despite her earlier certainty,
Mallory didn't know the answer to that
question. All her instincts told her that
Nathan was a faithful husband, but maybe
she'd only believed him innocent because
she couldn't bear not to.*

*"We've been apart so much," she said.
"Women offer themselves to you as a matter
of course. You'd be superhuman if you—"*

*Nathan was on his feet so suddenly that his
chair overturned, and his hand was hard
under Mallory's chin. "I'll tell you about
me, Ms. O'Connor!" he roared. "I love my
wife!"*

Dear Reader:

There is an electricity between two people in love that makes everything they do magic, larger than life. This is what we bring you in SILHOUETTE INTIMATE MOMENTS.

SILHOUETTE INTIMATE MOMENTS are longer, more sensuous romance novels filled with adventure, suspense, glamor or melodrama. These books have an element no one else has tapped: excitement.

We are proud to present the very best romance has to offer from the very best romance writers. In the coming months look for some of your favorite authors such as Elizabeth Lowell, Nora Roberts, Erin St. Claire and Brooke Hastings.

SILHOUETTE INTIMATE MOMENTS are for the woman who wants more than she has ever had before. These books are for you.

Karen Solem
Editor-in-Chief
Silhouette Books

Snowflakes on The Sea

Linda Lael Miller

Silhouette Intimate Moments

Published by Silhouette Books New York

America's Publisher of Contemporary Romance

SILHOUETTE BOOKS, a Division of Simon & Schuster, Inc.
1230 Avenue of the Americas, New York, N.Y. 10020

Copyright © 1984 by Linda Lael Miller
Cover artwork copyright © 1984 Lisa Falkenstern

Distributed by Pocket Books

ISBN: 0-671-50397-9

First Silhouette Books printing July, 1984

10 9 8 7 6 5 4 3 2 1

America's Publisher of Contemporary Romance

Printed in the U.S.A.

For my cherished parents,
Hazel and Grady "Skip" Lael . . .

Look—no hands!

Chapter 1

THE BARE SEMBLANCE OF A SMILE CURVED NATHAN McKendrick's taut lips as he stood at the living room windows looking down at the measured madness in the streets below. Cars fishtailed up and down the steep hills, and buses ground cautiously through the six inches of snow that, according to the doorman, had fallen since morning. The stuff was still coming down, in great lazy slow-motion flakes, like flour from a giant sifter.

Nathan sighed. The people of Seattle didn't really *believe* in snow—though they were certainly acclimated to rain—and they were always caught off guard when it came. The timid closed down their businesses and cowered at home, while the more adventurous braved the elements.

He focused his dark gaze on the distance. The harbor was invisible, through the swirling storm and the cloak of night, except for a few flickering lights, and the rugged Olympic Mountains beyond were blotted out entirely. The Space Needle, a modern tower commemorating a past world's fair, appeared as a patch of blue light in the gloom.

Depressed, Nathan turned from the scene and sighed again. The penthouse, sumptuously furnished in rich suedes and velvets, was close and confining that night, even though it occupied the entire top floor of the building and had been carefully designed to seem even more spacious than it was.

Where was Mallory? The question played in Nathan's exhausted mind and stretched his waning patience thin. He began to pace the empty living room in long, fierce strides, expending energy he didn't possess. A six-week concert tour, followed by the endless flight back from Sydney, had left him physically drained.

He paused, looking down at his travel-rumpled clothes—tailored gray slacks and a lightweight cream-colored turtleneck sweater—and grimaced. The garments felt scratchy against the lean, muscular length of his body, and the rough stubble of a new beard stood out on his face like tiny needles.

Though the penthouse boasted no less than four bathrooms, it hadn't occurred to him until that moment to take the time to shower, shave and change his clothes; he'd been too frightened, too desperate to find Mallory. Oblivious to everything except the state of his wife's health, he'd caught a cab at the airport and hurried to the hospital, where he'd been summarily informed that "Ms. O'Connor" had been treated and released.

The nurses had told him so little, and he hadn't been able to reach Mallory's doctor, Mallory herself or any of her friends. Finally, when he'd frantically dialed his sister's number, he'd gotten a recorded voice telling him cheerily that Pat couldn't come to the telephone at the moment.

Though he'd tried the penthouse number and gotten

no answer, he had hurried there hoping that Mallory might have left a note.

Now, having made all the same fruitless calls again and left a rather direct message on his sister's answering machine, he was nearly overwhelmed by weariness and frustration.

Softly, furiously, he cursed. Then, with consummate control, Nathan brought himself up short. Mallory was *all right*—Pat's cable had said that much, at least, and with characteristic certainty. Pat was never wrong about anything.

He ground his teeth and went back to the window, only to turn away again and stride toward the master bedroom and the sumptuous bathroom beyond. There, he stripped and stepped into a pulsing, steaming shower.

By the time he'd finished scouring his tense flesh, shaved and gotten dressed again, he felt better. He tried Pat's number once more and got the same mechanical spiel he'd heard before. Muttering a curse, he dialed the island house and was informed by a harried operator that the lines were down.

At that moment, the doorbell rang. Nathan bounded over the plush carpet and wrenched open one of the heavy double doors.

His sister stood impatiently in the hallway, glaring up at him. "You shouldn't say things like that on the telephone, Nathan!"

He remembered the colorful message he'd left for Pat and laughed gruffly. "And you should be at home when I want to talk to you," he retorted, arching one dark eyebrow.

Pat sighed, placated by his off-the-cuff comment. She looked tired as she ran one slender hand through the copper and gold strands of her long hair and blinked her wide cornflower blue eyes. "Could we start over here?" She smiled, stepping around her brother to enter the penthouse. And then, without waiting for an answer, she cleared her throat and began again. "Hello, handsome. Rough trip?"

Nathan shook his head distractedly. The grandfather clock in the living room chimed a soft reminder of the hour. "Pat, I'm going insane while you make small talk. What's the matter with Mallory, and where the hell is she?"

Pat stood on tiptoe to kiss her brother's freshly shaven chin. "Relax," she said gently. "Mallory is okay. After they released her from the hospital, I took her out to the island so she could have some peace and quiet."

He took his sister's arm, ushered her somewhat roughly toward the living room. "Why was she in the hospital, damn it?" he snapped, impatient and scared.

Pat settled herself on the suede sofa and crossed her shapely legs. "She collapsed on the set last night, Nathan, and they called an ambulance. Somebody from the show got in touch with me, and I cabled you as soon as I'd seen Mallory and talked to the doctor and everything."

Nathan stiffened, then leaned back against the long teakwood bar Mallory had bought in the Orient several years before, and folded his powerful arms in stubborn outrage. "I've been going out of my mind," he growled. "They wouldn't tell me anything at the hospital—"

Pat lowered her expressive blue eyes for a moment, regrouping, and then raised them intrepidly to her brother's face again. "Mallory's producer threatened them with mayhem if they gave out any information to anyone. Nathan, let it go."

With a harsh motion of one hand, Nathan reclaimed the brown leather jacket he'd tossed into a chair earlier and slipped his arms into it. Mallory was his first concern—at the moment, his only concern.

As he turned to leave, Pat rose from the couch and

caught his arm in one hand, gently but firmly. "Nathan, don't hassle Mallory about the name thing or the soap opera, all right? She's a wreck, frankly, and she doesn't need it."

"Right," Nathan agreed crisply.

Pat reached up to touch his dark still-damp hair. "One more thing, love—stop worrying. Everything is okay."

Nathan laughed, even though nothing in the whole damned world was funny, and walked away from his sister without looking back.

Mallory O'Connor loved the island house, though she didn't get back to it much, now that she was working in Seattle. Often, the sturdy, simply furnished structure seemed to be the only real thing in her life. Now, standing in the huge old-fashioned kitchen, with snow drifting past the polished windows, she drew a deep breath and allowed herself to feel the sweet, singular embrace of the one place that was really home. Then, comforted, Mallory began selecting fragrant, splintery lengths of kindling from the box beside the big wood-burning stove to start a fire. She'd slept for a while after Pat had raced back to the city, and now she was pleasantly hungry.

Pride filled Mallory as the blaze caught and began to heat the spacious kitchen. Her mother had been right— there *was* a certain satisfaction in doing things the old way, a satisfaction she'd never found in the posh Seattle penthouse she and Nathan shared between his long and frequent absences.

Mallory sighed. She loved Nathan McKendrick with an intensity that had never abated in six tumultuous years of marriage, though she couldn't have honestly said that she was happy. At twenty-seven, she was successful in her out-of-the-blue career, and Nathan, at thirty-four, was certainly successful in his. But there were elements missing from their relationship that caused Mallory to hunger even in the midst of opulence.

Money and recognition were pitiable substitutes for children, and the hectic pace most people considered glamorous only made Mallory's heart cry out for simplicity and peace.

Outside, in the silent storm, Mallory's Irish Setter, Cinnamon, began to howl for admission. Mallory smiled and went out onto the screened sun porch to welcome her furry and much-missed friend.

Cinnamon whimpered and squirmed in unabashed delight as Mallory greeted her with a pat on the head. "What do you say we just hide out here from now on, girl?" Mallory asked, only half in jest. "Nathan could go on with his concert tours—the darling of millions—and we'd exist on a diet of oysters and clams and wild blackberries."

The dog abandoned its mistress to sniff and paw at a large, unopened sack of dogfood leaning against the inside wall of the porch beside the screen door. Mallory began to pry at the stubborn stitching sealing the bag. "So much for living off the land," she muttered.

While Cinnamon crunched happily away on the dried morsels wrested from that recalcitrant bag, Mallory heated canned chicken soup on the cook stove. There was very little in the house to eat, but shopping could wait until morning—Mallory would get her car out of the locked garage then, and drive to the small store on the other side of the island.

The wooden telephone on the kitchen wall, actually a modern replica of the old-fashioned crank phone, rang in pleasant tones, and Mallory left the soup simmering on the stove to answer. When she and Pat had arrived, there hadn't been any phone service at all.

"Hello?"

Pleased feminine laughter sounded on the other end of the crackling line. "Mall, you *are* back!" cried Trish

12

Demming, one of Mallory's closest friends. "Thank heaven. I thought I'd fallen short in my dog-watching duties—I called Cinnamon until I was hoarse."

Mallory smiled. "She's here, Trish—safe and sound. I tried to call you, but the lines were dead."

Trish's voice was warm. "No problem. Actually, I should have looked at your house in the first place. Even when you're gone, Cinnamon is always dashing over there. What's going on, anyway? I thought you were all involved in taping that soap—er—daytime drama of yours, Mall."

Mallory sighed. "I'm having an enforced vacation, Trish. Brad isn't going to let me back on the set until I have a doctor's permission." She didn't add that she was relieved to have a respite from the crazy schedule; Trish wouldn't have understood.

There was a short silence while Trish considered the implications of Mallory's statement. "Honey," she said finally, concern ringing in her voice, "you're not sick, are you? I mean, you must be, but is it serious?"

Mallory touched the top of the yellow-enameled wainscotting reaching halfway up the kitchen wall and frowned at the smudge of dust that lingered on her fingertip. "I'm just tired," she assured her friend, glad that Trish couldn't see the dark splotches of fatigue under her eyes or the telltale thinness of her already slender figure.

For a while, the two women discussed the plot line of "Tender Days, Savage Nights," the first soap opera ever to be produced in Seattle. Brad Ranner, the show's dynamic creator and chief stockholder, had brought it out from New York a year before, partly because of lower production costs and partly because of a desire to use more outdoor scenes. The spectacular vista of sea and mountains and lush woodlands gave the program unique appeal.

Most of the original cast had balked at leaving New York, however, and open auditions had been held in

Seattle. On a whim, Mallory had gone, along with a horde of other applicants, to read for a part. Anxious to accomplish something strictly on her own, she had given her maiden name and prayed that no one would recognize her as the wife of a world famous rock singer.

No one had, and furthermore, Mallory had been selected, despite an embarrassing lack of acting experience, to play the role of Tracy Ballard, a troubled young woman who devoted boundless energy to destroying long-term marriages. The part had been a small one at first, but Mallory had played it with a verve that pleased sponsors and viewers alike. Her character on the show took on interesting dimensions, and suddenly, Mallory O'Connor McKendrick was a success in her own right.

And how empty it was.

She promised to visit Trish soon and rang off, frowning. Her hand lingered for a moment on the telephone receiver. Mallory was rich now and, in her own way, even famous, if "famous" was the proper word for a notoriety that caused strange women to confront her in supermarkets and department stores and even libraries, demanding that she stop interfering in this or that fictional marriage.

Nibbling at her lukewarm soup, Mallory considered her life and, for perhaps the ten-thousandth time, wished that it could all be different. Her hard-won teaching certificate had never seen a day's use, and she longed for a child of her own to love and nurture.

She was rinsing out her empty bowl and placing it in the orange plastic drainer beside the sink when a pair of headlights swung into the yard, their golden light speckled with glistening flakes of snow. Mallory leaned close to the cool, damp window, trying to recognize the car.

When that proved impossible due to the storm, she ran her hands down the worn red and blue plaid flannel

14

of her shirt front and hurried out onto the screened porch. Cinnamon danced at her heels and then wriggled gleefully against the legs of her jeans.

The slam of a car door echoed, mingling with the nightsong of the tide, and Cinnamon's magnificent tawny head shot up, suddenly alert. Before Mallory could grasp her collar, the dog propelled herself through the outside screen door and bounded into the ever-deepening snow, yipping hysterically.

Nathan laughed and reached down to greet Cinnamon with the customary pat-and-rub motion that made her ears flop about in comical disarray. "Hello, you worthless mutt," he said.

Mallory stood in the doorway, her mouth open, just staring. Would she never get over feeling as though she'd just been punched in the solar plexis whenever Nathan McKendrick came striding back into her life?

Standing in the stream of light coming from the kitchen, Nathan forgot the dog and raised his eyes to Mallory. They made their way over her trim, rounded hips, her small waistline, her high, firm breasts to settle at last on her face.

Mallory fell against the doorframe, watching him in stricken silence. Snow glistened in his unruly ebony hair and on the straining shoulders of his jacket, and he put his hands onto his narrow, powerful hips and stared back.

There was a charged silence between them for a long moment, threatening to melt the snow and raise steam from the buried earth. Mallory's traitorous heart caught in her throat. She'd known that he would come, known that Pat, ever the loyal sister, would contact him, alert him to the fact that his wife had been hospitalized. And yet she had hoped for more time, even as she had longed to be near him again.

Nathan executed a mocking bow. "Good evening— Ms. O'Connor," he said in a sardonic drawl.

As quickly as that, the strange spell was broken. Mallory lifted her chin in answer to his challenge and replied, "Good evening, Mr. McKendrick."

Nathan's jawline tightened with immediate annoyance, and some unreadable emotion glittered in his dark eyes as he strode toward her. Before Mallory could move, he had lifted her out of the doorway and over the two snow laden steps beneath it.

Her insides rioted with involuntary need as he held her, suspended, his face between her ripe, inviting breasts. Even through the heavy flannel of her shirt, she could feel the warmth of his breath.

Slowly, he lowered her, so that the throbbing fullness of her chest was crushed against the hard expanse of his own. Then, his hands cupping the roundness of her bottom, he pressed her to him, to the ready demand of his manhood and the granitelike wall of his thighs.

Good Lord, Mallory thought with remorse. *I'm as bad as any groupie—if he wanted to take me right here in the snow, I'd let him!*

Nathan must have known what havoc he was wreaking on her straining senses, but he said nothing. His mouth came down on hers in a kiss that was at once gentle and demanding. Deftly, his lips parted hers for the sweet invasion and searing exploration of his tongue. Mallory responded with hungry abandon, shivering violently in the force of her need.

Then suddenly, Nathan was thrusting her away, holding her at arm's length. His eyes glowed as they touched her lips and trailed, like the touch of a warm finger, to the pulsing hollow at the base of her throat. He turned her around and propelled her toward the house.

Mallory's face was hot as she turned to watch her husband enter behind her, Cinnamon rollicking exuberantly at his side.

Nathan closed the door quietly, his eyes working their singular magic again as they moved idly over

Mallory's body, assessing her, stirring primitive reactions as they passed. "I've missed you, lady," he said in a low voice.

Crimson color stained Mallory's cheeks, and her pride caused her to thrust her head back, so that her dark taffy hair flew over her shoulders in glossy profusion. Her round, thickly lashed eyes flashed with sea green fury born of his ability to inflame her so easily, and she did her best to scowl.

He laughed. "You *are* an actress, pumpkin," he allowed, approaching her slowly. One of Nathan's hands cupped Mallory's breast, the thumb stroking the bare nipple beneath her old shirt to hard and undeniable response. "Your body betrays you," he said hoarsely. "You don't hate me nearly as much as you'd like me to believe."

Of course I don't hate you! Mallory wanted to scream, but her pride wouldn't allow that, so she lifted her chin in stubborn, wordless defiance. But a small cry escaped her as Nathan's hand released her breast to undo one of her shirt buttons, and then another. Her entire body pinkened as he bared the rounded sweetness of her to his lazy inspection.

Mallory abandoned her act when her husband lowered his lips to one waiting nipple to nip at it, ever so gently, with his teeth. She moaned aloud and arched her back slightly so that he could feast upon her.

He chuckled in gruff triumph and flicked the rosy, pulsing center of her breast with the tip of his tongue, teasing. His hand slid between Mallory's legs to caress the taut, womanly secrets of her inner thighs.

"Bastard," she whispered, but there was a catch in her voice and a caress in the word itself. Her hands entangled themselves, without conscious instruction from Mallory, in the thick richness of his dark hair, pressing him closer. With sudden hunger, he devoured the freely offered breast, answering Mallory's groan of ancient pleasure with one of his own.

Presently, he turned to sample the other breast, again teasing and nibbling, again driving Mallory nearly insane with the need of him. She would not beg him—she *would not*—but even as she made this decision, desperate pleas were aching in her throat.

At last, Nathan pressed her against the wainscotting lining the wall, and the lean, inescapable hardness of his body joining hers revealed the force of his desire. He stood back only long enough to divest Mallory of her flannel shirt and kiss her flat, soft stomach in a tantalizing promise of further kisses that would drive her beyond passion into the paradise they had visited so many times.

He unsnapped her jeans, and she felt the zipper give way, the fabric slide down over her hips. She shivered as her panties, too, were lowered. Lips parted, she awaited loving that always bordered on the deliciously unendurable.

Nathan nuzzled the silken shelter of her womanhood; the warm promise of his breath and his searching lips made her tremble. One plea broke past her resolve, and it took the shape of his name.

Slowly, he revealed the small, yearning nubbin. In desperation, Mallory caught his head in both hands and thrust him to her. "Oh, God," she breathed, mindless now in her wanting. "Oh, God, Nathan, *please*—"

At the invitation he had purposely forced from her, Nathan partook hungrily of her, and his tender greed brought her to swift and searing release. She shuddered reflexively, her fingers moving in his hair, and moaned as he nibbled at her at his leisure, demanding a fiery encore to the performance just past.

Bared to him, and so deliciously vulnerable, Mallory whispered words of gentle, desperate encouragement as he tormented the bit of quivering flesh with soft kisses. She writhed, gasped with delight, when he took his pleasure yet again, bringing his tongue into play this time, sampling her and then suckling as though to draw some sweet nectar from her. "Don't—stop—," she pleaded, her wanting now as naked as her hips and her thighs and her stomach.

He drew back, just slightly. "Sweet," he whispered in a ragged voice, and then he enjoyed her in long, warm, delicious strokes of his tongue. Savage pleasure convulsed Mallory, and her triumph came in a cry that was half shout, half sob.

It was then that, in the snowy silence outside, an engine roared. One car door slammed, and then another.

Nathan swore harshly and straightened, while Mallory, cheeks burning, frantically righted her clothes. Feet were stomping heavily on the porch outside, and Cinnamon began to bark in somewhat belated alarm.

"Just a minute!" Nathan growled, closing his eyes in an obvious effort to control his roiling emotions and frustrated need.

As embarrassed as though the visitors had seen the impromptu love scene staged in the McKendrick kitchen, Mallory turned to the stove to hide her flaming face and occupy her hands with the task of brewing fresh coffee. After another moment of preparation, Nathan answered the door.

"Oops!" Trish Demming blushed, sizing up the situation with her usual gentle shrewdness. "Alex, I think we interrupted something."

Trish's good-natured, bespeckled husband pretended to rush for the door. He was Nathan's accountant and one of his closest friends.

"Sit down," Nathan ordered humorlessly, and Mallory felt his hot gaze touch her rigid back. Out of the corner of one eye, she saw Trish set a covered baking dish down on the counter.

It was several minutes before Mallory gathered enough composure to join the others at the kitchen table, and, even when she did, it was clear that Nathan wasn't going to give her an easy time of it. His dark eyes seared her breasts whenever the opportunity afforded itself, and lingered on her lips until she thought she'd shout with frustration.

Still, it was pleasant to spend time with dear friends, and Mallory genuinely enjoyed the lively conversation touching on everything from Nathan's last concert tour to the ban on gathering oysters along the island's rocky shores. Trish had brought one of her highly acclaimed peach cobblers, and they all ate a hefty slice with their coffee, Trish and Mallory bemoaning the astronomical calorie count.

Mallory was fairly trembling with hidden exhaustion and anticipation when Trish began to make sincere noises about leaving. Good-byes were said, and the Demmings bundled up in their practical island coats and braved the snow piling up between the house and their car.

Mallory and Nathan exchanged a look of resignation when they heard the car's motor grind half-heartedly, and then die. Nathan's eyes moved over Mallory's body in a sweep of hungry promise, and then he swatted her gently on the bottom and bent his head to nibble briefly at her earlobe. "I'll be back soon," he said, and strode out onto the sun porch, rummaging through the collection of battered coats that had belonged to her father.

Mallory needed to sink languidly into a warm, scented bath and go to bed. She was so tired that sleep would come easily, but not before she and Nathan had reached the breathless heights of love they always scaled after they'd been apart.

And we're apart so much, she thought, her weariness reaching new and aching depths.

A moment later, there was a stomping sound on the porch, and Trish reappeared, looking embarrassed and apologetic. "Nathan and Alex are trying to get the car started," she mumbled, unconsciously rubbing her chilled hands together. "Ace mechanics they're not."

Mallory grinned at her friend and firmly ushered her

closer to the stove. "It's all *right*, Trish," she cajoled. "There's still plenty of coffee, if you'd like more."

Trish shook her head, and her soft blond hair moved delicately with the motion. "We shouldn't have barged in here like that," she said ruefully, and then her blue eyes moved to Mallory's face. "I'm so sorry, Mall—it's just that I was worried about you, and, of course, we had no idea that Nathan was home."

Mallory hugged Trish warmly. "You were being thoughtful, as always. So stop apologizing."

Trish's pretty aquamarine eyes were pensive now, seeing too much. "Mall, you really look beat. Are you okay?"

Suddenly, Mallory had to look away; she couldn't sustain eye contact with this friend she'd known all her life and say what she meant to say. "I'm fine," she insisted after a short pause.

The tone of Trish's voice betrayed the fact that she was neither convinced nor mollified, but she spared Mallory her questions and gave her a gentle shove in the direction of the bathroom. "Go and take a nice hot bath and get yourself into bed, Mrs. McKendrick. I can look after myself until the men get our car going again."

Mrs. McKendrick. Mallory blanched, unwittingly giving away something she hadn't meant to reveal. She longed to be known by her married name again, and yet, it sounded strange to her, as though she had no right to resume it.

Trish laid a comforting hand on her shoulder. "Get some rest, Mall. We'll have a good, long talk when you're up to it."

There was much that Mallory needed to confide, but this was neither the time nor the place. "I—If you're sure you won't feel slighted—"

Trish's eyes were sparkling with warmth and controlled concern. "Just go, will you? I'm not such an airhead that I can't entertain myself for a few minutes!"

Mallory laughed, but the sound was raw and mirthless. Reluctantly, she left her friend to her own devices and stumbled into the bathroom, where she started running hot water in the tub.

While it ran, Mallory hurried through the doorway that joined that room to the master bedroom and began to search wearily through the suitcases Pat had packed for her earlier at the penthouse. There were jeans and sweaters, always necessary for winter visits to the island, but nothing even remotely glamorous had been included. Mallory thought of all the silken lingerie left behind in Seattle and sighed. She had so wanted to look especially attractive for Nathan, but Pat had either not foreseen that contingency or not considered it important.

With resolve, Mallory ferreted out her least virginal flannel nightgown and carried it into the steam-clouded bathroom. Over the roar of the water, she heard Trish and Alex's car start up.

Smiling to herself, Mallory stripped and climbed into the tub. The warmth of the scented water was heaven to her tired muscles, and she sank into it up to her chin, giving a soft sigh of contentment as total relaxation came at last.

Home, she thought happily. *I am home.*

The heavy enameled door of the bathroom squeaked open then, and, suddenly, Nathan was there, his dark eyes taking in the slender, heat-pinkened length of her body. Beneath the suntan he'd undoubtedly acquired in Australia, where it was now the height of summer, he paled.

"My God, Mallory," he swore. "How much weight have you lost?"

Mallory shrugged as she averted her eyes. "Maybe five pounds," she said.

Nathan was leaning against the chipped pedestal sink now, his arms folded, watching her. "More like fifteen," he argued, his voice sharpened to a lethal edge. "You were too thin when I left, but now—"

Mallory squeezed her eyes closed, hoping to press back the sudden and unaccountable tears that burned there. Was he saying that he didn't want her anymore, didn't find her physically attractive?

She felt his presence in the steamy bathroom, heard him kneel on the linoleum floor. When Mallory opened her eyes, she was not surprised to find him beside her, the knuckles of his powerful, gifted hands white with the force of his grasp on the curved edge of the bathtub.

"Mallory, talk to me," he pleaded hoarsely. "Tell me what to do—how to change things—how to make you really happy again."

One traitorous tear escaped, trickling down Mallory's slender cheek and falling into the bathwater. "I am happy, Nathan," she lied.

Nathan made a harsh, disgusted sound low in his throat. His eyes burned like ebony fire. "No," he countered. "Something is chewing you up alive, and the hell of it is, I can't do a damned thing about it if you won't trust me enough to be honest."

Mallory's voice was small and shaky with dread. "Do you want a divorce, Nathan?"

He was on his feet in an instant, turning his back on Mallory, shutting her out. His broad shoulders were taut under the soft gray fabric of his shirt.

Unable to bear the oppressive silence placidly, Mallory reached out and grasped the big sponge resting in an inside corner of the tub. Fiercely, she lathered it with soap and began to scrub herself so hard that her flesh tingled.

"I would understand," she said, when she dared speak.

Nathan whirled suddenly, startling her so badly that she dropped the sponge and stared at him, openmouthed. His face was rigid with suppressed fury and something very much like pain. He folded his arms in a gesture that, with him, signaled stubborn determination.

"Understand this," he said in a low and dangerous tone. "You are my wife and you will remain my wife. I don't intend to let you go, ever. And you will warm no one else's bed, my love—not Brad Ranner's, not anyone's."

Mallory felt the words strike her like stones, and it was all she could do not to flinch with the pain. "What?" she whispered finally, in shock.

Nathan's face was desolate now, but it was hard, too. "You've been wasting away ever since you signed on with that damned soap opera, Mallory. And there has to be a reason."

Mallory lifted her chin. There were reasons, all right, but Brad Ranner wasn't among them, nor was any other man.

"I've been faithful to you," she said stiffly. And it was true—she had never even been tempted to become intimate with another man, and she had come to Nathan's bed as a virgin. She couldn't bring herself to ask if he'd been as loyal; she was too afraid of the answer.

Nathan sighed, the sound broken, heavy. "I know, Mallory—I'm sorry."

Sorry for what? Mallory wondered silently, sick with the anguish of loving a man who belonged to so many. *Sorry for accusing me like you did, or sorry that you have a number of nubile groupies to occupy your many nights away from home?*

"I'm very tired," she said instead.

"I see. You weren't tired in the kitchen tonight, were you?"

The sarcasm in his voice made Mallory's cheeks burn bright pink. "That was a long time ago," she snapped, not daring to meet his eyes.

"At least an hour," Nathan retorted.

"Leave me alone!"

"Gladly," he snapped. Then, slowly, Nathan turned and left the room. When the door closed behind him, Mallory dissolved in silent tears of exhaustion and grief.

Nathan stood at the bedroom window, looking out. There wasn't much to see in the darkness, but the storm had stopped anyway. That was something. Behind him, Mallory slept. The soft meter of her breathing drew him, and he turned back to look at her.

The dim glow of the hallway light made her fine cheekbones look gaunt and turned the smudges of fatigue beneath her eyes to deep shadows. She looked so vulnerable lying there, all her grief openly revealed in the involuntary honesty of sleep.

Nathan drew a ragged breath. How could he have urged her to surrender her body the way he had, when she was so obviously ill? And what had possessed him to imply that she was attracted to Brad Ranner, knowing, as he did, that that kind of deceit was foreign to her nature?

Quietly, he approached the bed and pulled the covers up around her thin shoulders. She stirred in her uneasy sleep and moaned softly, intensifying the merciless ache that had wrenched at Nathan's mid section since the moment his press agent, Diane Vincent, had thrust Pat's cable into his hands after the last concert in Sydney.

The night was bitterly cold. Nathan slid back into bed beside his wife, and held himself at a careful distance. Even now, the wanting of her, the needing of her, was almost more than he could bear. Raising himself onto one elbow, Nathan watched Mallory for a long time, trying to analyze the things that had gone wrong between them.

He loved her fiercely and had since the moment he'd

seen her, some six and a half years ago. Prior to that stunning day, he'd prided himself on his freedom, on the fact that he'd needed no other person. Now, in the darkness of the bedroom, beneath the warmth of the electric blanket, he sighed. If he lost Mallory—and he was grimly convinced that he *was* losing her, day by hectic day—nothing else in his life would matter. Nothing.

She stirred beside him. Nathan wanted her with every fiber of his being and knew that he would always want her. But there was one thing greater than his consuming desire, and that was his love. He fell back on his pillows, his hands cupped behind his head, his eyes fixed on the shadowed ceiling.

Her hand came to his chest, warm and searching, her fingers entangling themselves in the thick matting of hair covering muscle and bone. "Nathan?" she whispered in a sleepy voice.

Despite the pain inside him, he laughed. "Who else?" he whispered back. "Sleep, babe."

But Mallory snuggled against him, soft and vulnerable. "I don't want to sleep," she retorted petulantly. "Make love to me."

"No."

Her hand coursed downward over his chest, over his hard abdomen, urging him, teasing. "Yes," she argued.

Nathan was impatient. "Will you stop it?" he said tightly. "I'm trying to be noble here, damn it."

"Mmmmmm," Mallory purred, and her tantalizing exploration continued. "Noble."

"Mallory."

She raised herself onto one elbow and then bent her head to sample one masculine nipple with a teasing tongue.

Nathan groaned, but he remembered her thinness, her collapse on the set in Seattle, the hollow ache visible in her green eyes. And he turned away, as if in anger, and ignored her until she withdrew.

Chapter 2

THE TELEPHONE WAS RINGING WHEN MALLORY AWAK-
ened the next morning. She burrowed down under the
covers with a groan, determined to ignore it. If she
waited long enough, Nathan would answer it, or the
caller would give up.

But the ringing continued mercilessly, and Mallory
realized that her husband wasn't nestled between the
smooth flannel sheets with her. Tossing back the bed-
clothes with a cry of mingled irritation and disappointment, she scrambled out of bed and reached
automatically for her robe.

The house was pleasantly warm, and Mallory smiled,
leaving the robe—and an aching recollection of Nathan's rejection the night before—behind as she made
her way into the kitchen and disengaged the old-
fashioned earpiece from its hook on the side of the
telephone. "Hello?" she spoke into the mouthpiece,
idly scanning the neat kitchen for signs of Nathan.

Except for the heat radiating from the big wood-burning stove, there was nothing to indicate that he'd been around at all.

"Hello," snapped Diane Vincent, Nathan's press agent. "Is Nate there?"

Mallory frowned. *Good question,* she thought ruefully. *And where the hell do you get off calling him "Nate"?*

"Mallory?" Diane prodded.

"He was here," Mallory answered, and hated herself for sounding so lame and uncertain.

Disdain crackled in Diane's voice. "One night stopover, huh? Listen, if he happens to get in touch, tell him to call me. I'm staying at my sister's place in Seattle. He knows the number."

Mallory was seething, and her knees felt weak. She reached out awkwardly for one of the kitchen chairs, drew it near and sat down. She despised Diane Vincent and, in some ways, even feared her. But she wasn't about to let anything show. "I'll relay your message," she said evenly.

Diane sighed in irritation, and Mallory knew that she was wondering why a dynamic, vital man like Nathan McKendrick had to have such a sappy wife. "You do that, sugarplum—it's important."

Mallory forced a smile to her face. "Oh, I'm sure it is—dearest."

Diane hung up.

Outside, in the pristine stillness of an island morning, Cinnamon's joyful bark pierced the air. Mallory hung up the phone and went to stand at the window over the kitchen sink, a genuine smile displacing the frozen one she'd assumed for Diane Vincent. Nathan and the enormous red dog were frolicking in the snow, their breath forming silvery white plumes in the crisp chill of the day. Beyond them, the towering pine trees edging the unpaved driveway swayed softly in the wind, green and snow-burdened against the splotchy sky.

Mallory swallowed as bittersweet memories flooded her mind. For a moment, she slid back through the blurry channels of time to a cheerful memory. . . .

"One of these days," her father was saying, snowflakes melting on the shoulders of his checkered wool coat and water pooling on the freshly waxed floor around his feet, "I'm going to have to fell those pine trees, Janet, whether you and Mallory like it or not. If I don't, one of them is sure to come down in a windstorm and crash right through the roof of this house."

Mallory and her mother had only exchanged smiles, knowing that Paul O'Connor would never destroy those magnificent trees. They had already been giants when the island was settled, over a hundred years before, and that made them honored elders.

With reluctance, Mallory wrenched herself back to the eternal present and retreated into the bedroom. There would be time enough to tell Nathan that Diane wanted him to call, she thought, with uncharacteristic malice. Time enough.

Mallory crawled into bed, yawned and immediately sank into a sweet, sound, dreamless sleep.

When she awakened much later, the sun was high in the sky, and she could hear the sizzle of bacon frying and the low, caressing timbre of Nathan's magical voice. Grinning, buoyed by the sounds and scents of morning, Mallory slid out of bed and crept to the kitchen doorway.

Nathan, clad in battered blue jeans and a bulky blue pullover sweater, stood with his back to her, the telephone's earpiece propped precariously between his shoulder and his ear. While he listened to the person on the other end of the line, he was trying to turn the fragrant bacon and keep an eager Cinnamon at bay at the same time. Finally, using a meat fork, he lifted one crispy strip from the pan, allowed the hot fat to drip off, and then let the morsel fall to the floor. "Careful, girl—that's hot," he muttered. And then he moved closer to the mouthpiece and snapped, "Very funny, Diane. I was talking to the *dog*."

Mallory stiffened. Suddenly, the peace, beauty and comfort of the day were gone. It was as though the island had been invaded by a hostile army.

She went back to the bedroom, now chilled despite the glowing warmth that filled the old house, and took brown corduroy slacks and a wooly white sweater from her suitcases. After dressing and generally making herself presentable, she again ventured into enemy territory.

Nathan was setting the table with Blue Willow dishes and everyday silver and humming one of his own tunes as he worked. Mallory looked at the dishes and remembered the grace of her mother's hands as she'd performed the same task, the lilting softness of the songs she'd sung.

Missing both her parents keenly in that moment, she shut her eyes tight against the memory of their tragic deaths. She had so nearly died with them that terrible day, and she shuddered as her mind replayed the sound of splintering wood, the dreadful chill and smothering silence of the water closing over her face, the crippling fear.

"Mall?" Nathan queried in a low voice. "Babe?"

She forced herself to open her eyes, draw a deep, restorative breath. Janet and Paul O'Connor were gone, and there was no sense in reliving the brutal loss now. She tried to smile and failed miserably.

"Breakfast smells good," she said.

Nathan could be very perceptive at times—it was a part, Mallory believed, of his mystique as a superstar. The quality came through in the songs he wrote and in the haunting way he sang them. "Could it be," he began, raising one dark eyebrow and watching his wife with a sort of restrained sympathy, "that there are a few gentle and beloved ghosts among us this morning?"

Mallory nodded quickly and swallowed the tears that

had been much too close to the surface of late. The horror of that boating accident, taking place only a few months after her marriage to Nathan, flashed through her mind once more in glaring technicolor. The Coast Guard had pulled her, unconscious, from the water, but it had been too late for Paul and Janet O'Connor.

Nathan moved to stand behind her, his hands solid and strong on her shoulders. It almost seemed that he was trying to draw the pain out of her spirit and into his own.

Mallory lifted her chin. "What did Diane want?" she asked, deliberately giving the words a sharp edge. If she didn't distract Nathan somehow, she would end up dissolving before his very eyes, just as she'd done so many times during the wretched, agonizing days following the accident.

He sighed and released his soothing hold on her shoulders, then rounded the table and sank into his own chair, reaching out for the platter of fried bacon. "Nothing important," he said, dropping another slice of the succulent meat into Cinnamon's gaping mouth.

Mallory began to fill her own plate with the bacon, eggs and toast Nathan had prepared. "Diane is beautiful, isn't she?"

Nathan glowered. "She's a bitch," he said flatly.

Mallory heartily agreed, in secret, of course, and it seemed wise to change the subject. "My contract with the soap is almost up," she ventured carefully, longing for a response she knew Nathan wouldn't give.

"Hmmmm," he said, taking an irritating interest in the view framed by the big window over the sink. The dwarf cherry trees in the yard looked as though someone had trimmed their naked gray branches in glistening white lace.

Mallory bit into a slice of bacon, annoyed. *Damn him, why doesn't he say that he's pleased to know I'll have time for him again, that we should have a child now?* "Well?" she snapped.

"Well, what?" he muttered, still avoiding her eyes.

Mallory ached inside. If she told him that she wanted to give up her career—it wasn't even a career to her, really, but something she had stumbled into—it would seem that she was groveling, that she hadn't been able to maintain her independence. "Nothing," she replied with a defeated sigh. She looked at the food spread out on the table and suddenly realized that the makings of such a meal hadn't been on hand when she arrived the night before. "You've been to the store."

He laughed at this astute observation, and at last he allowed his dark, brooding eyes to make contact with her green ones. "My dear," he imparted loftily, "some of us don't lounge about in our beds half the day with absolutely no concern for the nutritional needs of the human body. Which reminds me—" His wooden chair scraped along the floor as he stood up and reached out for a bulky paper bag resting on the kitchen counter. From it, he took six enormous bottles containing vitamin supplements. Ignoring his own rapidly cooling breakfast, Nathan began to shake pills from each of the bottles and place them neatly beside Mallory's orange juice. Finally, when there was a colorful mountain of capsules and tablets sitting on the tablecloth, he commanded sternly, "Start swallowing."

Mallory gulped, eyeing what amounted to a small meal all on its own. "But—"

Nathan merely leaned forward and raised his eyebrows in firm instruction, daring her to defy him.

Dutifully, his wife swallowed the vitamins, one by one. When the arduous task had been completed, Mallory had no appetite left for the food remaining on her plate, but she ate it anyway. Clearly Nathan meant to press the point if she didn't.

Once the meal was over, they washed and dried the dishes together, talking cautiously about things that didn't matter. As Mallory put the last piece of silverware into the appropriate drawer, however, she bluntly asked a question that had been tormenting her all along.

"Nathan, why didn't you make love to me last night?"

He looked at her, and their eyes held for a moment, but Mallory saw the hardening of Nathan's jawline and the tightening of his fine lips. He broke away from her gaze and once again took a consuming interest in the cherry trees outside.

"I was tired," he said after a long pause. "Jet lag, I guess."

Mallory was not sure whether what she felt was courage or just plain foolishness. "Are you having an affair, Nathan?"

He whirled, all his attention suddenly focused on Mallory's face. "No," he bit out, plainly insulted at the suggestion. "And in case you're wondering, I still find you as desirable as ever, last night notwithstanding, even if you are a touch too bony for my taste."

"Then what is it?" Mallory pressed, crumpling the damp dishtowel between her hands. "We haven't been together in six weeks and—"

Nathan pried the cloth out of her hands, tossed it aside and drew Mallory very close. The encounter of their two bodies, his, hard and commanding, hers, gently rounded and very willing, set off an intangible, electric response in them both. "You don't need to remind me how long we've been apart, pumpkin," he muttered, his lips warm and soft at her temple. "This last tour was torture."

Mallory throbbed with the dreadful, ancient need of him. "Make love to me now, Nathan," she whispered.

But he stiffened and held her away, and the only contact remaining was the weight of his hands on her shoulders. "No," he said firmly. "You're tired and sick. . . . I don't know what your doctor's orders were, but I'm sure they didn't include a sexual marathon."

Mallory's chin trembled slightly. Was he really concerned for her health? Or was he fulfilling his needs in someone else's bed? He'd denied having an affair, but it didn't seem likely that he would admit to anything of that sort when he knew his wife had been hospitalized only a few days before.

Taking no apparent notice of her silence, Nathan kissed Mallory's forehead in a brotherly manner and released his hold on her shoulders. "There's a nice fire going in the living room," he said, sounding determinedly cheerful. "Why don't you curl up on the couch and read or something?"

Mallory had several "or somethings" in mind for the living room sofa, but they certainly didn't include reading. With a proud lift of her chin, she turned and marched out of the kitchen without a word.

The living room was a warm and welcoming place, however, with its window seats and sweeping view of Puget Sound. Mallory couldn't help feeling soothed as she entered. She stood still for a long time, looking out at the water and the snowy orchard that had been her father's pride. When he wasn't piloting or repairing his charter fishing boat, Paul O'Connor had spent every free moment among those trees, pruning and spraying and rejoicing in the sweet fruit they bore.

Presently, the snow began to fall again. Mallory took a childlike pleasure in the beauty of it, longing to rush outside and catch the huge, iridescent flakes on her tongue. Too tired for the moment to pursue the yearning, she perched instead on a window seat, her knees sinking deep in its bright polka-dot cushions, and let her forehead rest against the cool dampness of the window glass.

She sensed Nathan's presence long before he approached to stand behind her, disturbingly close.

"I've got some business to take care of, pumpkin," he said quietly. "I'll be back later."

Mallory's shoulders tensed painfully, and she did not turn around to look at her husband. She had a pretty good idea of what kind of "business" he had in mind, but she would have died before calling him on it. If she was losing her husband, she could at least lose him with dignity and grace.

But she was entirely unprepared for the warm, moving touch of his lips on the side of her neck. A shiver of delightful passion went through her, and she was about to turn all her concentration on seducing Nathan then and there when he suddenly turned and strode out of the room.

Mallory closed her eyes and didn't open them again until she'd heard the distant click of the back door closing behind him. She cried silently for several minutes, and then marched into the bathroom and splashed cold water on her face until the tears had been banished.

On the back porch, Mallory exchanged her sneakers for sturdy boots and pulled on one of the oversized woolen coats that hung on pegs along the inside wall. The garment was heavy, and it smelled comfortingly of pine sap, saltwater and tobacco. Wearing it brought her father so near that Mallory almost thought she might turn around and see him standing in the doorway, grinning his infectious grin.

Outside, the tracks in the deep, crusted snow indicated that Nathan had brought his Porsche to the island the night before. The car was gone now, and so was Cinnamon.

Mallory crammed her gloveless hands into the pockets of her father's coat and frowned. "Rat fink dog," she muttered.

A stiff wind was blowing in from the Sound, churning the lazy flakes of snow that were still falling in furious white swirls. Mallory turned her back to the wind and started toward the wooded area that was the center of the island.

Here, there were towering pine trees, and more of

the Douglas fir that lined Mallory's driveway, but there were cedars and elms and madronas, too. Under the ever-thickening pelt of snow, she knew, were the primitive wild ferns, with their big, scalloped fronds.

Privately, Mallory thought that the ferns were remnants of the murky time before the great ice age, when the area might well have been a jungle. It was easy to picture dinosaurs and other vanished beasts munching on the plants while volcanoes erupted angrily in the background.

Mallory marched on. The mountains were minding their manners now, with the exception of one, but who knew when they might awaken again, alive with fiery violence? Unnerved by Mt. St. Helens, many scientists were pondering Mt. Rainier now, along with the rest of the Cascade range.

As Mallory made her way through the thick underbrush, a blackberry vine caught at her sleeve, eliciting from her a small gasp of irritation and then a reluctant smile. How many times had she ventured here as a child, armed with an empty coffee can or a shortening tin, to pluck the tart late-summer berries from their wicked, thorny bushes?

The thought made Mallory miss her mother desperately, and she hurried on. The motion did nothing, though, to allay the loneliness she felt, or banish persistent memories of Janet's warm praise at the gathering of "so many very, very fine blackberries." After the fruit had been thoroughly washed under cold water, Mallory's mother had cooked jams and jellies and mouth-watering pies.

At last, Mallory emerged on the other side of the island's dense green yoke, and Kate Sheridan's A-frame house came into view. She should have called before dropping in on this busy woman who had been her mother's dearest friend for so many years, she realized, but it was too late to consider manners now.

Kate was standing on the deck at the back of the house, smiling as she watched Mallory's approach.

She waved in her exuberant fashion, this trim, sturdy woman, and called out, "I *knew* I was right to wrench myself away from that wretched typewriter and brew some coffee!"

Mallory was warmed by this enthusiastic greeting, but she was chagrined, too. Kate Sheridan was the author of a series of children's mystery novels, all set in the Puget Sound area, and her time was valuable indeed. Pausing at the base of the snowy path, Mallory deliberated. "I could come back another time," she offered.

"Nonsense!" Kate cried, beaming. "I wouldn't dream of letting an interesting guest like you escape. But I warn you, Mallory—I intend to pump you for information about the things that nasty character you play is planning!"

Mallory assumed a stubborn look as she tromped up the wooden stairway leading to Kate's deck, but she knew that her eyes were sparkling. Her friend's undisguised interest in the plot line of the soap opera amused her deeply.

"My lips are sealed," Mallory said with appropriate drama, knowing all the while that she would tell Kate everything if pressed.

Kate laughed and hugged her, but there was a brief flicker of concern in her intelligent hazel eyes. "You look tuckered out, Mallory," she observed in her direct way.

Mallory only nodded and was infinitely grateful when Kate let the subject drop there and pulled her inside the comfortable house.

Kate Sheridan's home was a lovely place, though small. The opposite wall of the living room was all glass and presented a staggering view of the Sound. At night, the lights of Seattle were often visible, dancing in the misty distance like a mirage.

There was a small fireplace on the back wall near the sliding glass doors that opened onto the deck, and a crackling fire danced on the hearth. The furniture was as simple and appealing as Kate herself; the chairs and sofa were shiny brown wicker, set off by colorful patchwork-patterned cushions. Kate's large metal desk and ancient typewriter looked out over the water, an indulgence the gifted woman often bemoaned but never altered. She was fond of saying that she spent more time gazing at the scenery than working.

Of course, her success belied that assertion; Kate's writing obviously did not suffer for her devotion to the magnificent view. If anything, it was enhanced.

"Sit down," Kate ordered crisply as she took Mallory's bulky coat and hung it from a hook on the brass coat tree near the sliding doors. "Heavens, I haven't seen you since Christmas. It's about time you had some time off."

Mallory, settling into one of the wicker chairs, didn't point out that not even a month had passed since Christmas. She was comforted by the presence of things that were dear and familiar, and she watched Kate with overt affection as the woman strode purposefully into the tiny kitchenette to pour the promised coffee, looking terrific in her gray flannel slacks, white blouse and wispy upswept hairdo. The maroon sweater draped over her shoulders, its sleeves tied loosely in front, gave her a sporty look that suited her well.

"How is the new book coming?" Mallory called out, over the refined clatter of china and silver.

Kate's scrubbed face was shining as she carried two cups of coffee into the living room, placed them on the round coffee table and sat down in the chair facing Mallory's. "Splendidly, if I do say so myself. But tell me about *you*—why aren't you working?"

Mallory lowered her eyes. "They decided I was too tired."

Kate sat back in her chair and crossed legs that were

still trim and strong, probably because of her penchant for walking all over the island. "You do look some the worse for wear, as I said before. Is it serious?"

Mallory shook her head quickly. "I'm all right, Kate," she promised in firm tones.

The older, quietly elegant woman took a thoughtful sip from her coffee cup, watching Mallory all the while. "I don't think you are," she argued kindly. "You look about as unhappy as anybody I've ever seen. Mallory, what in heaven's name is wrong?"

Suddenly, Mallory's throat ached and her eyes burned with unshed tears. She lifted her chin. "Everything," she confessed, in a small, broken voice.

Kate raised a speculative eyebrow. "Nathan?"

"Partly," Mallory admitted, setting her own cup down on the coffee table and entwining her fingers. "Oh, Kate, our marriage is such a joke! Nathan is always away on tour or recording or something, and I'm working twelve and fourteen hour days on that stupid soap—"

"Stupid?" Kate asked, with no indication of opinion one way or the other.

Mallory's chin quivered. "I'm afraid I'm not very liberated, Kate," she confessed. "I wanted to prove that I could have a career, and that I could be important as someone other than the wife of a famous man. Now I've done that, I guess, but it isn't at all the way I thought it would be." She paused, reaching for her cup. It rattled ominously in its saucer, and she set it down again. "I'm so miserable!"

"I can see that," Kate replied calmly, resting her chin in her hands in a characteristic gesture. "What do you really want, Mallory?"

Mallory turned her head, not quite able to meet her friend's wise, discerning eyes, and examined the familiar scene in front of Kate's house. The beach looked strange under its blanket of snow, and the waters of the Sound were choppy. "I want to be a wife and a mother," she muttered. "And, maybe, someday, use my teaching certificate—"

"Rash thing!" cried Kate, with humorous, feigned outrage. "You want to be a card-carrying *woman!*"

Mallory was gaping at her friend, speechless.

Kate laughed. "You were right before, Mallory—you aren't very liberated. Liberation, you see, is the freedom to do what you really want to do, not some immovable directive requiring every woman on earth to carry a briefcase or wield a jackhammer!"

Mallory was still staring, but something very much like hope was beginning to flicker inside her. Kate Sheridan was the most "liberated" woman she'd ever known, and here she was, saying that wanting to make a home with the man you love was all right. "I thought—"

"I know what you thought," Kate broke in with good-natured irritation. "You thought it was your duty as a modern, intelligent young woman to set aside your real inclinations and devote all your energy to something that doesn't begin to please you."

Mallory reached for her coffee cup, this time successfully. Her thoughts were in a pleasant tangle, and she didn't try to talk.

Kate bent toward her, balancing her own cup and saucer on her knees. "Mallory McKendrick, you march to your own drumbeat," she ordered. "Your life won't be worth a damned thing if you don't."

Mallory laughed softly in relief; it felt so good to be addressed by her married name again. "I love you, Kate."

"I love you, too," the woman replied briskly. "But there have been times when I wanted to shake you. You do a creditable job as an actress, Mallory, but you weren't born to it. I've always seen you as a crackerjack mother, myself."

"Are you just saying that because you know it's what I want to hear?" Mallory challenged, grinning.

Kate laughed. "My dear, you know me better than that. Hot air belongs in balloons, not conversations between people who care about each other."

Mallory was pensive again. All right, she'd decided that she wanted a more settled life, children, maybe a chance to teach, when the time was right. But how would Nathan react to all this? They hadn't discussed any of the options, really, and they had grown apart since Mallory stopped accompanying him on tour to pursue a career of her own.

Kate's hand rested on Mallory's. "These things generally work out," she said with uncanny insight. "*Talk* to Nathan. He loves you, Mallory."

The two women chatted about less pressing things after that, and, when the snowstorm began to show signs of becoming really nasty, Mallory reluctantly took her leave. She was on automatic pilot during the walk home, her mind absorbed in all the things she needed to say to Nathan.

But as she came out of the woods and onto her own property, Mallory was jolted. Beside Nathan's silver Porsche sat Diane Vincent's bright red MG roadster.

Mallory paused, alarmed on some instinctive level that defied reason. All her assurances to herself that she was being silly blew away on the winter wind. After drawing a deep breath, she made her way purposefully across the yard and onto the screened porch, where she was met by a delighted Cinnamon.

"Don't tell me how glad you are to see me!" she admonished the squirming dog, even as she reached down to ruffle her lustrous, rusty coat. "You traitor!"

The back door squeaked open as Mallory was hanging her father's woolen coat. Nathan appeared in the doorway, his eyes even darker than usual, and snapping with challenge and controlled fury. "Where the hell have you been?" he demanded.

It seemed now that the sensible, reassuring conversation with Kate Sheridan had taken place in another lifetime. Mallory thrust out her chin. "I've been walking," she retorted.

"In this blizzard?" Nathan's jaw tightened in annoyance.

Mallory pressed her lips together, unable to shake the unsettling idea that Nathan's obnoxious mood had something to do with Diane Vincent's presence. Was he having an attack of conscience?

"Kate's house isn't that far away," she said. "And blizzard or no blizzard, Nathan McKendrick, I'll go wherever I want, *when*ever I want."

His granitelike features softened a little, and he even managed a half-hearted grin. "I'm sorry, Mallory—I was worried, that's all. Next time, will you at least leave a note or something?"

Too busy bracing herself for another encounter with Diane Vincent to answer him, Mallory simply brushed past her husband and entered the kitchen.

Diane looked sensational in her tailored pale blue slacks, white silk blouse and navy blazer. Her long, blond hair, so pale that it was almost silver, shimmered on her shoulders in a fetching profusion of curls, and her clear blue eyes assessed Mallory in a way that was at once polite and disdainful.

"Hello, Mallory," she said sweetly.

Mallory nodded. "Diane," she responded, already moving toward the stove. The kitchen was the heart of all island houses, and coffee was offered to every guest. Being a relative newcomer, Nathan had overlooked the gesture.

Diane seemed profoundly amused when Mallory raised the old-fashioned enamel coffeepot in question. "No, thanks," she said in a soft but cutting voice, one manicured nail tapping expressively at the less provincial drink Mallory hadn't noticed before. Diane's gaze swung fondly to Nathan, moving over his impressive frame like a caress.

Nathan scowled and tossed a beleaguered look in

Mallory's direction that brought his earlier one-word appraisal of Diane swiftly to mind. *Bitch.*

Mallory smiled, and for a while at least, she was no longer afraid of this woman, no longer in awe of her beauty and her sophistication and her undeniable charm. "Nathan?" she asked, again indicating the coffeepot.

He nodded, and Mallory grinned as she filled his cup and set it before him.

"That's bad for you!" Diane complained, frowning and reaching out to grasp Nathan's arm.

Nathan pulled free, raised the cup to his lips and winked at his wife. "Allow me this one vice," he said. "Since I'm temporarily denied my favorite."

Mallory felt her face flush, but she didn't look away. Nathan's gaze lingered at her lips for a long moment, causing her a sweet, singular sort of discomfort.

"So," Diane said, too cheerfully, "how is it that the notorious Ms. O'Connor isn't cavorting before the cameras?"

Mallory felt strong and confident for the first time in weeks, though she couldn't decide whether the quality had its roots in the long talk with Kate or the way Nathan was quietly making love to her with his eyes. Both, probably.

"The name is McKendrick," she said pleasantly, with a slight lift of her chin.

Something changed in Nathan's eyes; there was an earnest curiosity there, displacing the teasing hunger she'd noticed before.

Diane looked mildly upset. "I thought 'O'Connor' was your professional name," she said in an argumentative tone.

"O'Connor was my maiden name," Mallory replied sweetly, with a corresponding smile. "I *am* married, you know."

Nathan raised one eyebrow, but he said nothing. He merely toyed with the handle of his coffee mug.

Diane was obviously at a loss, but she recovered quickly. Leveling her devastating blue eyes at Nathan, she seemed to forget that Mallory was even in the room. "What have you decided about that television special, Nathan? I think it would be great to go back to Australia again, don't you? And the money is fantastic, even for you—"

Mallory suddenly felt bereft again, shut out. Those feelings intensified when she saw a sparkle in Nathan's dark eyes. What was he remembering? The beautiful, awe-inspiring Australian countryside? Walks along moon-kissed beaches with a warm and willing Diane?

"The people are so friendly," he mused aloud.

Especially the ones who wear Spandex jeans and lip gloss, Mallory thought bitterly.

Diane laughed with unrestrained glee and clapped her elegant hands together. Her whole face shone with appealing mischief as she smiled at Nathan. "I thought I would *die* when you were presented with that kangeroo!" she sang, and her voice rang like music in the simple, homey room.

Nathan grinned at the memory, but then his eyes strayed to Mallory, just briefly, and darkened with an emotion she couldn't quite read.

"They gave you a kangeroo?" Mallory put in quickly, in an effort to join the conversation. "What did you do with it?"

He shrugged, and his gaze was fixed on some point just above Diane's glowing head. "I gave it to the zoo."

"And then there was that great Christmas Eve party," Diane trilled, tossing a look of triumphant malice in Mallory's direction. "My God, the sun was coming up before *that* broke up—"

Nathan frowned, clearly irritated by the mention of the holidays. Or was he warning Diane not to reveal too much? "Ho, ho, ho," he grumbled.

Mallory lowered her eyes to her coffee cup. Her shooting schedule hadn't permitted her to join Nathan at Christmas, and while they hadn't discussed that fact in person, the subject had generated several scathing exchanges over long distance telephone. She said nothing.

But Diane went mercilessly on. "You can't imagine how *odd* it seemed, swimming outdoors on Christmas Day!" There followed a short, calculated pause. "What was it like *here*, Mallory?"

The shot hit dead center, and Mallory had to work up her courage before daring to glance at Nathan. His features were stiff with resentment, just as she'd feared.

"It was lonely," she said in complete honesty.

Diane was on a roll, and she knew it. Cloaking her animosity in sweetness, she smiled indulgently. "Now, Mallory, don't try to convince us that you sat at home and pined. Everybody knows what super parties Brad Ranner gives, and I read that you celebrated the holidays in a romantic ski lodge high in the Cascades."

Mallory had forgotten the write-up she'd gotten in the supermarket scandal sheets over Christmas week. One had born the headline, McKENDRICK MARRIAGE CRACKING, and linked Mallory to a country and western singer she'd never even met. Another had, just as Diane maintained, claimed that she had carried on an interesting intrigue in the mountains.

Neither claim was true, of course, but she still felt defensive and annoyed. Why did people buy those awful newspapers anyway? If they wanted fiction, books were a better bet.

Diane giggled prettily. "No comment, huh? Is that what you told the reporters?"

Mallory clasped her hands together in her lap, felt the color drain from her face as she glared defiantly at Diane. She did not dare to look at Nathan. "I didn't talk to any reporters," she said stiffly, hating herself for explaining anything to this woman. Inwardly, she realized that she was actually explaining, left-handedly, the facts to her husband. "Those stories were utter lies, and you damned well know it, Diane."

Diane sat back in her chair, apparently relaxed and unchallenged by Mallory's words. She shrugged. "Sometimes they get lucky and print the truth," she threw out.

Nathan's voice was an icy, sudden rumble. "Shut up, Diane," he said. "None of this is any of your business."

A smile quirked one side of Diane's glistening pink mouth. "They should have been watching *you*, shouldn't they? I can just see the headlines now. ROCK STAR CAVORTS DOWN UNDER."

Mallory flinched and bit her lower lip. She could feel Nathan's rage rising in the room like lava swelling a volcano. Any minute, the eruption would come, and they'd all be buried in ash.

"How about this one?" he drawled, leaning toward Diane with ominous leisure. "PRESS AGENT FIRED."

For the first time, Diane backed down. A girlish blush rose to pinken her classic cheekbones, and real tears gathered in her eyes. "I was only teasing," she said. "Where *did* you spend Christmas, Mallory?"

"In Outer Slobovia, Diane," Mallory replied acidly. "With fourteen midgets and a camel."

Nathan roared with laughter, but Diane looked affronted. "We could get along if we tried, you know," she scolded in a tone that implied crushing pain.

"I seriously doubt that," Mallory retorted. "Why don't you leave now?"

"Good idea," Nathan said.

Diane bristled. "Nathan!"

Nathan smiled and stood up, gesturing for silence with both hands. "Now, now, Diane—no more gossip. After all, the camel isn't here to defend himself."

Diane flung one scorching look at Mallory and stormed out, slamming the kitchen door behind her. A moment later, the outer door slammed, too.

"Thank you," Mallory whispered.

"Anytime," Nathan said, sitting down again.

"Those stories about me—"

He reached out, cupped her chin in one hand. "I know, Mall. Forget it."

Mallory couldn't "forget it"; there was too much that needed to be said. "I was here, Nathan—right here, on the island. I spent Christmas Eve with Trish and Alex, and the next day with Kate Sheridan. I—"

His index finger moved to rest on her lips. "It's all *right*, Mallory."

She drew back from him, more stung by some of the things Diane had implied than she would have admitted. "What did *you* do over Christmas, Nathan?"

He looked away. "I drank a lot."

"No Christmas tree?"

"No Christmas tree."

Mallory sighed wistfully. "I didn't put one up, either. But Trish had a lovely one—"

Suddenly, Nathan was staring at her. She knew he was thinking of the beautiful tree ornaments she'd collected in every part of the world, of the way she shopped and fussed for weeks before Christmas every year, of the way she always threw herself into the celebration with the unbridled enthusiasm of a child. "No tree?" he echoed in a stunned voice that was only part mockery. "No presents?"

Mallory had received a number of gifts—a silk blouse from Kate, books from Trish and Alex, a gold chain from Nathan's sister Pat—but she saw no point in listing them aloud. The package Nathan had sent was still stored in a guest room closet at the Seattle penthouse, unopened.

She lifted her coffee cup in a sort of listless toast. "Just call me Scrooge," she said.

Chapter 3

FORTUNATELY, NATHAN DROPPED THE TOUCHY SUBJECT OF that Christmas just past—the first Christmas since their marriage that the McKendricks had spent apart—and said instead, "Your turn to cook, woman."

Mallory glanced at the small electric clock hanging on the wall near the telephone, and started guiltily. Lunchtime was long past. "And cook I will," she replied.

In the next few minutes, Mallory discovered that her husband had done a remarkable job grocery shopping; the cupboards were full. She was humming as she assembled sandwiches and heated soup, regardless of the fact that she had absolutely no appetite.

While Mallory labored over that simple midday repast, Nathan fidgeted at the table. He looked almost relieved when the telephone rang, and moved to answer it with a swiftness that injured his wife. Was it so hard for him to talk to her that he was grateful for any excuse to avoid it?

"Hello," he muttered, and then, as Mallory watched, she saw him turn his back to her, saw the powerful muscles stiffen beneath his shirt. "Yes, Mrs. Jeffries," he said in a low voice. "Yes, Diane is supposed to stay there. The band is coming, too—they'll all be there before nightfall, I suppose. No, get extra help if you need it—"

Mallory set the sandwich plates down on the table with an eloquent *thunk* and whirled angrily to ladle hot soup into two bowls. Nathan was talking to his housekeeper, giving her orders to make Diane Vincent and the others comfortable in the sprawling Spanish-style villa on the other side of the island. *His* villa.

"Damn!" she muttered. She should have known that there would be no private time for the McKendricks—Diane and the band would see to that.

"Right," Nathan said, turning to scowl at Mallory, as though reading her inhospitable thoughts. "Hell, I don't care. Whatever's in the freezer—"

"What?" Mallory grumbled. "No lobster? No filet mignon?"

"Shut up!" Nathan rasped, and then he colored comically and glared at Mallory. "No, Mrs. Jeffries," he said into the telephone receiver, "I wasn't talking to you. Well, they usually bring their wives, don't they?"

"Whip out the satin sheets!" Mallory said, gesturing wildly with a soup spoon in one hand and a tuna fish sandwich in the other.

Nathan gave his wife an evil look and then grinned. "Oh, and one more thing, Mrs. Jeffries—put satin sheets on all the beds."

Mallory stuck out her tongue and sank into her chair at the table with as much visible trauma as she could manage.

Clearly, Nathan was enjoying her tantrum. She knew that she was behaving like a child but couldn't seem to stop. He ended the conversation with an additional order, meant to make his wife seethe. "We'll need lots of towels for the hot tub, too."

"We'll need lots of towels for the hot tub, too!" Mallory mimicked sourly. "God forbid that Diane Vincent should have to *drip dry!*"

Nathan was chuckling as he bid his housekeeper farewell and hung up. "Mellow out, Mall," he teased, grasping the back of his own chair in both hands and tilting his magnificent head to one side in a mischievous manner. "I'm not planning an orgy, you know."

"Why should you?" Mallory shot back. "The stage is already set for one!"

Nathan's eyes darkened, and the mischief faded from their depths, displaced by impatience. His voice was a sardonic drawl, and he made no move to sit down and share the lunch he'd all but ordered Mallory to prepare. "This is enlightening. I didn't think you *gave* a damn what went on at Angel Cove. You so rarely condescend to put in an appearance!"

Mallory swallowed miserably, all her saucy defiance gone. It was true that she avoided the magnificent house at Angel Cove—there were always too many people there, and there was always too much noise. "Sit down and eat," she said in a small voice.

Surprisingly, Nathan sat down. There was a short, awkward pause while he assessed the canned soup and slap-dash sandwiches. The fare was no doubt much more appetizing at Angel Cove.

Mallory mourned, feeling wearier than ever, as she dragged her spoon listlessly through her soup. She felt Nathan's gaze touch her, and involuntarily looked up.

"You didn't decorate a Christmas tree?" he asked incredulously.

There was no point in trying to skirt the issue; she had known it would come up again. She swallowed the pain that still lingered from that lonely holiday and answered the question honestly. "No."

"You?" Nathan pressed, no trace of his earlier irritation showing in his handsome, sensitive features.

Mallory nodded. "As far as I'm concerned, Christmas just didn't happen this year."

His eyes searched her face. "What about the things I sent? Did you get the package?"

Mallory managed a stiff smile. "I put them in one of the guest rooms, in a closet," she said, thinking of the large parcel she hadn't had the heart to open. "You got your gifts, didn't you? I mailed early—"

"Good Lord," Nathan breathed, shaking his head. It was clear that he either hadn't heard her question about the carefully chosen gifts she'd sent to him or didn't mean to answer. "Which closet?"

Mallory shrugged, though nonchalance was the last thing she felt. "You are a man of many closets," she remarked lamely.

"Mallory."

She frowned at him. "The room Pat sleeps in when she stays at the penthouse."

Nathan looked thoughtful, and a long silence followed. Finally, when both husband and wife had finished pretending to eat, he stood up, scraping his chair against the linoleum floor as he moved. "I don't think you're up to greeting the band," he said in a voice that was gruff and tender at the same time. "Not tonight, at least."

I'll bet you were counting on that, Mallory thought, but she only nodded, relieved that she could deposit the remains of her lunch in Cinnamon's bowl and spend some time gathering her scattered thoughts and emotions. "Say hello for me," she mumbled, holding back tears as Nathan bent to brush her cheek briefly with his lips.

When he was gone, Mallory ambled aimlessly into the living room where she went through the contents of several bookshelves and found nothing she wanted to read. She was being stubborn and stupid, and she knew it. Damn, anybody with any guts at all would have gone over to the villa on the other side of the island and—

And what?

Mallory flung out her arms and cried out with self-mocking drama, "God, I'm so depressed!"

There was no answer, of course, but Mallory's gaze fell on the video recorder hooked up to her portable television set, and she remembered her favorite remedy for depression—old Jimmie Stewart movies.

Five minutes later, she was curled up on the sofa, immersed in the opening, snowy scenes of *It's a Wonderful Life*.

The cold press of Cinnamon's nose awakened her with a start, and Mallory sat up on the sofa, alarmed. The house was cold and dark, and she knew without making even the most cursory search that Nathan was nowhere within its walls.

Patting the dog's head in quick reassurance, Mallory scrambled to her feet. She turned on a lamp and turned off the video recorder and the TV and saw by the glass clock on the mantel that it was nearly three in the morning.

Poor Cinnamon hadn't had any dinner at all.

"I am a dog abuser," Mallory said sleepily. Then, her thoughts churning, she made her way into the kitchen and quickly refilled Cinnamon's dishes with food and water.

Where was Nathan?

Mallory found her purse and rummaged through it until she found the medication her doctor had given her when she had been released from the hospital. She took one capsule into her palm, glared at it for a moment, filled a glass with water and assured herself of hours of deep, undisturbed sleep. If Nathan was at Angel Cove, making music with Diane Vincent, she didn't want to know.

* * *

It was late morning when Mallory awakened, and the house was filled with strange sounds and smells. It took her several moments to identify them. She sat up in bed, wide-eyed with disbelief. Turkey? The house definitely smelled of roasting turkey, and the lilting notes of Christmas music filled the air.

Mallory tossed back her covers, frowning in curious consternation. Deck the halls? What in the world was going on?

Wearing only Nathan's old football jersey, which she had put on in the wee hours of the morning after taking the sleeping medication, she made her way out into the kitchen. A glance at the window revealed yet another snowfall, this one lacking the fury of recent storms.

"Nathan?" Mallory ventured, still frowning. The kitchen table was littered with egg shells, onion skins, bread crumbs, wilted celery leaves and an assortment of dirty mixing bowls. "Nathan!"

The recorded Christmas music came to a sudden and scratchy halt, and Mallory wandered toward the living room to investigate. Her mouth fell open in wonder, and her third call of her husband's name died on her lips.

Nathan was standing in the corner beside a fully decorated Christmas tree, grinning like a little boy. With a flourish, he flipped a switch, and the tree was suddenly alight with colorful, glistening splendor.

"Merry Christmas, pumpkin," he said.

Mallory's sentimental heart twisted within her, and tears of delighted surprise smarted in her eyes. "Nathan McKendrick," she whispered, "it is the middle of January!"

He smiled, the Christmas tree switch still resting in one hand. "Not in this house it isn't. Aren't you going to open your presents?"

Mallory's blurred gaze dropped to the base of the fragrant evergreen tree and a number of brightly wrapped packages. In that instant, she knew where

Nathan had been during the night, and how badly she had misjudged him.

"You went all the way to Seattle!"

Nathan shrugged. "It seemed the logical thing to do."

"Logical!" Mallory choked, beaming through her tears. And then she raced across the room and flung herself into the arms of her own private Santa Claus.

Their embrace subtly changed the mood. The brief melding of their two bodies sparked a charge that lingered long after Mallory had opened the beautifully wrapped gifts that Nathan had originally mailed from Sydney.

Sitting cross-legged on the hearth rug, still clad in the oft-washed and somewhat shabby red football jersey, Mallory made a sound that fell somewhere between a chuckle and a sob. "There aren't any presents for you!" she mourned.

He arched one eyebrow and folded his arms, and a wicked grin curved his lips as he assessed her speculatively. "I can think of one," he teased. "And I can't wait to unwrap it."

Mallory turned the color of her football jersey, but her heart sang with the desire this man stirred in her. She looked at the glittering litter surrounding her, the sumptuous gifts, the Christmas tree. Finally, she dared to look at Nathan, who was perched on the arm of the old-fashioned sofa, looking even more handsome than usual in his dark blue velour shirt and gray flannel slacks.

"I love you," she said, as awed by the intensity of her feelings as she had been the day she first faced them, more than six years before.

Though he was a tall and muscular man, Nathan moved deftly. Within a moment, he was kneeling on the hearth rug, facing Mallory. Gently he traced the outline of her cheek with a warm index finger. His voice, when he spoke, was hoarse with emotion. "I hope you mean that, lady."

Mallory shifted to her knees with as much grace as possible, and wrapped her arms around Nathan's neck. Her answering pledge was in the kiss she gave him.

Tenderly, without breaking the kiss, Nathan pressed Mallory backward until she lay supine on the large oval rug. His right hand stroked her collarbone, the hollow of her throat, and then slid beneath the neckline of the jersey to close possessively over one warm, rounded breast. She groaned as his thumb brought the rosy center swiftly to a sensuous peak.

The kiss ended, and Nathan's lips strayed, warm, to the sensitive place beneath Mallory's ear and then to the pulsing hollow of her throat. She moaned once again as he drew the neckline of the jersey down far enough to expose a breast.

Idly he surveyed this first sweet plunder of his conquering, as though it were some rare and special confection, to be savored and then consumed slowly. After what seemed like an eternity to Mallory, he lowered his head and nipped gently at the peak awaiting him, causing his wife to writhe. She gasped with shameless pleasure as he softly kissed the pulsing morsel and then tasted it.

He laughed, his breath warm on the tender globe he fully possessed. "You like that, don't you, pumpkin?" he teased in a rich, baritone voice.

Mallory nodded feverishly, unable to speak.

Nathan circled the pink fruit of her bounty with a warm, tormenting tongue. "Ummmmm," he murmured as his right hand moved over Mallory's knee and then beneath the jersey to her firm, satiny thigh.

She squirmed, instinctively parted her legs in an early and desperate surrender. Her hands moved of their own frantic accord, to explore the muscular hardness of his back, beneath his shirt.

He shuddered with pleasure at her touch, and as his mouth closed hungrily over the breast that had grown warm and heavy for him he caressed her inner thighs with gentle fingertips and then tangled them in the nest of curls where sweet, ancient secrets were hidden.

Mallory whimpered as he parted the silken veil to pluck gently at the treasure sheltered there, bringing it to the same throbbing response as her distended nipple. "Yes," she gasped as he drew the football shirt ever upward, unveiling the spoils of his impending conquest. "Yes—"

And suddenly she was totally bared to him, the jersey flung aside. She was grateful when he wrenched off his shirt and hurled that away, too. She could touch him then, entangle her searching fingers in the crisp dark hair curling on his chest, feel the loving, countering warmth of him.

Easily he lifted her, so that she was sitting on the edge of the sofa. Then, kneeling, he gently parted her knees, stroked the tingling, delicate flesh along her inner thighs. A primitive groan of surrender escaped her as he lifted one of her feet, and then the other, placing them so that the heels were braced on the sofa. This accomplished, he pressed on the insides of her knees until she was totally, beautifully vulnerable to him.

This time it was Mallory who drew back the sheltering veil, baring her mysterious, aching self to him. She cried out in throaty ecstasy when she felt his breath, pleaded raggedly until he took timeless sustenance at the waiting feast.

Her fingers entwined in his thick hair, her breath coming in tearing gasps, Mallory reveled in his hunger, in the warm strength of the hands holding her knees apart, so that she could not close herself to him. As his tongue began to savor her in long strokes, Mallory shuddered and gasped a plea and loosed her fingers from his hair to again spread the veiled place for his full satisfaction and her own.

Tremors, both physical and spiritual, rocked Mallory's entire being as he brought her to a release so savage that she sobbed out his name. Quivering with molten aftershocks, she was too stricken to speak again, or even move.

"I love you," he breathed against the moist smoothness of her inner thigh.

Finally, after at least a partial recovery of her senses, Mallory met his eyes. She did not need to speak to relay her message; she wanted to be filled with him, to sheathe him in the rippling, velvety warmth of her and hear his familiar, rasping cries of need and violent, soul-searing satisfaction.

Understanding, his eyes dark with a wanting to match Mallory's own, Nathan moved back a foot or so, still kneeling on the floor, and moaned as his wife slid from the sofa's edge to face him. He trembled, closed his eyes and tilted his head back as she opened his slacks to reveal his straining manhood. For the next several minutes, Mallory enjoyed his magnificence at her leisure, with her eyes, her fingers, her mouth. Her spirit soared at his words of tormented surrender.

In a smooth motion born of passion and desperation, Nathan grasped Mallory's slender waist, lifted her easily and then lowered her onto the pulsing pillar that would make them each a part of the other.

They moved with a rhythm as old as time, increasing their pace as the swelling crescendo building within both of them demanded. When the explosion came, it rocked them, and they shouted their triumph in one voice.

They were still one person, still shuddering with their fierce mingling, when Cinnamon began to bark in the kitchen and they heard the back door open with a cautious creak. "Nathan!" called Eric Moore, the lead guitarist in Nathan's band. "Hey, Nate—I know you're in here somewhere! Mallory?"

Nathan cursed and scrambled to his feet. He was fully dressed again before Mallory had managed to wriggle back into the discarded football jersey.

"Stay where you are, Eric!" Nathan ordered in ominous tones as he strode out of the glittering, cluttered living room without so much as a backward glance. "And next time, knock, will you?"

Still sitting on the floor, Mallory cowered against the front of the sofa, trembling with resentment and a wild, inexplicable loneliness. The conversation taking place in the kitchen was couched in terse undertones, and she understood none of it. She sighed. Understanding the exact situation wasn't really necessary anyway. The fact was that, once again, Nathan's dynamic, demanding life was pulling him in another direction.

Mallory was thoroughly annoyed. She had been planning to give up her role in the soap opera in order to devote more time to a marriage she knew was failing. And all her efforts would mean nothing if Nathan could not or would not meet her halfway.

She stood up slowly, feeling hollow and broken inside. Was Diane really the threat she appeared to be sometimes, or was Nathan's career his real mistress?

Mallory stooped to recover the toy kangaroo that had been one of Nathan's gifts to her and then held it close. She could hold her own against a flesh-and-blood woman any time. But how could she compete with thousands of them? How could she hope to prevail against the tidal wave of adoration lavished upon Nathan McKendrick every time he sang his soul-wrenching compositions?

Still clutching the stuffed kangaroo, she sank to the sofa in dejected thought. Obviously the physical passion between her and her husband was as formidable as ever. Still, Mallory knew that a lasting marriage required more than sexual compatibility, more than romance.

She sensed, rather than saw or heard, Nathan's return to the room. He stood behind her, and though Mallory knew he wanted to touch her, he refrained. His voice was a low rumble and caused tremors in Mallory's heart like some kind of emotional earthquake.

"I've got to go to Angel Cove for a little while, Mallory," he said. "Diane is doing one of her numbers again. Do you want to come with me?"

Mallory did not turn to face her husband; she simply shook her head.

"Babe—"

Mallory held up both hands. "No—I'm all right. Just go and straighten everything out."

"We'll talk when I get back," he muttered, and Mallory could tell that he was already turning away. "Pumpkin, there is so much to say."

Yes, Mallory thought, *there is so much to say, and it is all so painful.* "I'll be here," she said aloud, wishing that she could crawl inside the pouch of the toy kangaroo and hide there forever. "Nathan?" she whispered, on the off-chance that he was still near enough to hear.

He was. "What?" he asked, somewhat hoarsely.

"I love you."

He came to her then, bent, brushed her temple with his lips. A moment later, he was gone, and the glistening beauty of the decorated room was a mockery.

Mallory sat very still for a long time, absorbed by her own anguish and confusion. It was only the smell of burning turkey that brought her back to her senses.

She took Nathan's awkward attempt at culinary competence from the oven before wandering into the bedroom to dress. When the telephone rang, she was standing in the kitchen, trying valiantly to salvage at least a portion of the incinerated fowl.

"Hello!" she snapped, certain that the caller meant to make yet another impossible demand on Nathan's time.

"It's me," said Pat, Nathan's sister, in a placating tone. "Mall, I'm sorry if I'm intruding—"

Mallory loved Pat, and regretted the tart way she'd spoken. "Pat," she said gently. "No, you're not intruding. It's just—"

"That plenty of other people are," Pat finished for her with quiet understanding.

"Right," agreed Mallory, who had learned never to try to fool her astute sister-in-law. At twenty-two, Pat was young, but her mind was as formidable as Nathan's. "Shall we start with the band, and progress to Diane Vincent, press agent *extraordinaire?*"

Pat sighed heavily. "Please," she retorted. "I just ate."

Suddenly, inexplicably, Mallory began to cry in the wrenching, heartbroken way she'd cried after losing her parents.

Pat drew in a sharp breath. "Mallory, honey, what is it? How can I help?"

The warmth in Pat's voice only made Mallory sob harder. She felt stupid, but she couldn't stop her tears, and she couldn't manage an answer, either.

"Sit tight," Pat said in brisk, take-charge tones. "I'm on my way."

Mallory sank into one of the kitchen chairs and buried her face in her hands. The telephone receiver made an accusing clatter as it bounced against the wall.

It was a full fifteen minutes before Mallory regained her composure. When she had, she dashed away her tears, marched into the bathroom, ran a tubful of hot water and tried to wash away all the questions that tormented her.

Was Nathan's casual dislike for Diane Vincent really part of some elaborate ruse designed to distract Mallory and everyone else from what was really taking place?

"Diane is doing one of her numbers again," Nathan had said just before he dashed off to handle the situation.

Mallory slid down in the hot, scented water to her chin, watching the slow drip fall from the old-fashioned faucet. Diane wasn't really the issue, she reminded herself. It was just easier to blame her, since she was so obligingly obnoxious in the first place.

Grimly, Mallory finished her bath and, wrapped in a towel, walked into the adjoining bedroom. As she rummaged through her drawers for clean clothes, she regretted not asking Pat to stop by the penthouse for more of her things.

Once dressed in a pair of jeans and a soft yellow sweater, Mallory went to the bedroom window and pushed back the brightly colored cotton curtains to look outside. The snow was still falling, already filling the tracks left by Nathan's car.

Mallory returned to the bathroom to brush her teeth and comb her hair and apply a touch of makeup. Unless she was on camera, she needed nothing more than a dab of lip gloss. Her eyelashes were thick and dark, requiring no mascara, and, normally, because of her fondness for the outdoors, her cheeks had plenty of color. Now, staring at herself in the old mirror over the bathroom sink, Mallory saw the pallor that had so alarmed her friends and co-workers of late. Because she hadn't brought blusher from the penthouse, she improvised by pinching her cheeks hard.

In the living room, the lights on Nathan's Christmas tree were still blazing, and with a sigh, Mallory flipped the switch. The glorious tree was dark again, and the tinsel dangling from its branches whispered in a draft.

Mallory closed the door leading into the living room as she went out. The January Christmas was a private thing, and she did not want to share it with anyone other than Nathan—not even Pat.

In the kitchen, she sliced off a piece of turkey and gave it to an appreciative Cinnamon, but she had no appetite herself. She cleaned up the mess Nathan had left behind and put the half-charred bird into the refrigerator.

Mallory was brewing fresh coffee when she heard the sound of a car motor outside. Knowing better than to hope that Diane's crisis, whatever it was, had been resolved so soon, thus freeing Nathan, she didn't bother to rush to the window and look out.

The visitor was Pat. Her trim camel's hair coat glistened with snowflakes as she rushed into the kitchen, shivering. "Good Lord," she complained, hurrying to stand beside Mallory at the stove. "It's *cold* out there!"

Mallory laughed, somewhat rawly, and began to divest her sister-in-law of her coat and knitted scarf. When the things had been put away, the two women sat down at the kitchen table to sip coffee and talk.

Pat's shimmering blond hair was swept up into an appealing knot on top of her head, and she looked slim and competent in her tailored black suede suit and red silk blouse. Her blue eyes searched Mallory's face as she warmed her hands on her coffee mug.

"You were pretty shook up when I called, Mall. Are you okay now?"

Mallory nodded. She was tired of all the solicitude, and besides, there was really nothing Pat could do to help. In any case, she had no intention of complaining about Nathan's demanding life to his sister. "I—I'm all right, Pat—honestly. And I'm sorry if I frightened you. C—Couldn't we talk about something mundane—like the weather?"

Pat gave her a cynical look, but she wasn't the type to pry; that was one of her most endearing qualities. "You and Nathan assured me," she said, arching one golden eyebrow, "that the weather on Puget Sound was *mild*. Do you realize that it has been snowing for almost a week?"

Mallory shrugged, grinning. "What can I say in our defense? Every few years somebody up there forgets that it isn't supposed to snow much here, and we get buried in the stuff. Seattle must be wild."

Pat rolled her eyes. "We are talking blatant insanity here!" she cried. "When I drove onto the ferry, I was amazed that I'd made it through town in one piece. People are slipping and sliding into each other over there, with and without cars."

"You like Seattle, Pat," Mallory challenged kindly. "You're not fooling me one bit."

Suddenly Pat was beaming. Her cornflower blue eyes sparkled, and her face glowed. "You're right," she confessed. "I love it! The water, the mountains, the trees—"

Mallory laughed. "Not to mention the fresh raisin bagels they sell at Pike Place Market."

Pat shook her head. "I've sworn off bagels, along with lottery tickets and cigarettes."

"How about Roger Carstairs?" Mallory teased. "Have you sworn off him, too?"

Pat seemed to shine like the Christmas tree hidden away in the living room at the mention of the handsome young attorney she'd met while acquiring property for Nathan's growing corporation. Since then, Roger's name came up a lot. "No way. I don't make a habit of swearing off hunks, Mallory."

Mallory's green eyes danced with mischief. "Patty McKendrick, you're in love!"

The guess was correct; Pat blushed slightly and nodded her head. "Don't tell Nathan, though. I don't want him doing one of his Big Brother numbers—demanding to know Roger's intentions or something."

Mallory laughed. That would be like Nathan; he was fiercely protective of his sister, partly because their parents, like Mallory's, were no longer living. "I promise not to breathe a word!"

"Good," Pat said. "How is Nate, by the way? He looked pretty undone at the penthouse the other night."

Mallory laid her hand on Pat's, quick to reassure her. "He's fine." *I'm the one who might have to be carted off in a padded basket.*

Like her brother, Pat could be uncannily perceptive at times. "Mall," she began cautiously, "I love you, but you really look like hell. Have you told Nathan that you're thinking of dropping your contract with the soap?"

Mallory's eyes strayed to the window, and she pretended an interest in the incessant snow. "No."

"Why not?"

Cinnamon came to lay her head in Mallory's lap and whimpered sadly. Probably she was feeling abandoned, since Nathan had left her behind this time. Her mistress patted her reassuringly. "I'm not sure how he'll take it, Pat."

"What do you mean, you're not sure how he'll take it? You know he hates the demands the show makes on you, and, well . . ." Pat paused, and when Mallory glanced back at her sister-in-law, she saw a reluctant look in her eyes. "Mallory," she went on at last, "it hurts him that you don't use his name anymore."

"I know," Mallory nodded, thinking back to Diane's visit the day before, when she had announced her intention to drop "O'Connor" and call herself Mallory McKendrick again. She hadn't had a chance to explain her decision to Nathan—or was it that she hadn't had the courage? Now, she wasn't sure which was really the case. "I guess, in the back of my mind, Pat, I'm afraid that taking back my married name isn't going to matter to Nathan. His life is so fast-paced, and I'm not sure I can keep up anymore."

"*Talk* to the man, Mallory. Make him listen, even if

you have to throw a screaming fit or insult his band to do it!"

It was the only sensible course of action, and Mallory knew it. Too many times, all during her marriage to Nathan, she had stepped aside when other demands were made on him, however intrusive and unreasonable, content to wait her turn. A hot blush of anger crept up from her collarbone into her cheeks, and she drew a deep breath.

Her turn had come.

"I see I've gotten through," Pat said, rising purposefully from her chair. "He's over at the other house, I assume?"

Mallory nodded, the high color of outrage still pounding in her cheeks.

Pat collected her coat and scarf from the hall closet and came back into the kitchen. "I'll spend the night over there, since I can't quite face fighting my way through downtown Seattle tonight. And you, Mrs. McKendrick—you get Nathan on the phone and tell him to get over here, in no uncertain terms!"

Mallory felt some of her determination drain away. Nobody *told* Nathan McKendrick to do anything, and Pat knew it as well as she did. "But if he's busy—," she wavered, hating herself all the while. *Busy doing what?* taunted a voice in her mind. *Holding Diane's trembling hand? Soaking in the hot tub?*

Pat pressed her lips together in undisguised annoyance. "Stop with the peasantlike awe, will you, Mallory?" she snapped. "Nathan is a man, not a god. It's high time he turned some of his energy into his marriage, and if you don't tell him that, I will!"

Mallory bit her lower lip, but she was already making her way to the telephone when Pat left the house. Her hands trembled a little as she dialed the number that would connect her with her husband.

One of the band members answered in a lazy drawl. "Yeah?"

"This is Mallory," Mrs. McKendrick said bravely. "I would like to speak to Nathan, please."

"Oh—Nate. Yeah. Well, he's not around right now."

Mallory felt a growing uneasiness quiver in the pit of her stomach. "Where is he?" she asked stiffly.

There was a long, discomforting pause. "Diane was freaking out, so he took her back to Seattle."

Mallory drew a deep breath and let her forehead rest against the kitchen wall. "What do you mean, 'Diane was freaking out'?"

"I don't know—like, she was just losing it, you know? Really coming undone."

"There must have been a reason," Mallory insisted.

Another pause. "Like, I'll have Nate call you when he gets back, all right?"

"Don't bother," Mallory snapped. And then, without pausing to give the matter further thought, she left the telephone receiver dangling, strode into the bedroom, and began flinging the few things she'd unpacked back into her suitcases.

Twenty minutes later, with Cinnamon sitting happily in the back seat, Mallory drove her sleek black and white Mazda onto the passenger ferry that would carry her back to Seattle.

The huge vessel, capable of transporting both pedestrians and motorists, had always reminded Mallory of an old-time riverboat, with its railed decks and dozens of windows. Normally she loved to stand on the highest deck, watching the magnificent scenery pass and feeding chunks of snack-bar cinnamon rolls to the gulls, but today it was bitterly cold and she didn't even bother to get out of the car and climb the metal stairs leading to the lower deck. She simply sat behind the wheel, Cinnamon patient behind her, and stared beyond the other cars parked in the bowels of the craft to the water ahead.

The snow was still falling, and Mallory watched in aching silence as the huge, intricate flakes, so beautiful and perfect, came down to the salty waters of Puget Sound and were dissolved. The snowflakes, like the love she and Nathan shared, were at once breathtakingly beautiful and temporal.

Mallory lowered her head to the steering wheel, and she didn't lift it again until the great horn sounded, announcing that Seattle was just ahead. When the ferry docked, Mallory collected her scattered emotions and concentrated on the task of driving. Navigating in the storm-plagued city would require all her attention.

Pat had certainly been right about the traffic conditions, and the next half hour was harrowing. Mallory was pale with exhaustion when she finally drew the small car to a halt in front of the expensive apartment complex in the city's heart and climbed from behind the wheel.

The doorman, George Roberts, rushed toward her. "Ms. O'Connor! I thought you were on the island—"

With an effort, Mallory returned the man's warm smile. She saw no need, the way things stood, to correct his use of her name. "Is Mr. McKendrick at home?" she asked, hoping that the vast importance of the matter didn't show in her face.

George shook his head, and wisps of powdery snow flew from the brim of his impeccable visored hat and shimmered on the gold epaulets stitched to the shoulders of his coat. "No, ma'am, he isn't," he answered, stealing an unreadable look at Cinnamon, who was whining to be let out of the car.

Mallory turned her head to take one more look at the busy, storm-shrouded Sound. *Snowflakes on the sea,* she thought, aching inside.

Chapter 4

MALLORY HOOKED CINNAMON'S LEASH TO HER COLLAR and flipped the seat forward so that the dog could leap out onto the paved driveway and wriggle in the joy of sudden freedom. "If you would?" she said to George, indicating the car.

George Roberts nodded, smiling. "I'll have it parked for you, Ms. O'Connor. Is there any luggage?"

Mallory was already leading a delighted Cinnamon toward the well-lighted, posh lobby of the building. "There is," she called over one shoulder. "But please don't worry about it now. I'll get it in the morning."

No one inside the building looked askance at Mallory and her canine companion, and no comments were made during the elevator ride either, though there were a surprising number of people crowded inside. Mallory liked to think that they were being kind—pets other than birds or tropical fish were strictly forbidden by general agreement—but she knew the real reason was simply deference to Nathan. After all, he owned the building.

On the top floor, Mallory fumbled with the keys for several seconds, her hands numbed by the cold outside, and then managed to open the double doors leading into the penthouse. She paused in the lighted, marble-floored entryway, her eyes rising to the polished antique grandfather clock opposite the door. It was still very early—what was she going to do with the rest of the evening?

Mallory sighed as Cinnamon whimpered beside her; in her turmoil she'd forgotten how very inconvenient the high-rise apartment building would be for the poor creature, who was used to roaming the island at will. With glum resignation, Mallory locked the penthouse again and pushed the button that would summon one of the two elevators serving the building.

The doorman raised a curious eyebrow when Mallory and Cinnamon stepped out into the snowy night so soon after going in. But he said nothing.

Mallory walked Cinnamon until she could bear the stinging cold no longer, and then went home again. After feeding the dog two cans of liver pâté in the enormous kitchen, Mrs. Nathan McKendrick marched down the hallway to the plush master bedroom and began shedding her clothes.

Looking up at the huge skylight over the bed, at the shifting lace of glistening snow, Mallory felt tears smarting in her eyes. How many times had she and Nathan made love in this bed, with the sky stretched out above them like a beautiful mural? She swallowed hard, tossed back the covers of the oversized round bed and crawled between icy satin sheets. Cinnamon settled companionably at her feet with a canine sigh, her nose resting on her red, shaggy paws, her great weight causing the mattress to slope slightly.

In spite of everything, Mallory laughed. "You lead a

tough life, dog," she said, reaching out to switch off the lamp beside the bed. "Sorry we were out of caviar, but such is life."

Cinnamon made a contented sound and went to sleep.

Mallory, however, spent several hellish hours just staring up at the moving patterns of eiderdown snow on the skylight. She'd been wrong to leave the island without a word to anyone; she knew that now and guessed that she'd known it all along.

The thing was, she just hadn't been able to face another night of waiting for Nathan.

So what do you call this? she asked herself ruthlessly. *Aren't you waiting, even now, for him to call or show up? Preferably with some convincing reason for leaving the island with Diane and not even bothering to let you know first?*

Mallory turned restlessly onto her side. Why should she have left word for him? Hadn't he been equally thoughtless?

Her stomach twisted into a painful knot. It was possible that Nathan wouldn't even know she was gone for hours yet, and that was the hardest thing of all to bear.

She buried her face in the smoothness of her pillow and cried until her throat was raw. Then, fitfully, she slept.

Nathan glanced at the clock on the Porsche's dashboard and grimaced. Damn, it was late.

Diane flung a petulant, sidelong look in his direction as he guided the car down the ferry ramp and into the still-crazy Seattle traffic. Her face was pale and pinched with residual shock, and her hands were clasped, motionless, in her lap.

High drama, Nathan thought bitterly. *God, she should have been an actress.*

"This is all a bad dream," she said in a stricken, whispery voice.

Nathan shifted gears and reminded himself that she'd had a hard night. She'd been so upset by his decision that he'd taken her from the island to Tacoma, where her parents lived, thinking that she needed to be close to someone who cared about her. But her parents had been away, and they'd missed the connecting ferry to Seattle finding that out.

He sighed. "Listen, Diane—I'm sorry you had to hear the news from the guys in the band. I really am—"

Diane drew in an audible breath calculated to inspire guilt and lifted her chin in theatrical acceptance of a cruel fate. "One way or the other, we're all fired. I don't see what it matters that I heard it from them and not you."

Nathan had no answer for that; he concentrated on the road ahead. The traffic lights were mere splotches of red or amber or green, dimly visible in the swirling snow, and the tires of the Porsche weren't gripping the pavement all that well.

"You're doing this for Mallory, aren't you, Nathan?" Diane demanded, after some moments of silence.

Nathan stiffened but didn't look away from the traffic. "Mallory is my wife," he replied flatly.

Diane made a disdainful sound. "Wife! Good Lord, Nathan, you're insane to give up your career for *her!*"

Nathan tossed one scathing look in Diane's direction. "Watch it."

She subsided a little. "Why? Nathan, just tell me why. If she loved you, she—"

"I'm tired, Diane," he broke in, and his tones proved it. "I've got more money than I can spend in a lifetime, and I've done everything I set out to do, musically, at least. Now I intend to straighten out my marriage."

"You have no marriage!" Diane cried in a hoarse, contemptuous whisper. "You and Mallory are a joke!"

Nathan's fingers tightened dangerously on the leather-covered steering wheel, but he maintained control. "Your opinion of my marriage couldn't matter less to me, Diane."

There was still a tinge of hysteria in her tone when she spoke again. "So you're doing the farewell concert here, and that's it? No television specials, no tours, no records?"

"I'll record, and I suppose I'll write songs, too. But I'm through chasing fans all over the world."

"How do you plan to make records without a band?" Diane demanded, her voice rising.

Nathan sighed. "If the guys are available, we'll work together." He looked again at Diane and saw exactly what he'd feared he would—hope. Why couldn't she just find another job and let the thing drop? She was a gifted press agent, and she wouldn't be out of work long. Although Nathan had always disliked her on a personal basis, her recommendation would be a good one.

"Then I could keep doing your press work—"

"No."

Diane seethed in electric silence as Nathan guided the car up a slight hill into the residential section where her sister lived. Because Diane's work kept her in Los Angeles most of the time, she didn't need a permanent place in Seattle.

When he drew the Porsche to a stop in front of her building, he faced her. "Good night, Diane. And I'm sorry."

Diane's lower lip trembled, and she tossed her magnificent head of hair in a kind of broken defiance. The motion filled the chilly interior of the car with the flowery, somewhat cloying scent of her perfume. "Not half as sorry as you're going to be, Nathan McKendrick," she vowed.

Nathan rested his head against the back of the car seat, sighed and glowered up at the leather upholstery in the roof. "What is that supposed to mean, pray tell?"

There was a note of relished power in her tone. "I built you up, Nathan. I can tear you down."

"How melodramatic," he retorted in sardonic tones. "For all the world like a scorned lover."

Diane wrenched open the car door and scrambled out to stand, trembling, on the snowy sidewalk. Her eyes glittered, scalding Nathan in blue fire. "How long do you think that naive little wife of yours will last under a full-scale press attack, darling?"

An explosive rage consumed Nathan's spirit, and his jaw tightened until it ached. Still, he managed to keep his hands on the steering wheel and his voice even. "If you do anything to hurt Mallory, Diane—*anything*—you'll spend the rest of your shallow little life regretting it."

Diane smiled viciously. "Or savoring it. Good night, handsome."

Wondering why he hadn't fired Diane years ago, Nathan watched until she had disappeared inside her sister's apartment building. Then another glance at the dashboard clock made him groan.—Why the hell hadn't he called Mallory before leaving the island? God knew what she was thinking by now.

Turning the Porsche back toward the waterfront in a wide, deft sweep, he swore under his breath. He could stop and call now, however after-the-fact the gesture might be. But Mallory was probably asleep. No, he would just get back to the island as soon as he could and they would talk in the morning.

Seething, Diane Vincent unlocked her sister's front door and stormed into the apartment, not even bothering to turn on a light. In the room Claire kept just for her, she flung down her purse, wrenched off her coat and angrily punched out a familiar number on the telephone beside the bed.

"I know it's late!" she hissed, when the recipient of her call grumbled about the time. "Did you find someone?"

The affirmative answer made Diane smile. Without even saying good-bye, she hung up.

Cinnamon awakened Mallory early the next morning, bounding up and down the length of the big bed and occasionally plunging an icy nose into her mistress's face.

Grumbling, Mallory crawled out of bed and stumbled into the bathroom. It was as large as the living room in the island house with its garden tub, hanging plants, cushioned chairs and gleaming counters.

After a quick shower, Mallory dressed in gray wool slacks, a red turtleneck sweater and boots. Two more cans of pâté were sacrificed to Cinnamon's hearty appetite, and then it was time for another walk.

The telephone on the hallway table rang as they were going out, but Mallory didn't answer. In fact, she didn't even look back. But a half an hour later, with Cinnamon's morning walk accomplished, Mallory found herself at loose ends. Still shivering from the bite of the winter wind, she choked down one slice of whole wheat toast and a cup of tea.

After that, she went into the study, a spacious room equipped with two glass desks that faced each other, and flipped on the television set. "Tender Days, Savage Nights" was on, and she watched herself steal a diamond bracelet and the heroine's husband, all in the space of an hour.

And then Cinnamon was hungry again. She stood by, watching, as the beast happily consumed two cans of imported lobster.

"This will never do, you know," she informed the Setter as she poured scalding water over the dish the dog had eaten from and placed it inside the dishwasher.

"So don't expect gourmet fare. From here on out, it's good old canned dogfood, all the way."

Cinnamon whimpered and tilted her beautiful red-gold head to one side, as if to protest this projected change in the menu.

Mallory reached down to pet the dog and sighed. She'd kept all thoughts of Nathan carefully at bay, but now they were suddenly streaming into her mind and heart like some intangible river.

She wandered into the mammoth living room, with its massive ivory fireplace and thick silver-gray carpeting. Snow drifted past the slightly rounded floor-to-ceiling windows overlooking Seattle's beleaguered downtown area and the waterfront.

Her thoughts spanned the angry waters to the small island, invisible in the fury of the day. Surely Nathan was there, angry but safe—

The shrill jingle of the telephone made Mallory start. She steeled herself.—This time, she would have to answer it.

The walk to the telephone table beside Nathan's favorite chair seemed inordinately long.

"Hello?" she ventured, turning the cord nervously in her fingers.

"Hi, babe," Brad Ranner greeted her, his voice full of pleased surprise. "How long have you been back in the big city?"

Mallory swallowed, sank onto the sturdy suede-upholstered arm of Nathan's chair. "Since last night. Why?"

"Mallory, haven't you heard? There isn't any phone service to the island, and the ferries aren't running either. I called on the off-chance that you might have come back to town earlier than you planned."

Mallory felt a swift stab of alarm. Except during labor strikes, the ferries *always* ran.

Brad seemed to sense her agitation. "Relax," he

said. "You're back in civilization yourself. That's what counts."

His insensitive comments taxed Mallory's strained patience. "Brad, I have a number of friends on that island, and I think Nathan is there, too. What if someone is sick or—or—"

Brad's tone was soothing. "Honey, take it easy. The Coast Guard will check things out. You know that."

Mallory did know, and she was comforted. Besides, the islanders were independent sorts, and they would look after one another. "How are things on the set?" she asked in order to change the subject.

"Everybody is excited. Mall, I have *great* news. That's one of the reasons I called. I'd like to tell you in person, though. Is it all right if I brave the treacherous roadways and drop in?"

Mallory closed her eyes for a moment, summoning up her courage. "Brad, about the show—I—"

"We'll talk when I get there," Brad broke in cheerfully. And then, before she could say a word in response, he hung up.

Will we ever, Mallory thought, one hand still resting on the telephone receiver. *And you're not going to like my end of the conversation at all.*

Two minutes later, Mallory was in the bathroom, applying makeup. No sense in greeting Brad with her wan, tired face and having to endure the inevitable you-haven't-been-taking-care-of-yourself lecture.

The cosmetics transformed Mallory from a very pretty woman to a beauty, but they could do nothing to mask the weariness in the depths of her green eyes. In hopes of drawing attention away from them, she brushed her lustrous dark-taffy hair and pinned it up into a loose Gibson-Girl.

Once again, she felt pain and remorse; Nathan loved her hair in that particular style.

Where was he now? Stranded on the island, with no

idea where his wife had gone? Lying in some love-rumpled bed with Diane Vincent? Mallory brought herself up short. She had enough trouble without borrowing more.

She went back into the bedroom and sat down on the edge of the neatly made bed, hurriedly dialing the number of the house at Angel Cove. Maybe Brad had been wrong about the telephone service's being out. But an operator broke in to say that emergency line repairs were being made.

So Brad had been right, after all. Frustrated, Mallory wandered back to the living room and distractedly petted a whimpering Cinnamon. She had wanted so badly to reach Nathan, to hear his voice, to apologize. Now, it might be hours, or even days, before she reached him.

Mallory went to the windows and, for the first time in her life, cursed the snow.

Cinnamon made a low, whining sound in her throat, and then barked uncertainly. A moment later, Mallory heard the opening and closing of the front doors. She turned, frowning, from the windows, expecting to see the woman who came in to clean twice a week.

Instead, she was confronted with a scowling, disheveled, unshaven Nathan. His dark eyes swept over her, leaving an aching trail wherever they touched.

"I chartered a boat," he growled, neatly dispensing with the first question that rose in Mallory's mind. "What are you doing here?"

Mallory's throat closed and, for a moment, her mind went blank and she honestly didn't know what she was doing there. "I—I—," she stammered.

Nathan slid out of his suede jacket and ran one hand through his rumpled hair. "Damn it, Mallory, what is going on with you? Everybody on the island is out of their mind with worry—"

Suddenly, Mallory found her voice. Hot color

pounded in her cheeks. "Was that before Diane's latest crisis, or after?" she snapped.

Some of the fierce anger drained from Nathan's lean, towering frame, and he sank into a chair. "Is that why you did the disappearing number, Mallory? Because of Diane?"

His tone was so reasonable that Mallory felt ashamed of her outburst. She dared not approach him, but she did try to match his decorum with her own. "Yes," she admitted. "I called y—your house—at the Cove. One of the guys said you'd taken Diane back to Seattle. I—I know I was hasty, but—"

Nathan thrust himself out of his chair and made a hoarse, contemptuous sound in his throat. "Spare me, Mallory. I'm tired and mad as hell and I really don't think this is a good time to discuss your paranoia about Diane."

Mallory was instantly furious. Her *paranoia!* How dare he shift all the blame to her, when none of this would have happened if he hadn't been so quick to come to Diane's aid! "Damn you," she swore. "Nathan McKendrick—"

But he was striding around her, on his way toward the bedroom. By the time she recovered enough composure to storm in after him, he was in the shower.

Outraged, Mallory pounded at the thick, etched glass doors with both fists. Through the barrier, she could see the shifting blur of his tanned flesh.

"Nathan!" she yelled, in anger and in pain.

Suddenly, the shower doors slid open and, with a lightning-quick motion of his hand, Nathan pulled Mallory under the pounding, steaming spray. Water plastered his ebony hair to his face and dripped, in little rivulets, down over his muscular, darkly matted chest. Mallory dared look no further.

"You wanted to talk," he shouted over the roar of the shower. "So talk!"

Mallory's makeup was smeared, and her hair clung to her neck. Her sweater, slacks and boots were all drenched. She threw back her head and shrieked in primitive, unadulterated fury.

Gently, Nathan thrust her backward against the inside wall of the shower and out of the spray of water. His hand caught under her chin and lifted. "So I *can* make you feel something, lady—even if it is rage."

Mallory stared up at him, stunned by his words, by the situation, by the alarming proximity of his naked, beautifully sculptured frame. Her throat worked painfully, but she could say nothing.

Nathan bent his head to kiss her, and the sea-breeze scent of his wet hair caught at her heart. His lips moved gently on hers, at first, and then with undeniable demand. She trembled as his tongue laid first claim to total possession. "Mallory," he rasped, when the devastating kiss broke at last. "I want you."

Mallory stiffened and thrust him angrily away, even though a desire equal to his was raging inside her. She turned, let her forehead rest against the water-speckled tiles lining the inside of the shower stall. "Don't, Nathan. Don't touch me—don't talk—"

But his hands were hard on her shoulders as he turned her back to face him. "Listen to me, Mallory. We've played this game long enough. I didn't spend the night rolling around in Diane Vincent's bed!"

Mallory arched one eyebrow and looked up at him in silence.

His muscular shoulders moved in a defeated sigh. "I was wrong not to call you and let you know what was going on, and I'm sorry."

Mallory believed him. She looked down at her soaked clothes and laughed, at herself, at Nathan, at the ludicrous insanity of the situation.

And he kissed her again.

The ancient heat began to build in Mallory's slender

body, just as she knew it was building in Nathan's powerful one. She trembled as he removed her sodden garments, her boots, the few pins that had held her hair in place, and discarded them in the separate world beyond the shower doors.

Nathan surveyed her waiting body for a long moment, missing nothing—not the full sweetness of her firm breasts, the narrow tapering of her waist, the trim but rounded lines of her hips and thighs. Making a sound low in his throat that must have dated back to the beginning of time, he reached out for her again.

His tongue traced the pink hollow of her ear, flicked briefly at her lobe. Mallory shuddered with reflexive pleasure as he nibbled at the softness of her neck and kissed the tender hollow of her throat. She arched her back and cried out when the warmth of his mouth strayed over the rounded top of her breast and then claimed the waiting nipple. With one hand, he cupped the breast he was consuming, with the other, he sought the very core of her womanhood. When he knelt, Mallory entwined both her hands in the thick darkness of his hair to keep herself from soaring away on the crest of her own fiercely undeniable need.

Her release was so savage in its force that it nearly convulsed her.

She was in a spell as Nathan turned off the spray of the shower, as they dried each other with soft, thirsty towels, as her husband lifted her into his arms and carried her into the adjoining room to the bed, where the final and most intimate sharing would take place.

They lay facing each other, naked and still warm from the shower, and Nathan groaned as Mallory circled one masculine nipple with a mischievous tongue. She worked her own magic, loving him fully, savoring the responses she stirred in him.

When the outer boundaries of ecstasy had been reached, she lay back to await his claiming. A low moan escaped her as he parted her legs with one knee and poised above her, and she saw the reluctance in his eyes, along with a fathomless need.

"Mallory, if you don't feel—"

She shook her head, almost feverishly, and clasped his taut buttocks in her hands, urging him to her. She gasped with delight as their two bodies became one.

Nathan's control was awesome, his entry and withdrawal calculated to prolong the sweet misery for them both.

When she could bear the waiting and the needing no longer, Mallory lifted herself to him, prevented his retreat with strong, desperate hands. The steady rhythm of her hips caused him to plead with her in a soft, ragged voice.

Mallory's passion flared within her like fire, compelling her on to a fulfillment she couldn't have escaped even if she'd wanted to. In one glimmering moment, shattering release was upon them, flinging them as one beyond the charted regions and into a world of streaming silver comets and crimson suns. They drifted downward slowly, linked spiritually as well as physically among the fragments, their mingled cries of triumph echoing around them like music.

The insistent buzz of the doorbell signaled their return to the real world.

Nathan groaned, and Mallory laughed, soft and pliant beneath him, smoothing his damp hair with a tender hand. "Our public," she said.

Nathan swore, stood up and wrenched on a hooded maroon velour robe. "I'm coming!" he shouted angrily, and Mallory dissolved in a fresh spate of giggles.

If Brad Ranner had any idea what he'd interrupted, he did an admirable job of hiding the knowledge. When Mallory and Nathan emerged from the bedroom, one at a time and as subtly as possible, he made no comment. Of course, he couldn't have helped noticing that Nathan, now clad in jeans and a red T-shirt, had answered the door in a bathrobe.

His shrewd blue eyes did catch, just momentarily, the flush in Mallory's cheeks, before moving on to politely assess the silken lines of her pink and gold caftan.

Brad was a short, stocky man, and the uninitiated usually took him for a serious young accountant or a budding corporate lawyer. In truth, he was a dynamic and innovative entrepreneur, noted for his skill, insight and artistry.

"Mallory," he began without preamble, raising his glass in a dashing toast, "we're about to talk business, you and I. *Big* business."

Nathan folded his arms and raked the unflappable Brad with a scorching look. Then he nodded curtly in Mallory's direction, as though they hadn't soared in each other's arms only minutes before, and muttered, "This is obviously private. Later."

The crisp words and his immediate departure for the study made Mallory blush slightly. She was still floating in the warm glow of Nathan's lovemaking, though it appeared that her husband had already forgotten their brief, fiery union. Besides, she'd wanted him to hear the things she meant to say to Brad.

Brad pretended an almost clinical interest in his drink. There was no love lost between the two men, but they usually managed a sort of cold civility. "If you'd told me Mr. Superstar was here," he said softly, "I would have stayed away."

Mallory lifted her chin and offered no reply. When Brad offered, with a gesture, to make a drink for her, she nodded.

There was a short, stiff silence, broken only by the clink of crystal, as Brad poured Mallory's customary white wine. Cinnamon, fickle to the end, had left the room with Nathan.

Mallory sighed as Brad handed her her drink and sat down on the sofa beside her. "So what's the big news?" she asked without any real interest, wondering how he was going to take her announcement that she had no intention of renewing her contract with the show.

Brad grinned and took a slow sip from his whiskey. "Cable," he said.

Mallory frowned. "Cable?"

"The show is being picked up by a cable network, Mallory, and they're opening with a two-hour movie. It will mean more money and extra exposure."

Mallory tensed, staring at her producer. "Exposure is certainly the applicable word. Brad, have you *seen* those cable soaps? Everybody is naked—"

Brad's eyes moved almost imperceptibly to Mallory's fine bustline, and then back to her face. "You don't have anything to worry about on that score," he said. "If you'll pardon the expression, love, you'd stack up against the best of them."

Mallory shot to her feet, and some of her wine sloshed over the rim of her glass and fell onto the rug. "My God, Brad—I can't believe you're asking me—do you really mean—I *wouldn't*—"

As usual, Brad was totally unruffled, absorbing her outburst without evident effort. "Calm down, Mall. It's true that cable soaps have nude scenes, but they also have some really challenging scripts. This is your chance to grow as an actress—"

"*No.*"

"Why not?" Brad asked reasonably, raising one eyebrow. "Think of it as an art form."

Mallory was pacing now, her glass clasped in both hands. "Art form! Bull chips, Brad. My God, Nathan would—"

Brad set his drink aside and folded his hands casually around one knee. "There we have it, don't we, Mallory? Nathan. Couldn't Mr. Macho handle the competition?"

Mallory stopped her pacing, too stunned to move. She gaped at Brad, who was watching her implacably, and then snapped, "This is *my* body we're talking about, Brad. Don't try to shift the blame onto Nathan. *I'm* the one who doesn't want to flash for America!"

Brad sat back, sighing a little. From his manner, they might have been discussing some mundane, everyday matter. "Bull," he said pleasantly. "You're afraid of what Nathan will say—or do."

Mallory's heart was pounding with anger, just as it had pounded with passion such a short time before, and her breath burned in her lungs. "Damn it, Brad, I wouldn't do what you're asking even if I were single!"

Brad stood up, walked to the teakwood bar, and set the drink he had just reclaimed down with a thump. When he turned to face Mallory again, his eyes were snapping, even though his voice was low and evenly modulated. "Mallory, we are talking about big, *big* money here—millions."

"I don't care."

"Damn it, I do!" Brad retorted. "If we have to recast your part, production will be delayed."

"Then production will be delayed!"

"Mallory—"

"No. Damn it, Brad, *no*. I wasn't planning to renew my contract as it was—"

Brad swore roundly. Then, without another word, he grabbed his overcoat and stormed out of the penthouse, slamming the doors behind him.

Having been wrenched, in just one morning, from one emotional extreme to the other, Mallory folded. She sank into Nathan's chair, set her drink on the table beside it and wept softly into both hands.

She caught Nathan's clean, distinctive scent just as he drew her up out of the chair and into his arms.

"What did that bastard say to you?" he wanted to know, but his tones were infinitely gentle.

Mallory could only shake her head and cry harder.

"Okay," Nathan conceded softly, his hand warm and strong in her hair, his lips brushing her temple. "We'll talk about it later. But if I see that guy again, he may have to order new knees."

Despite everything, Mallory giggled into the fragrant warmth of Nathan's red T-shirt.

Her husband caught one hand under her chin and tenderly urged her to look up at him. Briskly, he kissed the tip of her nose. "I believe we were conducting a rather interesting reunion before we were so rudely interrupted."

Sniffling and smiling through her tears and already warming to the hard, insistent nearness of this man she loved so fully, Mallory nodded.

Nathan laughed softly. "I'll be with you in a minute —just let me make a sign for the front door."

Mallory lay in bed, looking up at the black velvet expanse of the skylight. The snow was melting, leaving shimmering beads of water in its place. Beside her, warm and solid, Nathan slept the sleep of the exhausted. Tenderness welled up inside Mallory as she turned to look at him, to gently trace the outline of his strong jaw, his arrogant chin, his neck. He stirred but did not awaken.

Mallory smiled. Nothing would disturb his desperately needed sleep—nothing. If need be, she would have fought tigers to see to that.

Gently she kissed the cleft in his chin. "I love you, Nathan McKendrick," she said softly. Then, snuggled close to him, she slept.

The bright warmth of undiluted sunshine awakened Mallory the next morning, aided by the cold, wet nuzzling of Cinnamon's nose in her face. The dog whimpered as Mallory sat up, wriggled impatiently as she crept out of bed without awakening Nathan.

"Shh," she ordered, raising an index finger to her lips. "I know you need to go outside."

Cinnamon whined as Mallory scrambled into her

clothes, again wishing that she'd left the dog behind on the island. Keeping the poor creature in a penthouse was inexcusable.

In the outer hallway as Mallory and Cinnamon waited for an elevator, Mallory made up her mind to correct the mistake that very day. Provided the ferries were running again, she would take the dog home.

Outside, the glaring brightness of the day greeted them, as did the inevitable clamor of a big city. Horns honked, boat whistles whined and cars rushed helter-skelter through the glistening slush on the roads.

Cinnamon was terrified.

In a grocery store some blocks away, Mallory bought two cans of dogfood, having left Cinnamon to wait bravely on the sidewalk.

Because the weather was so beautiful and Cinnamon seemed calmer, Mallory decided not to go directly back to the penthouse. Even though Nathan would be there, the blue and gold day was simply too appealing to be abandoned so quickly.

They walked, woman and dog, back toward the waterfront. On Pike Street, where the road was paved with worn red bricks and merchants offered every sort of fish, fresh vegetable and pastry from open stalls, they bought bagels and cream cheese.

On the Sound, a passenger ferry sounded its horn, as if to remind all and sundry that no storm could stay it for long.

Mallory drew a deep, salt-scented breath. "We'll go home today," she said, as much to herself as to Cinnamon. "All of us."

Cinnamon yipped, as if in celebration, and then strained at her leash as a tame seagull ventured too near, waddling over the brick street in search of scraps. Mallory was restraining the dog when she felt a hand come to rest on the sleeve of her windbreaker.

She turned, smiling, expecting a friend or someone who had been following her misadventures on the soap.

Instead, she met the snapping azure gaze of Diane Vincent.

After a moment, Diane allowed her eyes to sweep contemptuously to the dog, who still wanted to investigate the intrepid seagull foraging nearby. "Hello," she said, her voice trimmed in sweet malice. "Out walking your—dog?"

"Obviously," Mallory replied.

Diane smiled acidly. She did look splendid, though, in her casual tweed blazer, yellow silk blouse fetchingly open at the throat and tailored designer jeans. "Let's have coffee, Mallory. How long has it been since we really talked, you and I?"

Not long enough. Mallory managed a stiff smile, though she couldn't have said why she made the effort. "I really don't have time, Diane." She patted the shopping bag resting in the curve of one arm, still holding Cinnamon's taut leash in the other hand. "When Nathan wakes up, he's going to be hungry, and—"

Diane tossed her head, so that the sun caught in her magnificent hair. "He's still sleeping—well, after last night, that figures."

Mallory visualized headlines in her mind. SOAP OPERA VILLAINESS MURDERS REAL-LIFE RIVAL. . . .

"Diane," she said at length, and with commendable control, "if you've got something to say about last night, why don't you just say it?"

Nathan's beautiful press agent shrugged, and a hint of a malicious smile curved her lips and then shifted to her eyes. "We'll get together another time, Mallory," she said. "Give my regards to Nathan."

With that, the woman turned and walked away, leaving Mallory to stare after her, all her questions unanswered.

Chapter 5

WHEN CINNAMON BEGAN TO TUG ANXIOUSLY AT HER leash, probably bored with the seagull and ready for breakfast, Mallory, stunned, snapped out of her mood and started off in the direction of the apartment complex. When she reached the building, her earlier high spirits still tarnished by the encounter with Diane, Mallory found that the lobby was uncommonly crowded.

"What's going on, George?" she asked of the harried doorman, who was scowling at the bevy of reporters and photographers milling about.

George's suspicious glance turned to one of worried recognition. "Ms. O'Connor—they'll recognize you—." Before she could find out more, Mallory was being shuffled into the building manager's cluttered office, out of view, Cinnamon following cheerfully behind.

Inside Mallory frowned and set her shopping bag

down on the desk usually occupied by the woman Nathan retained to look after the building. "Where's Marge? George, what in the world?—"

"They're after Mr. McKendrick, from what I gather," George confided, looking very much like a beleaguered general barely able to stave off attack. "Marge is upstairs, talking to Mr. McKendrick."

Annoyed, Mallory reached for the telephone on Marge's desk and punched out the number for the penthouse. Oddly, it was Marge who answered. "Yes?" she demanded coldly.

"Marge, this is Mallory—I'm downstairs. Will you put Nathan on, please?"

"Are you in my office?" Marge blurted after a sharp intake of breath. "For God's sake, stay there—." For a moment, the middle-aged woman's voice sounded farther away as she spoke to someone else. "Yes, she's here—I don't think so—"

A moment later, Nathan was on the line, and the strange timbre of his voice frightened Mallory. "Mallory, listen to me. I want you to stay inside that office until I come for you. All right?"

Something shivered in the pit of Mallory's stomach. "Nathan, what's happening? There are reporters and—"

He broke in brusquely. "I'll explain it all in a few minutes, Mallory—*just don't leave that office.*"

"But—"

"Mallory."

"Nathan, you've got to tell me—"

"Do I have your promise or not?"

Even more alarmed, Mallory sighed in frustration. "All right, damn it, I promise."

"Good," Nathan snapped, and then the line went dead.

Just then, the office door burst open, and an avid-looking man was standing there, his small eyes raking over Mallory as though she were some curious museum piece, meant to be thoroughly examined. "Did you know about the girl, Mrs. McKendrick?" he blurted out, as an angry George lumbered toward him. "Has your husband admitted to an affair with her?"

Mallory could only stare at the man, and the office spun around her as George pushed the man out and quickly locked the door. The doorman was grumbling as he turned to face the woman he had so wanted to protect.

Apparently alarmed by the sight of her, he sputtered, "Now, Mrs. McKendrick—Ms. O'Connor—don't pay any mind to that scum! He's probably with one of those papers they sell in the supermarket—."

Mallory couldn't answer; her head was full of echoes. *Did you know about the girl, Mrs. McKendrick? Has your husband admitted to an affair with her?*

George caught her arms, thrust her gently into the chair behind Marge's desk and brought her a Styrofoam cup brimming with hot, strong coffee. Five minutes passed, ten. Mallory managed the occasional sip of coffee, but only because George looked so worried. The stuff was like bile in her mouth.

Suddenly, she heard an unmistakable shout of annoyance in the area outside the office, followed by a terse invective that the reporters would probably choose not to print. George opened the door to admit a livid Nathan.

"Will you get rid of those creeps?" snapped Mallory's husband, addressing the doorman.

"I'll try," George promised somewhat uncertainly, making a hasty exit.

Nathan swept Mallory's trembling frame with dark, furious eyes, and then turned to lock the door again. Her hand shaking, she set aside what was left of her coffee and braced herself.

After a rather drawn-out battle with a very simple

lock, Nathan turned to face his wife. "Are you all right?"

Mallory could manage nothing more than a nod. If he didn't explain what was happening, and fast, she would explode in a fit of shrieking hysteria.

Pale beneath his tan, Nathan took a newspaper Mallory hadn't noticed before from under his arm and thrust it at her. Despite what the reporter had said to her, cold, sickening shock turned her stomach as she read the headline. SINGER NATHAN McKEN-DRICK NAMED IN PATERNITY SUIT.

Mallory closed her eyes and swallowed the burning sickness that scalded in her throat. *These things happen all the time,* one part of her mind argued calmly. *It's gossip, it's trash—*

"Mallory." Nathan's voice broke through the fog of pain and betrayal that surrounded her. *This is no cheap scandal sheet. It's an important newspaper—*

"*Mallory!*"

She felt the angry, frightened strength of Nathan's hands as he grasped her shoulders, and opened her eyes to see the torment in his face. "Who is she?" she whispered.

Nathan flinched as though she'd struck him, and drew back. Head down, he thrust his hands into the pockets of his gray flannel slacks, and an awesome tension tightened the muscles in his shoulders. "I don't know."

"What do you mean you don't know?" Mallory cried out, wounded. Then, remembering the reporters who were no doubt still lurking outside, anxious to grasp any tidbit, she lowered her voice. "Nathan, damn you, start talking!"

As if insulted, he thrust the newspaper at her. "Read it for yourself," he snarled. "And then you'll know as much about it as I do!"

Hoping that she could trust her hands, Mallory

unfolded the newspaper, winced inwardly as she read the headline again, and then turned her attention to the picture and article beneath it. The photograph showed Nathan standing in a crowd of delighted girls, clad in the flowing silk shirt and fitted trousers he customarily wore on stage. His arm curved easily around the waist of one particularly voluptuous young lady, and he was smiling.

Mallory forced herself to read the words printed below. *Eighteen year old Renee Parker, of Eagle Falls, Washington, has named singer Nathan McKendrick in a paternity suit, claiming that she and McKendrick have been intimately involved on a number of occasions. This alliance, says the attractive young waitress, has resulted in the conception of . . .*

Mallory could read no further. A soft cry of outraged pain echoed in the room, and she realized that it was her own.

"Read the rest of it," Nathan ordered, his voice a taut, anguished rasp, his arms folded across his chest.

She shook her head. "No—no, I can't."

"It ends with, 'Mr. McKendrick was unavailable for comment, according to his press agent, Diane Vincent.' Mallory, does that tell you anything?"

The tumult outside the office seemed to be building to a crescendo, rather than waning. Apparently, George had been unsuccessful in his efforts to get rid of the press.

"Eighteen," Mallory whispered, as though Nathan hadn't spoken. "Oh, my God, Nathan, she's only *eighteen.*"

Nathan's magnificent features were flushed with out-raged color, and a vein at the base of his throat pulsed ominously. "God in heaven, Mallory, you don't seri-ously think—"

Before he could finish, there was an imperious knocking at the door, and Pat's voice rang out over the clamor in the lobby. "Nathan—Mallory! Let me in!"

After one scathing glance at Mallory, Nathan un-locked the door, easily this time, to admit his sister.

She spared a sympathetic look for her brother and then turned her attention to a stricken Mallory. "I see this morning's fast-breaking news story didn't go over well. Nate, I've talked to the press. They'll let Mallory pass if you'll answer some of their questions. If you don't, they're prepared to hang around until Nixon gets reelected."

Nathan's dark eyes, charged with fury only a moment before, were dull with pain as they linked again with Mallory's. "Tell them they have a deal," he said, in a voice his wife hardly recognized. "Just get Mallory out of here."

Five minutes later, Mallory and a very confused Cinnamon were in the safe confines of Pat's bright yellow Mustang, on their way to her condominium overlooking Lake Washington.

Pat looked pale as she navigated the slushy streets, and her knuckles were white where they gripped the steering wheel. "You know, I hope," she ventured, after they'd traveled some distance, "that that newspa-per article is libelous?"

Libel. Mallory might have laughed if she hadn't felt as though everything within her was crumbling. "That's no gossip rag, Pat," she said brokenly. "It's a responsi-ble, highly respected newspaper."

Pat said a very unladylike word. "You innocent. Are you telling me that you *bought* that garbage?"

"I don't know," Mallory admitted honestly, her eyes fixed on the blurred houses and businesses moving past the car window. And it was true—at that moment, she couldn't have said whether she believed Nathan to be innocent or guilty. She was still in shock.

There was a long, painful silence. Pat finally broke it with an impatient, "Do you want to go to the island, Mallory? To Trish or Kate? I could take you there right now—"

Mallory shook her head quickly. The island might have offered sanction during any other crisis, but, for the moment, it held no appeal at all. She wouldn't be able to think clearly there or in any other place she'd lived with Nathan. "You could do me one favor, though," she said tentatively, and the softening in Pat's face was comforting.

"What's that?"

Mallory reached back and patted the fitful dog filling the car's back seat. "Take Cinnamon back to the island. Trish will look after her."

"Are you sure you'll be okay—while I'm gone, I mean? Nathan might be busy for a while."

"I need some time alone," she said, and knew that her eyes were imploring Pat. "C—Could you keep Nathan away f—for a few days?"

Pat sighed as she turned into the driveway of her condo. "I'll try, Mallory. But he knows where you are, and he's going to be very anxious to settle this."

Glumly, Mallory nodded. "I know, but I don't want to talk to him now. I've got to think—"

"You can't run away from this, Mallory," Pat said not unkindly as she turned off the car's engine and pulled the keys from the ignition. "Rotten as it is, it's real, and avoiding your husband won't make it go away."

"Three days," Mallory pleaded. "Please—just three days."

Pat shrugged, but her blue eyes were filled with worry and reluctance. "All right, Mall—I'll plead your case. Just remember that I can't promise he won't come storming over here to have it out with you."

Half an hour later, Mallory had her wish—temporarily, anyway. She was alone in Pat's airy, sun-brightened condo, without even Cinnamon to disturb her churning thoughts.

She paced the sumptuously carpeted living room for

some minutes after Pat's departure, looking blindly out at the view of Lake Washington. Despite the miserable weather of the past few days, or perhaps because of it, the azure water was dotted with the colorful sails of several sleek pleasure boats.

Mallory was honestly surprised to discover that there were tears sliding down her face. Angry with herself, she brushed them away and approached the telephone. After a short, awkward conversation with a discerning Trish (surely the newspaper article was common knowledge on the island, too, by now) she replaced the receiver and wandered to the sofa. Bless her, Trish had asked no questions, probably sensing that Mallory couldn't bear to talk about the impending lawsuit just yet, and she'd promised to look after Cinnamon.

The telephone rang shrilly, startling Mallory, and she debated whether to answer it or ignore it. She didn't want to talk to Nathan yet, and she certainly didn't want to speak with any reporters, but this was Pat's telephone and it was most likely that the call was unrelated to Mallory's personal problems.

She answered with a spiritless, one-word greeting, and nearly hung up when she heard Nathan's voice.

"Babe, are you all right?"

Oh, I'm wonderful. You've made some groupie pregnant and she's telling the world and who could ask for anything more? "I'm fine," she lied. "How about you?"

He made an irritated, raspy sound. "I don't need the light repartee right now, sweetheart," he replied tartly. "I know what you're thinking."

"Then you know I need time, Nathan. Time and space."

"I'm not the father of that girl's baby, Mallory."

Tears were coursing down Mallory's face again, and she was glad of only one thing in the world—that Nathan couldn't see her crying. She wanted so desperately to believe him, but she was afraid to; it would be too shattering to find out later that he'd lied. "D—Don't, Nathan—not now. I'm so tired and so confused—"

His sigh was a broken, despondent sound. "All right. All right—just don't forget that I love you, Mallory, and that I don't sell out people who trust me."

Mallory nodded, realizing that he couldn't see her. "I'll call you in a few days, Nathan—I promise."

"Is there anything you need?"

She thought for a moment—it was so difficult to accomplish even the simplest mental processes with her mind in such a turmoil. "My car. Could you have George bring my car?"

"Sure," he said, and Mallory was grateful that he didn't offer to deliver it himself. "Take care, pumpkin."

"I will," Mallory whispered, and her hand shook as she replaced the telephone receiver.

Twenty minutes later, George delivered Mallory's Mazda, handed over the keys without comment and left again in a taxi. Mallory made her way to Pat's guest bath, took a shower and appropriated a cozy looking chenille bathrobe from her sister-in-law's bedroom closet.

She was curled up on the living room sofa again, trying to read, when Pat returned. With typical thoughtfulness, she'd stopped at the penthouse for a suitcase full of Mallory's clothes.

"Did you hear from Nathan?" she asked without preamble, setting the suitcase down at Mallory's feet.

Mallory nodded, but was, for the moment, speechless. Why in hell did she feel so guilty, when it was Nathan who had stirred up an ugly scandal, Nathan who had been the betrayer? Or had he? She saw an angry defense of him brewing in Pat's dark blue eyes.

"He was in pretty bad shape when I left him a few minutes ago, Mall."

Mallory felt a swift and searing fury flash through her

battered spirit, but the emotion was tempered with self-doubt. Suppose Renee Parker's paternity charge was trumped up, as so many such cases involving celebrities were? Suppose Nathan was as innocent a victim as Mallory herself?

"Be more specific, Pat. 'Pretty bad shape' is a broad phrase."

Pat pulled off her coat in angry motions and tossed it aside. Then she sank into a chair facing Mallory's and glared at her sister-in-law. "Will 'dead drunk' do? Damn it, Mallory, you're putting the man through hell for something he didn't do!" Sudden tears brimmed up in the blue eyes and then spilled over. "He's my brother and I love him and I can't stand what this is doing to him!"

Mallory shivered. Nathan, drunk? She'd never seen him intoxicated even once, in all the time that they'd been married, and she couldn't begin to imagine how he would look or sound in such a state. "Pat," she asserted, "you're not being fair! I'm not trying to hurt Nathan—"

Quickly, Pat reached out, caught Mallory's hand in her own. "I know, Mall—I know. It's just that—well—"

"I understand. A—Are you sure he was drunk?" In her mind, Mallory was remembering the day she and Nathan had talked about their Christmas apart from each other, and he'd said, *"I drank a lot."*

A rueful, sniffly giggle escaped Pat. "He was on his lips, Mallory."

"Was he alone?"

Instantly, Pat was on the defensive again. "Did you think he'd send for Renee Parker, Mallory? Of course he's alone!"

"He shouldn't be."

Hope gleamed in Pat's misty eyes. "You'll go to him, then?"

Mallory shook her head. "I can't, Pat—not yet. But he shouldn't be by himself. Alex Demming is his best friend—I'll call him."

"Forget it," Pat said sharply, disappointment clear in her voice. "I'll ask Roger to go over there."

Mallory looked down at her hands, clasped painfully in her lap, startlingly white against the deep blue of the borrowed chenille robe, and wondered if she was being selfish in avoiding Nathan now when he obviously needed her. She did her best not to hear Pat's tearful conversation with her boyfriend and felt deep gratitude when Nathan's sister informed her, after hanging up the phone, that Roger was on his way to the penthouse.

It was a long night. Mallory soon gave up on the idea of sleep and got out of bed to pace the guest room, torn between the fact that she loved Nathan McKendrick with all her heart and soul, no matter what he might have done, and the counterpoint: her own pride.

No matter how deeply she loved that impossible, arrogant, wonderful man, she would never live with him again if he'd betrayed her. There would be no trust, and without trust, love meant nothing.

The sun was barely up when Mallory crept out of Pat's condo, yesterday's newspaper tucked under one arm. Sitting behind the wheel of her Mazda, she scanned the article just once more, to confirm her plans.

The girl's name was Renee Parker, and she lived in Eagle Falls, a small town about an hour from Seattle. Mallory had been in that community once, years before, with her parents.

And now she was going there again.

Nathan rolled over in bed and moaned. Nausea welled up in his middle, and blood pounded in the veins beneath his skull. He swore.

Roger Carstairs, Pat's boyfriend, appeared in the bedroom doorway, his healthy looks annoying. He was wearing the housekeeper's apron and stirring something in a mixing bowl. "Breakfast?" He grinned, his green eyes alight with malicious mischief.

Nathan swore again. "How much did I drink last night?"

"Let's just say I wouldn't throw a party, if I were you, without replenishing your liquor supply."

The telephone on the bedside table rang suddenly, jarring Nathan's throbbing head. "Hello!" he barked obnoxiously into the receiver. If it was a reporter, he'd—

It was Pat, and she sounded worried. "Nate, is Mallory over there?"

Nathan's jaw was suddenly clenched so tightly that it ached. "No—." He paused and looked questioningly at Roger. "Mallory didn't drop by, did she?"

Roger shook his head.

"No," Nathan repeated. "My lovely wife is not here, soothing my tortured brow. Did you call her place on the island, or Angel Cove?"

"Yes. I called Kate Sheridan and Trish Demming, too, and they haven't seen her either."

Though he was trying to be angry, Nathan was actually scared. Mallory hadn't been in the best state of mind before the paternity charge, and the pain and confusion she had to be feeling didn't even bear thinking about. God, she might have left, might have walked out of his life forever. And the hell of it was that he was innocent; whatever other sins he might have committed, he had been a faithful husband from the first.

"She must have said something, Pat—*anything*."

"She said very little, Nathan. Her clothes are still here, if that's any comfort."

It wasn't. Mallory had enough credit cards to buy all the new ones she wanted. Forgetting his incredible hangover, Nathan threw back the covers on his bed and sat up, still cradling the receiver with his shoulder. He was reaching for a pair of jeans when he barked, "Damn it, if she's left me—she *promised*—"

"Oh," Pat marveled in the tones of one who has just had a revelation. "I think I know where she is."

"Spare me the dramatic pause, Pat!" Nathan snapped, struggling into the jeans. *"Where?"*

"Eagle Falls."

"Eagle what?"

"That little town where your alleged lover lives, dummy. Eagle Falls. Mallory went there."

The thought made Nathan sick. "What makes you think she'd do a stupid thing like that? What the hell could she hope to accomplish?"

"I'd do that, if I were in her shoes—that's what makes me think it. Nathan, you have been straight with me, haven't you? She's not going to walk into some hideaway filled with romantic mementos and candid snapshots of you, is she?"

Nathan was balancing the telephone receiver between his shoulder and his ear, and wrenching on his socks. "On the basis of our long-standing relationship, sister dear, I'm going to let that question pass. It's too damned low to rate an answer!"

"All right, all right. So what do we do now?"

Instantly deflated and stung on some primary level, Nathan sank back to the bed, abandoning his previous hasty efforts to get dressed. He ignored Pat's question to continue angrily, "She *believes* it. God, after everything we've been through together, *she thinks I'd go to bed with someone else.*"

"Nathan—"

Rage and hurt made his voice harsh. "Damn her, she knows better!"

"Does she? Nathan, how would you have felt if that story had been about her? Well, I'll tell you how you would have felt, Bozo!"

Nathan calmly laid the receiver down on the bedside table and walked away, and his sister's tirade was audible even from the doorway leading into the bathroom.

He heard Roger speaking placating words into the phone as he reached into the shower and turned the spigots.

Eagle Falls was smaller than Mallory remembered. In fact, it boasted only one gas station, one cafe and one grocery store. Behind this one-block business section, about two dozen shabby houses were perched on the verdant hillside, along with a post office, a tiny school and a wood-frame church. Remembering that Renee Parker was, according to the newspaper article, a waitress, Mallory headed for the cafe.

Inside that dusty, fly-speckled kitchen, she was informed by an eager-eyed fry cook that Renee lived in the pink house next door to the church. Like as not, the man imparted further, she'd be home, since she wasn't working in the cafe anymore.

Mallory nodded politely and left. What was she going to say to this Renee person, anyway, once they came face to face?—"Pardon me, but have you been sleeping with my husband?"

Angry tears were stinging her eyes when she slid back behind the wheel of the car, and it was a moment before she dared start up the engine again and drive. Damn it, she didn't *know* what she was going to say to the bimbo, but she had to see her. One look at her and she would know whether the stories were true or not. Just one look.

I could say I'm the Avon lady, she thought five minutes later when she drew the car to a stop in the crunchy snow rutting the street in front of Renee Parker's modest house. After drawing one deep breath, Mallory got out of the car and strode toward Renee's front door, exuding a confidence she didn't feel.

There was smoke curling from a chimney in the roof of the small house, and the front door was open, the passage blocked only by a rickety screen door. Inside, a young, female voice was lustily singing along with one of Nathan's records.

And in that moment, inexplicably, Mallory froze. Nathan was innocent. She was about to force her rigid muscles to carry her back down the crumbling walk when the screen door opened suddenly and a pretty girl appeared on the porch. "Ray—"

Mallory assessed Renee Parker—she looked much as she had in the newspaper picture—and mentally kicked herself. The girl was cute, and obviously pregnant, but she was too young to hope for more than passing notice from a man like Nathan. He was far more likely, if he strayed, to choose someone like Diane Vincent.

Renee paled, then her brown eyes darkened. "Tracy Ballard!" she gasped, reaching wildly for the handle of the screen door behind her. "Mom, Tracy Ballard is out here—"

Mallory lifted her chin. All this and a fan of the soap in the bargain. She nearly laughed. "I'm not really Tracy Ballard, Renee," she said, with dignity. "I'm Mrs. Nathan McKendrick."

Renee laid one unsteady hand on her protruding stomach. "Oh."

"Yes. Could we talk, Renee?"

The girl's eyes were suddenly very round. "I'm not taking back any of the things I said!"

Mallory advanced a step, trying to look ominous, though she hadn't the vaguest idea what she'd do if Renee called her bluff.

Fortunately, Renee didn't. She leaped behind the screen door, pulled it shut and flipped the hook into place, as though fearing for her very life. "This baby belongs to your husband!" Renee cried, "and that's the truth!"

"We both know it isn't, Renee," Mallory said evenly. "Who paid you to file that lawsuit?"

"Nobody paid me! Nathan was in love with me, he—"

"I see. Did you know he's planning to file a counter-suit, Renee? This is slander, you know. His lawyers will make you appear in court, and it will be harder to lie there. You'd be committing perjury, and they can put you in jail for that."

"*Jail?*"

"Jail," Mallory confirmed, feeling profoundly sorry for the frightened girl before her. "Who put you up to this?"

Renee shook her head. "Nobody—nobody!"

"Very well. Then I'll see you in court. Good-bye, Renee."

With that, Mallory turned regally and walked back to her car. She was starting the engine when Renee appeared at the window on the driver's side, her face pinched and pale with fear. "C—Could you wait a minute? Could we talk?"

Mallory managed a nonchalant shrug, betraying none of the jumbled nerves that were snapping inside her like shorted electrical wires. "I thought we'd said everything."

"J—Just wait here—just for a minute—please?"

"I'll wait," Mallory promised, and when Renee had scurried back inside the small pink house, she allowed her forehead to drop to the steering wheel. Good God, what had she done? Nathan had never said anything about filing a countersuit against Renee Parker. What if Renee called Mallory's bluff?

Seconds later, when Mallory had composed herself again, Renee reappeared. She was holding a battered *TV Guide* cover in one hand, and there was a pinhole in the top, as though it had been affixed to a wall.

Mallory took the cover and was assaulted by her own smiling face. She had forgotten that interview; even though they'd used her picture on the cover, most of the writer's questions had been about Nathan. She looked up at Renee, truly puzzled. "What?—"

"Would you autograph it? Would you write, 'To Renee, from Tracy'?"

For a moment, Mallory could not believe what she was hearing. Was it possible that this girl would ruin her life, shake the very foundations of a marriage she treasured and then blithely ask her for an autograph? "You've got to be kidding."

Renee looked hurt. "I watch your show all the time—"

Mallory drew a deep breath, then fumbled through her purse for a pen. "Tell you what, Renee. I'm going to write a phone number on the back. If you decide to tell the truth about your baby, you call me."

"D—Did you leave Nathan?"

Mallory lifted her chin. *In the lurch*, she thought. *Like a fool.* "I love him, Renee, and he loves me."

One tear glistened in the corner of Renee's eye as Mallory handed her the worn *TV Guide* cover, now boasting Tracy Ballard's signature and several phone numbers on the back. "I didn't mean to—it was so much money—"

Mallory's throat ached so badly that she couldn't speak. She could only look into this young woman's face and hope.

The girl bit her lower lip and stepped back. "I might call you soon, okay?"

"Okay," Mallory managed.

Renee looked down at the magazine cover in her hands and beamed. "Oh, boy, just *wait* till I show this to my mom—"

Mallory stopped herself from offering the girl a check that would exceed whatever she'd been paid to lie about Nathan and calmly drove away.

When she came to the gas station, however, she pulled up beside the rest rooms, ran inside the appropriate chamber and was violently ill. Afterward, she splashed her face with the tepid water that trickled from the spigot marked "cold" and returned to her car. Again, she considered paying Renee.

She shuddered. If she did that, people would say she'd bought the girl off, and believe ever after that Nathan had indeed fathered Renee Parker's child. *Nathan.*

The name was like a plea, torn from her heart. *Forgive me,* she thought. *Oh, forgive me—*

He'd tried to tell her, and she hadn't listened to him—she hadn't *listened.* She picked up the newspaper, still resting on the seat, and read the article again, objectively.

And the last line quivered, jagged, in her mind, like a wounding spear. *Mr. McKendrick was unavailable for comment, according to his press agent, Diane Vincent.*

"Fool," she whispered brokenly. "Oh, Mallory, you *fool!*"

With that, Mrs. Nathan McKendrick started the journey back to Seattle, and self-recriminations dogged her every inch of the way. Again and again, she heard Nathan recite that last line of the article, heard him say, *"Mallory, does that tell you anything?"*

She was crying when she surrendered the Mazda to a worried-looking George and rushed into the one elevator that would take her all the way to the penthouse.

Her hands trembled as she unlocked the door and stepped into the entry hall, and she knew that Nathan wasn't there long before she called his name and got no answer at all.

Pacing the study in his house at Angel Cove, Nathan was drawn to the telephone again and again. Where was Mallory now? What was she thinking? Feeling?

God knew what kind of reception she'd gotten from Renee Parker, whoever the hell she was. What if there had been some kind of ugly scene and Mallory was shaken up and driving? What if she'd been hurt? What if, even now, she was in some ditch along the road, bleeding—

He caught himself on one raspy swearword, and started when the telephone rang.

"She's back," Pat said coolly. "I just talked to her, so why haven't you?"

Nathan sighed, sank into his desk chair and twisted the phone cord in his fingers. "She knows where I am," he bit out, his relief at knowing that Mallory was all right completely hidden by his tone.

"Nathan, you ass. Will you call the woman, please?"

"Hell, no. She wanted time—she gets time. *I*, as it happens, want time."

"For what?"

"To think."

"About what?"

"About whether or not I want to stay married to a woman who obviously has such a low opinion of my morals."

"It's your *brain* that I hold in question. Nathan, do you love your wife or not?"

He sighed as a savage headache gripped the nape of his neck. "You know I do."

"Then why don't you act like it?"

"Because I'm mad as hell right now, that's why."

"Poor baby," Pat crooned in an obnoxious manner that conveyed all her scorn. "Damn you, Nathan, *grow up!*"

Having imparted this message, Pat hung up with a resounding crash. Nathan glared at the receiver in his hand for a moment, and then chuckled ruefully. The hell of it was, he reflected as he replaced it in its cradle, that she was right. He was sulking.

Ten minutes later, Nathan was on board the ferry and on his way to Seattle.

After imbibing two glasses of white wine and stalking back and forth across the penthouse living room until she thought she'd shout with frustration, Mallory fell on the telephone that waited beside Nathan's chair and forced herself to dial his number. One ring, two, three—no one was there, not even Mrs. Jeffries.

Tears smarted in Mallory's eyes as she hung up and then tried the other number in desperation—the one that would ring in her own house on the other side of the island. There was no answer there either.

Mallory ached inside. *Good Lord,* she thought, hugging herself in her anxiety. *If I don't talk to somebody, I'll die.*

Just then she heard a key in the lock and stiffened in sudden panic. As desperate as she'd been to reach Nathan, she didn't know what she would say to him now. She hurried to the bar and refilled her wineglass, and when she turned around, he was there, his dark eyes piercing her. But were they accusing, or pleading?

His name caught in her throat and came out as an unrecognizable sound.

He came to her in long strides, removed the glass from her hand and set it on the bar with an authoritative thump. "Take it from one who knows, pumpkin— that stuff won't solve your problems."

"I—I saw her today—I talked to her," Mallory faltered miserably, needing to speak rationally with this man standing so disturbingly close. "Renee, I mean."

Nathan raised one dark eyebrow, his expression unreadable. "Does she have two heads?"

"S—She's a child, really. Scared—"

He was being stubbornly silent; refusing to make the conversation easier, to reach out. He stood still, his arms folded over his chest, waiting.

Mallory lowered her eyes. "I'm sorry," she whispered.

"Are you?" he drawled, and there was no love in the words, no warmth. "What, exactly, transpired in Eagle River?"

"Eagle Falls," Mallory corrected him, still unable to

meet his eyes. "Nothing much happened. She insisted the baby was yours to the end. She also hinted that someone had paid her to say so."

"A contradiction in terms," Nathan observed blandly, still keeping his distance.

Mallory made a sound that might have been a chuckle or a sob, and dashed at the tears burning her eyes with the back of one hand. "Renee is nothing if not a walking contradiction. Would you believe she asked me to autograph that old *TV Guide* cover? She wanted me to write, 'To Renee, from Tracy.'"

Nathan placed his hands gently on her shoulders, drawing her close. His lips were warm in her hair. "Did you?"

Mallory began to tremble violently, and hysteria bubbled up into her throat and escaped in a series of wracking sobs. Nathan lifted her into his arms, carried her to a chair and sat down, holding her in his lap like a shattered child. He continued to hold her until long after the sobs had subsided and the trembling had stopped.

"We're in a lot of trouble, you and I," he said, at length.

"I know," Mallory responded, her head resting against his shoulder. And she knew he wasn't talking about the paternity suit or Renee Parker, but about the chasm that had grown between them.

As the sun went down, they agreed to separate.

Chapter 6

EVEN THOUGH THE INITIAL STIR HAD DIED DOWN, THERE were a few press people posted in the lobby that evening when Nathan and Mallory set out for the island. Nathan was coldly uncommunicative; he had never, under the best of circumstances, been overly fond of reporters. But Mallory recognized a number of these people, and considered them friends. There wasn't much she could say without betraying things that were necessarily private, but she did manage a few polite, if inane, words, and she kept her chin high and her shoulders square.

On board the ferry, Mallory and Nathan remained in the Porsche, dealing in silence with their thoughts and feelings. Mallory's car would be delivered in the morning.

The silence looming between them had reached ominous levels by the time Nathan drew the luxurious, high-powered automobile to a stop in front of the house they both thought of as Mallory's.

Was there nothing that was not specifically his or hers, but theirs? Mallory wondered brokenly.

Still at the wheel of his car, Nathan flexed his hands and sighed, his eyes carefully avoiding his wife's. "I still love you," he said, his voice so low that it was almost inaudible.

"And I love you," Mallory replied.

He turned his head slightly to study her with eyes that were both wounded and angry. "Then what the hell are we doing?"

Mallory couldn't answer. She got out of the car, thus forcing Nathan to do so, too, and her gaze locked with his over the black vinyl expanse of the vehicle's roof. Her throat worked painfully, and she swallowed.

"Is it okay if I come in for a little while?" Nathan asked gruffly, again avoiding her eyes.

Mallory nodded, despairing, and wondered why she couldn't talk to this man, why things couldn't be straightened out with a few rational words.

The next half hour was a tense time, and Mallory was grateful for the mechanics of reopening the house. While Nathan started a fire in the stove, she unpacked her clothes.

Though her back was to the door, Mallory knew immediately when Nathan entered the bedroom. She stood very still and did not turn around to face him.

He said nothing, and the silence again seemed infinite and eternal.

Mallory was both stricken and relieved when Nathan withdrew and busied himself in the living room. She could not bear to follow, but she knew that he was dismantling the January Christmas tree.

Long after the unpacking was finished, Mallory ventured as far as the kitchen. She was grateful that Nathan hadn't made coffee; it gave her something to do. All the same, an unbearable sadness clutched at her heart as she grappled with the small task.

Beyond the window, the dwarf cherry trees looked grim without their lacy trimming of snow, and the sky was a bleak and threatening gray. Mallory was sure that she would carry a jagged and hurting piece of that sky in her heart forever.

She was sitting at the kitchen table, sipping coffee, when Nathan came in. Without a word, he set the gifts he'd given Mallory on the far end of the counter and folded his arms.

Since even a screaming fight would be better than this blasted silence, Mallory said the first thing that came into her mind, and her voice was brittle. "Why do you suppose Diane didn't try to head off those reporters?"

Nathan went to the stove, poured himself a cup of coffee. "I fired Diane."

Mallory closed her eyes. So he did lay Renee Parker's lawsuit at Diane's feet. She wondered why that knowledge didn't make her feel better. "Oh," she said woodenly, when she wanted to scream, *Don't leave me, don't let this happen, I love you.*

"No cries of joy?" he pressed, without apparent bitterness, but Mallory was angered all the same.

For a moment, she forgot her anguish, her desperate need to make peace. "What you do with your employees is your business," she parried coldly.

Nathan came to sit at the table across from her, his hands cupped around his coffee mug, his dark, accusing eyes fixed on Mallory's face. "How long are we going to keep this up, Mallory?"

Mallory looked down at her own coffee; it was half gone and she hadn't tasted it at all, had no conscious memory of drinking it. "How long are we going to keep what up?" she retorted.

Nathan spat a swearword, tilted his head back, closed his eyes. "Mallory, I didn't fire Diane for the reason you're thinking," he offered, in the tones of one offering sanity to a raving maniac. "I don't need her anymore."

"Define 'need,' if you don't mind," Mallory ventured, aware of the caustic note in her voice but unable to alter it.

The dark eyes were suddenly riveted to her face, hurting where they touched. "Damn it, talking to you is like sparring with a shadow! And kindly stop trying to switch this conversation off into all my imagined transgressions!"

Mallory sat back in her chair, folded her arms stubbornly across her chest and waited.

Nathan gave an irritated sigh and shook his head. "I'm trying to tell you that I don't need Diane because I don't need a *press agent*. I'm retiring, Mallory."

Nothing he could have said would have startled her more. Mallory's coffee spilled onto the tablecloth as she put it down with a jolt. *"Retiring?"* she choked. "Nathan, why didn't you tell me?"

He scowled, his gaze fierce, challenging. "If you hadn't rushed out of here in a huff, I would have. And then at the penthouse, if you'll remember, we weren't into heavy discussions."

Mallory remembered all right, and she yearned for that stolen, glorious time. Perhaps, even if their marriage somehow survived this agreed separation, they would never soar like that again, never share souls and bodies quite so fully. She was mourning when she spoke again. "Aren't you a little young to retire?"

"Why shouldn't I retire?" he shot back sharply. "Do we need the money?"

Mallory might have laughed if the situation hadn't been so serious. Nathan had been wealthy long before their marriage, and money had never been an issue. "What do you intend to do with your time?" she hedged.

Nathan's eyes were brooding, defying her to discuss

the subject they were skirting. "I didn't father that baby, Mallory," he said bluntly.

Mallory knew he hadn't; the confrontation with Renee Parker had convinced her of that much. But something inside her insisted that she deny what she knew to be truth, that she use the issue to keep Nathan at a safe distance.

"Mallory."

She met his eyes. "Assuming that someone really paid Renee to file that suit—"

"Assuming? Mallory, she as much as told you someone did! And that someone was, undoubtedly, Diane Vincent."

"She might have been scared—Renee, I mean—"

"The baby *isn't mine!"*

"Okay," Mallory said in a voice that was at once agreeable and frantic.

Nathan was obviously frustrated. "My God, you still don't believe me, do you?"

Suddenly, despite her earlier certainty, Mallory didn't know the answer to that question. All her instincts told her that Nathan was and always had been a faithful husband, but she could not fully trust them. Wishful thinking, in a situation like that one, was an easy trap to fall into. Maybe she'd done just that that morning, when she'd sought out Renee. Maybe she'd only believed Nathan innocent because she couldn't bear not to.

"We've been apart so much, Nathan," she said reasonably, sanely. "Women offer themselves to you as a matter of course. You'd be superhuman if you—"

But Nathan was on his feet so suddenly that his chair overturned with a crash, and his hand was hard under Mallory's chin. "I'll tell you about me, Ms. O'Connor!" he cried in a controlled roar. "I love my wife! And while I may have been tempted to bed down the occasional groupie, I never have!"

Instantly furious herself, Mallory thrust his hand aside and stood up. "Damn it, Nathan. Stop!" she screamed. "You would hardly confess to an indiscretion when you have every reason to believe that I would fall apart before your very eyes!"

Something violent contorted Nathan's big frame; Mallory could feel it even though they weren't actually touching. When it passed, he spoke again, in ragged tones. "If I were callous enough to sell you out like that, Mallory, I wouldn't care how you reacted, would I?"

Hot tears were smarting in Mallory's eyes. "Maybe you just didn't plan on getting caught!"

A muscle moved in Nathan's jaw, and ominous rage made his throat work, but he said nothing. He turned away from Mallory and stormed out of the house, slamming the door behind him.

Mallory sank back into her chair and dropped her head to her trembling arms, too shattered to cry. The separation of the McKendricks was off to a less than tender start.

Probably unable to refrain any longer, Trish knocked on Mallory's kitchen door bright and early the next morning. One look at her friend's tear-swollen face brought her scurrying across the uneven linoleum floor to offer an embrace.

Mallory cried, and so did Trish. But neither spoke until they had left the house and walked down the muddy path through the orchard to the Sound. The tide was in, and it did much, in its ancient and dependable way, to soothe Mallory.

After an interlude of reflection, Trish bent, slender in her worn blue jeans and red windbreaker, to pick up a small piece of driftwood and fling it into the bubbling surf. "What happened, Mall?"

Mallory overturned a barnacle-covered rock and

watched dispassionately as the tiny sand crabs living beneath it rushed in every direction. "I'm not sure," she said.

"What the hell does that mean?"

Mallory abandoned the pandemonium she'd created in the sand to sit down on a bleached-out log and wriggle the toes of her sneakers in a tangle of wet kelp. "You read about the paternity thing?"

Trish nodded, letting the low tide surge around her ankles. "You must know that's a crock," she observed, squinting in the springlike sun.

Mallory swallowed miserably. "The crazy thing is, Trish, I *do* know that. I think I knew it from the time the story broke. But instead of saying that, and standing my ground, I drove up to Eagle Falls and confronted her."

Trish sighed. "I guess I would have done that, too," she conceded finally, though she clearly disapproved. "Was Nathan upset about it?"

"He saw it as a lack of trust on my part."

"And?"

"And we can't seem to talk about it without fighting, Trish. My God, even when I wanted to say that I believed in him, I couldn't. It was as though that part of me had been shoved aside."

Trish came to sit beside Mallory, her hands cradling her knees. "Do you love him?"

Mallory nodded glumly.

Trish's soft blond hair danced around her face as she studied her friend. "But still you wanted to keep him at a distance, didn't you, Mallory?"

Mallory's mouth dropped open, but before she could say anything, Trish went bravely on.

"You know what I think, Mall? I think you're trying to hold onto your old life—the life you had when your parents were still alive. Look at you—you're married to a millionaire, for God's sake, and you *insist* on living in that little crackerbox of a house because that way you won't have to let go of Mommy and Daddy."

Mallory shot to her feet, her cheeks crimson, her throat closing and opening spasmodically over a surging fury. "That's a lie!"

"Is it, Mallory? You've been married to that man for over six years and I'll bet you haven't spent more than two or three nights at Angel Cove in all that time! And if it weren't for that damned soap opera, which everyone knows makes you *miserable,* you probably wouldn't set foot inside the penthouse either! And then there's your name—"

"Shut up!" Mallory shrieked.

Trish stood up calmly, faced her friend. "Your parents are dead, Mallory. Dead. Gone. And, baby, it's forever!"

Mallory was trembling; she wanted to turn and run away from Trish, from all the hurtful things her friend was saying, but she couldn't move. It was as though she'd become a part of that beach. Tears coursed down her cheeks, and her throat ached over screams of protest.

And Trish hugged her. High in the azure sky, a lone gull squawked in comment.

Mallory sniffled inelegantly and moved to dash at her tears. "How can you—say such—things?—"

Trish shrugged, her hands firm on Mallory's shoulders. "Mallory, grow up. You love Nathan—fight for him."

Drawing deep restorative breaths, Mallory shook her head. "We've agreed to separate for a while, Trish. And I th—think we need the time apart."

Trish shook her head in angry wonder. "You've had too *much* time apart already, don't you see that? Go to him, tell him everything you're feeling—contradictions and all."

But Mallory was drawing back inside herself, refusing to hear the reason in Trish's suggestion, refusing to think that she didn't belong in the small house beyond the orchard anymore.

And after that, there was no reaching her.

Nathan stood at the living room windows in his own house, looking out over the peaceful vista of sea and sky and mountains. Angel Cove itself was sapphire blue and sun-dappled that day, and boats with brightly colored sails bobbed in the distance. Beyond them rose Mt. Rainier, snowy and impervious even as she favored lesser beings with a rare view of her rugged slopes.

"Mr. McKendrick?"

He started slightly, having forgotten that he wasn't alone. Even though the band was gone for the time being—some of them hadn't taken the news of his retirement any better than Diane had—the housekeeper was always in residence.

Mrs. Jeffries stood in the center of the spacious room now, carrying a china coffeepot with steam curling from its spout and looking nervous. The stains in her cheeks, no doubt, were the result of the scandal and shame served up by the ever-vigilant press.

"What is it?" Nathan demanded, none too politely.

"Th—There's a man at the door, asking to see you."

"Who?"

Mrs. Jeffries actually shuddered, and the coffeepot was in peril. "I think he's a process server!"

Nathan sighed, exasperated and weary. "Show him in, please. And put down that coffee before you burn yourself!"

The housekeeper obeyed, then scurried out into the hallway again.

Nathan looked at the coffee and distractedly shook his head, even though there was no one to see. He'd had too much coffee during the long night, and his nerves were crackling under his skin like high-voltage wires.

A moment later, a man in a sedate business suit

entered the room and looked at Nathan with obvious recognition. "Nathan McKendrick?"

Irritated, Nathan simply held out his hand.

The visitor extended a folded document and then fled.

After parting with Trish, Mallory made her way back toward the house alone. Cinnamon met her in the middle of the orchard path, bounding and yipping in greeting.

The pat Mallory gave the animal was half-hearted, at best. Reaching the house, she filled Cinnamon's bowl from the dogfood bag on the screened porch and set it down near the door.

The telephone rang suddenly, and the sound of it reverberated through Mallory's body to her very spirit. She crossed the kitchen floor with such speed that she bruised her knee on one corner of the big wood-burning stove, and tears of physical pain were brimming in her eyes. "Hello!"

"Hi," Brad Ranner said, as easily as though they'd never argued, never shouted at each other over cross purposes. "How's life in the wilds of Puget Sound?"

Mallory's disappointment was crushing; she had hoped, desperately, unaccountably, that the caller would be Nathan. "Wild," she answered in a peevish, dispirited whisper.

"I'm sorry about that scene at the penthouse the other day, Mallory—I really blew it. Forgiven?"

Mallory sighed, rubbing her throbbing knee and grimacing. "Brad, I haven't changed my mind. I'm still leaving the show."

Brad's voice was as smooth and warm as the fresh butter Mallory's mother had always served with steamed clams. "In view of Nathan's latest escapade, I'm surprised."

Mallory closed her eyes tight, but the gesture was no

help against the sudden knotting pain in her stomach and the ache beneath her skull. "Brad," she responded evenly, "I don't care if my husband impregnates a *hundred* groupies—I'm still not going to take my clothes off on national television."

"Maybe we could work around that."

Mallory bit her lower lip and tried to think clearly, but she was simply too tired and too confused.

"Mall?"

She drew herself up, summoned all her flagging strength. "I'm here. Listen, Brad—I'm not really an actress, you know? The show was a kind of a—well—a lark for me. But now I'm tired and I can't think and—"

"Babe, this paternity thing has really leveled you, hasn't it?"

Why lie? "Yes. And I'll thank you not to make any more remarks about Nathan's alleged escapades, Brad."

He sighed. "I was out of line, and I'm sorry."

Even though she knew he couldn't see the gesture, Mallory nodded. "C—could we talk another time, Brad?"

"Of course, sugar. You'll think about renewing your contract, won't you?"

Mallory McKendrick was not sure of many things at that point, but she was sure about one in particular. She hated memorizing lines, standing under bright lights and before cameras, getting up before dawn to go to the studio to be smothered in makeup. "No, Brad. I'll finish out my commitment, but that's all."

"Fine," Brad said, his calm manner gone. "You're fired!"

"Thank you very much."

"Mallory!"

Mallory replaced the telephone receiver gently. She had no more than stepped back from it when she felt a wild relief. For all the things that were wrong in her life, she'd taken one positive step. Once the few episodes she was legally bound to do had been taped, she would be free.

Maybe too free, she thought as the fact that Nathan was living in one house and she in another displaced her momentary pleasure.

She turned, looked around the humble kitchen, and saw that it looked almost exactly as it had when her mother had walked out of it for the last time. Was Trish right? Was she trying to cling to two people who no longer existed?

I'm on some kind of psychological roll here, she thought with grim humor. And she knew then that, on some subconscious level, she'd been waiting here, all this time, for parents she knew could not return to her.

Mallory wiped away the tears that had welled up in her eyes and reached resolutely for the telephone again.

Mrs. Jeffries spoke in crisp answer, her voice harried and sharp. Undoubtedly, people had been calling from all over the world, shocked by the news of Nathan's retirement. Not to mention Renee Parker's accusation.

"This is Mrs. McKendrick," Mallory said wearily, her pride thick in her throat as she swallowed it. "May I please speak with my husband?"

There was a pause, perhaps to give the loyal housekeeper time to decide whether Mallory was really Nathan's wife or just some brazen fan. "He isn't taking calls now, Mrs. McKendrick—"

Mallory felt crimson fury pounding in her cheeks. It was bad enough to grovel, without being turned away like some salesperson or irksome reporter. "I want to talk to him *now!*"

Mrs. Jeffries reconsidered, and, a full two minutes later, Nathan ventured a cautious greeting into the phone.

Mallory didn't know where to begin; they'd made

such a tangle of things that any one of half a dozen conversational threads could have been picked up. She drew a deep, shaky breath, closed her eyes and took the plunge. "Do you think we could go back to square one and start over, Nathan?"

There was a silence on the other end of the line, and then a rasped, "I'll be right over."

Mallory remembered the things Trish had said to her that morning on the beach, and the sense of it all was undeniable. "No. I'll come there."

His voice was hoarse, broken. "Mallory—"

She swallowed painfully, knowing how troubled he was, regretting every moment she hadn't spent at his side. "Shh. We'll talk when I get there."

"But—"

Mallory hung up the telephone.

The villa overlooking Angel Cove was of graceful, Spanish architecture, and Mallory admired it anew as she approached. It was enormous, boasting a terra cotta roof and some twenty rooms in addition to a swimming pool and a plant-bedecked sun porch with its own hot tub. Holly trees grew in the yard, and the house looked out over the Sound and the private wharf where Nathan's boat, the *Sky Dancer,* bobbed on the water.

Mallory was so caught up in the ambiance of the place that she was startled by her husband's voice.

"Hi," he said, and she looked up to see that he was waiting on the front step. For all his strength, he looked so vulnerable in that moment that Mallory's heart constricted.

"Hi," she replied, when she could speak.

He was standing up, striding toward her. When they were face to face at the base of the long flagstone walk, he brought gentle hands to her shoulders and bent to kiss her forehead. "I would have killed the fatted calf, but we don't have one."

Mallory smiled up at him, feeling shaky inside. What if they ended up hurting each other again? What if—

Firmly she caught herself. "I'd settle for a glass of white wine and a dip in your hot tub," she said.

He laughed. "You're on. The phones are unplugged, and Mrs. Jeffries has stern orders to tell any visitors that we're lost in the Cascade Mountains."

As they walked toward the magnificent house, Mallory tucked under Nathan's arm and wondered how to begin straightening things out. She ventured a serious statement. "No sex, though—okay? Every time we try to talk, we end up making love and nothing gets settled."

He held up one hand, as if to swear an oath. "No sex," he promised. And then an evil light flashed behind the pain in his dark eyes. "For now," he added.

Less than five minutes later, they were both in the swirling waters of Nathan's hot tub, Mallory sipping the requested white wine. The black and white swimsuit she wore was one she'd left behind one summer day, and she was grateful that it was her own; she wasn't quite sure she could have dealt with all the questions that would have arisen in her mind if it hadn't been.

Nathan, his strong, tanned forearms braced against the tiled edge of the hot tub, watched her for several long seconds before he ventured, "Mallory, I was served with the summons today—it's official."

She wanted to avert her eyes, to look down at the warm water bubbling around her or stare into her wineglass. But she didn't. She forced herself to meet his gaze squarely. "I'm sorry."

He sighed, and his voice, when he spoke, was low and rough. "My lawyers want me to settle out of court."

"Do you plan to?"

Nathan shook his head quickly, but he didn't look affronted by the question. "No. That would mean an admission of guilt."

Mallory swallowed. "Nathan, you know you're not guilty, and I know you're not. Maybe it would be easier if you did settle."

Nathan brought one gentle hand to Mallory's shoulder, and his eyes searched her face. "Do you, Mallory? Do you believe I'm telling the truth?"

She nodded. "I guess I was just hysterical or something. I don't know. Trish made me see that I might be—well, kind of holding out on you and on our marriage—trying to keep one foot in the life I had with my parents and one in the life you and I share."

He said nothing; clearly, he was waiting for her to continue. She drew a deep, shaky breath.

"I—I never realized it before, but I think Trish had a point. I mean, I kept on calling myself 'Mallory O'Connor' and then there's the house—"

Nathan smiled, traced the curve of her right cheek with an index finger. "Lots of women are using their own last names now, Mallory. It's a sign of the times."

"Well, I don't feel comfortable with it."

"The choice is yours, Mallory. With your career and everything, it makes sense to call yourself 'O'Connor.'"

Mallory flushed slightly at his mention of her acting; here was another subject they hadn't even touched on. She'd been shocked to hear that he planned to retire, and now he'd be shocked, too. Dear heaven, when had they stopped telling each other their plans and their hopes and their dreams? "I'm not renewing my contract with the soap, Nathan."

He raised one dark eyebrow. "That's news to me. Did you get another offer or something?"

She could see by the expression on his face, guarded as it was, that he was hoping she hadn't. "No. I just don't *like* acting. If I did, it would be different."

He looked away for a moment, pretending an interest in the fuchsias, ferns and healthy ivy plants thriving along one wall of the steamy room. "So what do you plan, as you asked me, to do with your time?"

Mallory took another sip from her wineglass, then set it aside. "The first thing I want to do," she began softly, her hand rising, of its own accord, to his muscle-corded shoulder, "is my part to make our marriage work. Nathan, we've grown so far apart. We don't share anymore—we don't act like married people."

He laughed, and it was a gruff sound, a sound of agreement. "That is truly an understatement, my love. You should have been the first to know that I planned to retire."

"And you should have been the first to know that I did, too. Oh, Nathan, what happened to us? Why did things change?"

"Change is inevitable, Mallory. As much as I'd like to be a part of you, we're two separate people and we've simply gone our own ways."

"Do you think we can find each other again?"

"I know we can. But it's going to take work, Mallory, and time—not to mention understanding and patience."

"Then maybe it's a good thing our careers won't be pulling us apart." She paused to touch his steam-dampened, fragrant hair, and then frowned. "I'm sure quitting the soap is best for me, but I'm not so certain about your leaving the music business. Nathan, it's a part of you."

He shrugged, then drew her close, so that their bodies were touching beneath the lulling churn of the water in the hot tub. "Lady, for you I would quit the *breathing* business. Besides, I'm tired—for the time being, all I want is you and one hell of a lot of rest." He bent his magnificent head, sipped mischievously at her lips. "Admittedly, those two objectives are about as compatible as oil and water."

She laughed, drew back slightly in his embrace, and looked up at him with dancing eyes. "No sex, remember?"

He groaned, made his case by nipping seductively at her lower lip.

"Nathan."

He stepped back, looking comically chagrined. "Just how long did I agree to abstain?" he demanded.

She was trembling with a desire that equalled or even surpassed his, but she managed a flippant toss of her head. "At least long enough to get upstairs. People don't make love in hot tubs, after all."

He chuckled and then made a growling sound in his throat as he wrenched her close again, trailed searching lips along the length of her tingling neck. "Don't they? Mallory, Mallory—you innocent."

She gasped involuntarily as his hand rose to cup her breast; it was a proprietary gesture, for all its gentleness, and it made her traitorous body yearn to offer itself in unqualified surrender. "P—Please—stop—"

But Nathan drew down her strapless, elasticized swimming suit top to reveal just one delectable breast. The nipple pulsed as his thumb stroked it to an inviting hardness, and the tender flesh surrounding that pink nubbin was being caressed not only by his hand, but by the warm, soothing water.

Mallory tried to protest, but all that came out of her mouth was a sound that was part croon, part whimper.

"Please, Mallory," he whispered, his lips burning at her ear like fire. "Let me see you—all of you. Let me touch you—"

"M—Mrs. Jeffries—," she reminded him breathlessly.

He drew the swimsuit down deftly, baring her other breast, her stomach, her abdomen. She stepped out of the garment and immediately forgot that it had ever existed, as a pulsing, insistent warmth surged through

125

her. She cried out softly as he closed hungry lips around the nipple of one breast, drew teasingly at its tip.

Her legs were wrapped around his waist almost before she knew what was happening, and she groaned as he took his leisurely pleasure at her breasts, leaving one only to devour the other.

Presently, he released her and set her back on her feet. She caught both thumbs under the top of his swim trunks and drew them down until he was as naked as she. Then, with gentle hands, she caressed him.

Nathan gasped with pleasure and stood with his feet planted wide apart so that he could be still more vulnerable to Mallory's touch. The passion she saw in his taut features made her want him desperately.

When he could bear the sweet torment no longer, he lifted Mallory out of the hot tub, climbed out himself and tenderly pressed her down onto a thickly padded chaise longue. He placed her feet gently onto the tiled floor, one on one side of the chaise, and one on the other.

She gasped and arched her back as he caressed the silken vee at the junction of her thighs, trailed soft, warm kisses over her rib cage, her stomach, the tingling flesh beneath her breasts.

He nibbled at the sweet peak of one breast. "Tell me what you want, Mallory."

She didn't have the breath to answer him; her body was doing that without words. Her hips moved in rhythm with the delicious torment of his fingers, and her hands clutched desperately at the ebony richness of his hair.

He mounted her gently, entered her just far enough to tease. "Mallory," he rumbled, his lips moist and commanding where her neck and shoulder met. "Tell me."

"I—I want you to f—fill me—"

Her reward was a swift thrust of his hips as he

plunged deep inside her, filling her, possessing her and yet, at the very same moment, surrendering. They moved as one person, both gasping words that made no sense.

Finally, Nathan lifted Mallory's hips, so that his shaft stroked the very core of her womanhood as it entered and withdrew, entered and withdrew. And then she cried out, shuddering, as the crescendo of their loving convulsed her, took primitive pleasure in his echoing groan of total release.

When, at last, they had both caught their breath and drawn apart, albeit unwillingly, there was a timid knock at the door leading into the kitchen.

"What?" Nathan barked irritably, as Mallory blushed profusely and plunged back into the hot tub in search of her discarded swimsuit.

"L—Lunch is ready," dared Mrs. Jeffries meekly, from beyond the door.

Mallory began to giggle unaccountably as she struggled into her suit, and the sound softened the awesome tension in Nathan's face and finally caused him to grin lopsidedly.

"We'll have it in the master bedroom," he replied, his eyes sparkling as he watched another blush rise in Mallory's cheeks. At last clothed—if somewhat more scantily than she would have liked—Mallory found Nathan's trunks and flung them at him furiously.

He caught them, but made no effort to put them on again. His grin widened as Mrs. Jeffries called out something and then went back to her duties.

Mallory bit her lower lip, annoyed with Nathan, annoyed with herself. "We'll have it in the master bedroom!" she mimicked.

Nathan laughed. "No doubt we will."

"I meant—oh, damn you—"

He arched one eyebrow. "Must be some kind of mating ritual," he mused.

Mallory crossed her arms over her breasts and stood stubbornly in the middle of the hot tub. "What are you talking about?"

"The way we always fight—before and after making love. It must have *some* significance."

"Why?" Mallory demanded sourly, her feet still firmly planted on the floor of the hot tub.

Idly Nathan pulled on his swim trunks, his eyes still full of mischievous musing. He slid easily into the bubbling, surging water again and approached her. "Why what?" he countered. "Why do our fights have significance, or why did I tell Mrs. Jeffries to serve lunch in the bedroom?"

Mallory retreated a step, wide-eyed and suddenly wary. "B—Both, I guess," she faltered, stalling.

He grinned, and advanced toward her cautiously. "I think we fight because when we make love we both become so much a part of the other person that it scares us. And I want lunch in the bedroom because I want *you* in the bedroom."

Mallory trembled. There was much truth in what he'd said about their lovemaking; they were both strong-willed people, both fierce individuals. And when their bodies joined in the throes of passion, she often felt as though she'd lost herself in the consuming fire, as though her separate identity had somehow been forged to his, creating a third person that neither of them really knew.

It wasn't surprising, really, to find out that Nathan had felt the same way. But as he drew too near, she was again aware of his incredible power over her, and she stepped back once more. "I—I for one intend to eat my lunch," she babbled inanely, trying to keep him at a distance. "I'm h—hungry and—"

He laughed, closed the space between them and caught her shoulders in strong, gentle hands. "Don't worry, pumpkin—you can eat undisturbed. I have, after all, a vested interest in seeing that you keep up your strength."

Just as he had probably intended her to, Mallory colored profusely. "Don't you ever think about anything besides sex?"

"Only rarely," he confessed in a gravelly tone that sent fresh desire stirring through her like warm butter. "Where you're concerned, it's a compulsion."

In spite of everything, she laughed into his damp, strong shoulder; in spite of everything, she listened as he told her, in gruff, sensuous tones, all that he meant to do to her in his bed.

And where he led, she followed.

Chapter 7

THEY SAT FACING EACH OTHER IN THE CENTER OF THE huge, love-rumpled bed, Nathan clad only in a pair of cutoff jeans, Mallory wearing a lace-trimmed teddy that was, like the swimsuit, a remnant of some other visit to her husband's house.

A dozen feet away, a fire crackled romantically on the hearth of a small, ornate ivory fireplace, and a new snow was drifting past the windows over the head of Nathan's bed. Still dazed from the lovemaking that had consumed the whole afternoon, Mallory sighed with warm contentment.

"What do we do now?" she asked, stifling a yawn.

An evil light sparkled in Nathan's dark eyes, but then he laughed at her sudden blush. "You're as pink as that delectable bit of silk you're wearing. What is that thing, anyway?"

Mallory laughed and scooted back a little, as though to withhold herself from this man who could take her whenever and wherever he pleased. "It's a teddy—don't you know anything?"

He grinned, and with a warm, exploring finger traced the snow white lace edging Mallory's bodice. "I know it drives me crazy. What I don't know is whether I like it better on or off."

"Lecher."

Nathan tilted his head to one side and chuckled. His finger slipped with tantalizing prowess into the warm, shadowed cleft between her breasts, then coursed upward, slowly, along the satiny length of her neck, to the supersensitive place beneath her right ear.

Mallory shivered, though she'd never been warmer in her life, and then glared at her husband. "Will you stop that, you sex fiend?"

He laughed, withdrew his tormenting hand and bounded suddenly off the bed. The light from the fire shifted and danced in fascinating patterns on the sun-browned, muscular expanse of his naked back as he went to a closet and began rummaging through a variety of items stacked on the top shelf. "All right," he conceded in a teasing voice that set Mallory to wanting him all over again, "I am a man of my word. No sex for at least three hours."

"That is so big of you," Mallory retorted, somewhat petulantly, her eyes still fixed on the splendid play of the muscles in his back and his powerful thighs.

"Noble is my middle name," he said.

"Albert is your middle name," Mallory countered, an obnoxious grin curving her lips.

Nathan whirled from the shelf, a Monopoly box clutched in both hands, his face a mockery of outrage. "And if you ever tell, I'll shave your mink jacket," he threatened, approaching the bed with long, ominous strides.

"Rash words," she shot back, reaching out and grabbing the game from his hands. "You forget how many charge cards I have."

The bed sloped a little as Nathan returned to his former position, facing Mallory, his long legs crossed at the ankles, Indian-style, and opened the Monopoly box. "You have me there," he said. "But Monopoly is another matter. I'm warning you, woman—if you buy Park Place and Boardwalk again and jam them with hotels, it's over between us."

Mallory smiled evilly and arched one eyebrow. "Is that so, fella?"

He rummaged through the little metal gamepieces tucked into a nook in the box. "Furthermore," he said, as though she hadn't challenged him at all, "I want the racecar this time, and that's it."

Mallory sighed with mock resignation and reached into the box to claim her personal favorite, the tiny Scottie dog. "Look out," she said fiercely, and, within fifteen minutes, she owned both Boardwalk and Park Place.

"I'm having an underwear party," Trish announced briskly, her voice warm with humor. "It's this afternoon at two and you'd better be there, McKendrick."

Mallory yawned into the telephone receiver and snuggled down into the warm vacancy on Nathan's side of the bed. Hearing him singing in the shower, she smiled to herself. "Underwear?" she echoed, her mind still fogged by last night's lovemaking.

"You rich people call it 'lingerie,' daaahling," Trish teased. "It's that silky, sexy stuff you wear under your clothes."

Mallory laughed, yawned again and stretched languidly in the warm bed. "Oh, *that*," she said in the tones of one who suddenly understands a consuming mystery. "Isn't this short notice for a party? I'm trying to conduct a reconciliation here, you know."

As if on cue, Nathan came out of the master bath, wrapped in a precariously draped towel, the water from the shower beaded on his powerful shoulders, an evil grin on his face.

"Okay, so I didn't give you two weeks and an engraved invitation," Trish retorted. "Just be here, will you? I booked the thing so Candy Simpson could get a bathrobe for half price, and most of my guests are only coming because they think you'll be here!"

Mallory gasped as Nathan tugged teasingly at the covers, revealing one sleep-warmed breast, and then circled the nipple with a wanton finger. "A—bathrobe —for—half price?"

Nathan replaced the exploring finger with his tongue, causing Mallory's nipple to harden in eager surrender, and she moaned.

"What the devil's going on over there?" Trish demanded, never in her life having been accused of subtlety.

Mallory arched her back and swallowed a contented purr as Nathan nibbled mercilessly at her breast. "It would serve you right if I told you, Trish Demming—"

"T—Two o'clock!" Trish sputtered in an obvious rush of understanding. "Candy's bathrobe is at stake!"

Nathan pulled the receiver from Mallory's hand and replaced it without interrupting his other enterprise at all.

There was a very becoming blush rising in Trish's cheeks as she opened her front door to Mallory that afternoon, but her blue eyes were sparkling with mischief. "How goes the reconciliation?" she whispered. "As if I needed to ask."

Mallory laughed. "Despite repeated interruptions, it goes well," she threw back.

Trish's modestly furnished living room was filled with familiar faces, including Kate Sheridan's.

"Did she give you that line about Candy Simpson's bathrobe, too?" Kate demanded from the leather recliner where Alex usually sat.

Mallory flashed a look of mock suspicion at Trish and nodded. "Was it just a ploy to get us here?"

"Of course it was," Trish confessed buoyantly. "Candy Simpson has more sense than the rest of us. She's in Hawaii, lounging in the sun and sipping Mai Tais."

Mallory shook her head as she shrugged out of her warm, snow-speckled jacket and thrust it into Trish's hands. "You rat. I thought I was on a mission of mercy!"

"You *are*," Trish imparted dramatically. *"I'm* the one who wants to get a bathrobe at half price!"

Despite the fact that she missed Nathan, despite the carefully veiled curiosity in the eyes of the half-dozen women in Trish's living room, Mallory enjoyed the lingerie party immensely. It felt good, after the rush of taping the soap every day for so many months, to participate in something so ordinary and frivolous.

"Have you heard about Trish's new business enterprise?" Kate Sheridan queried, once the party was over and she and Trish and Mallory sat alone in the Demmings's spacious kitchen, drinking coffee.

Mallory raised her eyebrows and assessed her younger friend with teasing interest. "Don't tell me they've recruited you to sell underwear!"

Trish laughed, but her eyes were full of sparkling, earnest dreams. "I passed my real estate exam, Mall."

Admiration and genuine pride caused Mallory to reach out and touch her friend's arm. "Congratulations! Good heavens, I didn't even know you were studying for it."

Trish rolled her bright blue eyes. "It was a beast, but I managed. Starting next Monday, I'll be talking the tourists into cozy island hideaways."

"Great," Mallory said, honestly delighted. There was only one real estate agency on the island, but they did a brisk business among the summer people. "Are you going to give Soundview Properties a run for their money?"

Trish shook her head. "Heck no, I'd have to be a broker to do that. I'm working for them."

"Sensational. I'd like the honor of being your first client."

Trish leaned forward, nearly spilling her coffee, and widened her eyes. "What?"

Mallory looked from Trish to Kate and grinned at the startled expressions playing in both their faces. "I want to sell my house," she said bluntly.

Trish emitted an undignified whoop, and Kate beamed her approval.

"It's about time," observed the latter. "If I were married to a hunk like Nathan, I'd ride around in his hip pocket!"

Mallory laughed. "Kate Sheridan, I'm *shocked!*"

"That's progress," Kate retorted with tart good humor. "You've stepped up from stupid."

"Thanks a lot!"

Trish giggled conspiratorially and hunched her shoulders beneath her pink velour shirt. "Mall, you were terrific this afternoon! Those women were positively *eaten up* with curiosity, but you didn't give them one damned thing to talk about."

"They'll make things up to fill the void," Mallory said somewhat ruefully, turning her empty coffee cup in one hand.

"Who cares?" Kate demanded. "They would anyway."

Trish's hand closed over Mallory's, warm and reassuring. "I really think you're doing the right thing, Mall. You love Nathan—I know you do."

Mallory nodded distractedly; suddenly, it was as though Renee Parker had joined the women sitting around that homey table, and the glow of the afternoon just past was somewhat tarnished by her unseen presence.

"You and Nathan ought to go away somewhere," Kate interjected quickly. "Now that he's retiring—"

Mallory shook her head, drew a deep breath and forced a brave smile to her face. "We can't—not yet, anyway. It would look as though we were running away. Besides, he still has that farewell concert in Seattle next month. If I know him, rehearsals will begin any minute."

"After that, then," Kate persisted, a small, worried frown creasing the space between her eyebrows.

Mallory shrugged. "I can't think that far ahead. I still have an obligation to Brad, for one thing."

"Brad!" Kate scoffed dismissively. "That creep is half your problem, if not all of it. Break your contract, Mallory, and see Alice Jackson over at the elementary school. They're looking for substitute teachers to fill in whenever the regulars are sick."

Mallory was gaping at Kate. "Break my contract? I can't do that!"

"Why not?" Trish asked cautiously. "You said you didn't want to act anymore."

"Well, there is such a thing as loyalty, you know." Mallory bridled stiffly. "A contract is a promise!"

"There are exceptions to every rule," Kate said with staunch persistence. "And besides, I'll lay odds that Brad Ranner is behind this paternity suit."

Mallory was stunned; until that moment, she had placed all the blame for Renee Parker on Diane. "W—Why would he do that?" she managed after a long, difficult pause.

Kate and Trish exchanged looks of exaggerated impatience before the younger of the two replied, "Mall, you dummy—Brad looks at you like you're made of spun sugar! If he thought he could get Nathan out of the picture, he'd do anything."

Mallory had known that Nathan was jealous of Brad Ranner, though she'd never understood why. Their relationship was harmless—almost like that of a brother and sister. And yet, Brad had been so outraged that she meant to quit the show—

But that was business, of course. She glared at Trish and Kate in turn and lifted her chin. "Diane Vincent got Renee to say those things about Nathan," she said firmly. "Brad wouldn't do a thing like that!"

"Wouldn't he?" challenged Kate, who seldom interfered in the problems of other people. "Wake up, Mallory. I've seen him and Nathan together, and they look like two lions about to do battle over the same quarry."

"Diane did it because Nathan fired her!" Mallory insisted, almost desperately.

"When was that?" Trish pressed. "Yesterday? The day before? It takes longer than that to arrange a lawsuit, Mallory—this thing has been in the works for weeks."

"It could still have been Diane!"

Kate shrugged. "Maybe they arranged it together," she said. "I wouldn't put anything past that she-cat either. Just watch your step around Ranner, because he's not what he seems to be."

Mallory felt sudden, unaccountable tears smarting in her eyes. Why was it so important to her to blame Diane? Kate and Trish weren't meddlers, and they were both extremely intelligent. Had they noticed something in Brad's manner that she'd missed?

God, why did she have to think about Renee Parker and that stupid paternity suit anyway?

Trish's pretty face crumpled with shared pain and deep concern. Unceremoniously, she dragged her chair closer to Mallory's and wrapped her friend in comforting arms. "I'm sorry, Mall. I should never have brought this up—"

Mallory sniffled, returned Trish's hug and drew back a little. "It's okay," she said bravely, dashing away the tears on her face. "You'll call me about putting the house on the market?"

Tears gleaming in her own eyes, Trish bit her lower lip and nodded.

Kate rose briskly from her chair. "Well, I've spent half of my next advance on lacy geegaws no man will ever see. I trust you earned your damned bathrobe!"

Both Trish and Mallory laughed, and the tension in that cozy room was broken, just as Kate had probably intended it to be. She laid a motherly hand on Mallory's shoulder.

"Come on, Mrs. McKendrick—I'll drive you home. If I know you, you walked over here."

Trish pretended to be very busy gathering up the coffee cups and spoons on the table. "Blizzards don't stop her. She has herself confused with the postal service. How does that go?—'neither snow nor sleet nor gloom of night—'"

"You pitiable innocent," Kate broke in. "When was the last time you mailed anything?"

Mallory laughed. "Don't let Kate disillusion you, Trish. She has a running war with the post office."

Kate was shrugging into a heavy woolen sweater-coat. "Only because they deliver my manuscripts by skateboard. Let's get out of here before I *really* get on my soapbox!"

Knowing Trish's house as well as she knew her own, Mallory said good-bye and went off to find her jacket again. Kate was waiting in her car a few minutes later when she went outside.

The snow was falling in the gray twilight by then, and the air was bracing, but not really cold. Mallory almost regretted agreeing to the offer of a ride home; it would have been nice to walk.

"You're serious about selling your house?" Kate asked as she eased the small car out of Trish's driveway and onto the main road.

Mallory nodded. "I realize now that I've been using it as a hideout, rather than a home."

"You were happy there once. Naturally, you're fond of it."

Again, Mallory nodded. She wondered what advice her parents would have given her if they'd been alive. Would they have believed that Nathan deserved her trust and loyalty, or would they have urged her to cut her losses and run?

The answer was easy. Janet and Paul O'Connor had liked and respected their son-in-law, after an initial wariness stemming from his unusual occupation, and they'd never been big on quitting.

"You're wondering what your parents would have thought about this paternity mess, aren't you?" Kate asked quietly.

Mallory chuckled. "Sometimes you amaze me. If you ever get tired of writing books, you could always become a mind reader."

"I'd probably make more money," Kate retorted with a wry grin. "I trust I can spare you the lecture about how you're a grown woman now and you should think for yourself?"

"I would be grateful if you did," Mallory said.

Kate's attention was fixed on the snowy road. "We didn't mean to upset you, Mallory—Trish and I. We just don't want you to be hurt anymore."

"You've never doubted Nathan since this thing started, have you, Kate? I don't think Trish has either. Tell me, why do you have so much confidence in him?"

Kate flipped on her windshield wipers and peered out at the snow-dappled night. "He wears his heart where his tie clasp should be," she said. "Love is an obvious thing, and I've never seen a more flagrant case than Nathan McKendrick's."

Mallory swallowed and looked out the window on her side of the car. "I wish I could be so sure as you are. S—Sometimes I think he loves me, and other times—"

"Yes?" Kate prodded gently.

"Other times I think he can't possibly be interested in someone as ordinary as I am."

"Then the fault lies in you, not in him. You need to believe in yourself, Mallory."

Since no point on the small island was very far from any other, it didn't take Kate long to reach Angel Cove. During that brief time, however, Mallory seriously considered what her friend had said. It was true that she didn't have much confidence in herself.

The question was, why? Paul and Janet O'Connor had been wise parents—they'd raised Mallory to believe she could do anything. And she hadn't made such a bad showing. She'd gotten excellent grades in college, graduated with a teaching certificate, walked onto the set of a soap opera and landed a promising part.

In the warm confines of Kate's practical car, Mallory sighed. Nothing she might accomplish seemed very impressive beside the glittering success that attended Nathan's every move. But, then, who did she need to impress?

"Won't you come in for a few minutes?" Mallory asked a few minutes later when Kate drew the car to a stop in front of the brightly lit house at Angel Cove.

Kate shook her head firmly. "I'd like to, but chapter seven awaits. Besides, the last thing you and that young man need is company."

Mallory laughed and opened the car door to get out. After thanking her friend and saying good-bye, she bounded up the snow-dusted walk to the front door.

Nathan was just coming down the stairs when she walked in, and the house was deliciously quiet without the numerous members of his entourage. He grinned, as though he'd read her thoughts, and she blushed at the images his closely fitted jeans and soft, white sweater inspired.

"Hi," he said. "Where's your underwear?"

Mallory gaped at him, having forgotten all about the sales party she'd just left. "I beg your pardon?"

Nathan laughed, approached his wife and placed gentle hands on her shoulders. "I wasn't getting personal, pumpkin. Didn't you go to some kind of party at Trish's?"

Feeling foolish and oddly electrified by this man who had been her husband for six full years, Mallory nodded. "It's not underwear, it's lingerie. And you don't bring it home the same day like you would if you shopped in a store. You just order it."

His gifted fingers were kneading her tense shoulders, and she could feel their warmth, even through her jacket. "Thank you for clearing that up. I'll rest easier knowing the straight scoop about underwear parties."

Mallory gave him a slight shove, although the last thing she wanted at the moment was distance between them. "You're incorrigible. And by the way, you'd better give Alex a raise."

He lifted one eyebrow. "Yeah? Why?"

"Because the only reason Trish gave this party was to get a bathrobe for half price."

Nathan laughed. "Could we please drop this conversation? I've got a candlelight dinner all laid out in the dining room, and you're standing here talking about cut-rate bathrobes."

Mallory unbuttoned her jacket, and her flesh tingled pleasantly beneath her clothes as Nathan took the coat from her with practiced hands. "A candlelight dinner, is it? And we don't have to eat it in the bedroom?"

He feigned shock. "What? Eat on the very site of my ignoble defeat at Monopoly? Never."

Mallory smiled, wishing that their lives could always be this way—unhurried, romantic—and private. "Tell me about this candlelight dinner. Did you cook it?"

"Yes," he said, guiding her out of the entry hall and through the doorway that led to the imposing formal dining room. "Mrs. Jeffries is in Seattle, visiting her sister. Therefore, I had no choice but to venture into the wilds of her kitchen and concoct a culinary delight unmatched even by your canned soup and tuna sandwiches."

"Was that a dig?"

Nathan pointedly ignored the question and ushered Mallory to a chair at the long mahogany table that was usually lined with band members, their wives and girlfriends, and an accumulation of diverse hangers-on. Candles flickered elegantly over a repast of hot dogs, white wine, and limp french fries.

Mallory sat down with dignity, biting her lower lip to keep from laughing out loud. The ploy was unsuccessful.

Nathan, seating himself next to her, looked properly wounded. "You have no appreciation for fine food."

"What on earth did you do to those french fries? They look positively anemic!"

He arched one eyebrow. "I put them in the microwave," he answered defensively.

"After taking them from the freezer, no doubt?"

"Of course."

"I see. Well, they're far more appetizing if they're browned in the regular oven."

"Thank you, Julia Child."

Mallory laughed and dutifully began to eat, and even though the french fries were still partially frozen and the hot dogs weren't much warmer, she couldn't remember a better meal.

"I'm selling my house," she announced, once the fare had been consumed, her eyes on the kaleidoscope colors the candles were casting into her wineglass.

There was a short silence, followed by the inevitable, "Why?"

Mallory swallowed, though she had yet to touch her wine, and met her husband's dark gaze. "Because it's foolish to hang around over there, waiting for my childhood to come back."

Nathan's hand gently covered both of Mallory's.

"The place means a lot to you," he said, and she couldn't tell whether he was opposing her plans or approving them.

"I need to do it, Nathan—it feels right."

"Then do it."

"W—We have too many things that are yours or mine, and so few that are ours."

"Everything I have is yours, Mallory—I thought you knew that."

She felt tears burn in her eyes as she looked around at the huge dining room, with its elegant furnishings, its twin chandeliers, its oriental rugs. "I—I've spent so little time here, I feel like a guest."

"You still don't like this house, either, do you, Mallory? You're only here to please me."

She shook her head quickly. "I love this house, Nathan. It's so spacious and airy and elegant. It's just that usually—well—"

Nathan finished for her. "Usually, there are too many people here."

Glumly, Mallory nodded.

"That will change now," he said, and his gaze shifted from Mallory's face. "I'm retiring, remember?"

Though she knew that he hadn't meant her to, Mallory heard the reluctance in his voice. If he was reluctant now, how would he feel in a few weeks, a few months, a year? His career was understandably important to him. Would the loss of it make him bitter?

"I think one unemployed McKendrick is enough. Don't give up music because of me, Nathan. I couldn't bear to be the cause of that."

His eyes returned to her face now, but their expression was unreadable in the dim light. "I love you, Mallory—and I need you. Our marriage is more important to me than anything else in my life, including music."

"But you really don't want to quit, do you?"

He left his chair to stand beside hers, and his hand was gentle under her chin. "I'm not sure, Mallory. The only thing I really have a handle on right now is that our marriage is on shaky ground."

Mallory nodded in sad agreement and searched his face with wide, anxious eyes. "Nathan, please don't retire because of me. There has to be some other way."

He tilted his head to one side. "We need time, babe. Besides, do you think you're the only one who ever gets tired?"

Mallory had been to dozens of Nathan's concerts, and she was suddenly conscious of the incredible energy he expended when he performed. Add to that the constant travel and the endless rehearsals, and the formula for physical and emotional exhaustion was complete. "Then take six months off," she said quickly, "or even a year."

He looked away, considering. "A year," he said, finally. "I'll take a year off. At the end of that time, we'll talk again, Mrs. McKendrick."

Mallory offered a handshake to seal the bargain, but Nathan did not return the gesture in the usual way. Instead, he turned her hand and kissed the delicate, supersensitive skin on the inside of her wrist.

She trembled involuntarily, and Nathan chuckled in gruff amusement.

"Ummmm," he teased. "A year of candlelight dinners and lovemaking—I may never go back to work."

His tongue found the inside of her palm, teased it ruthlessly. "You'll—be—bored," Mallory managed, between gasps of helpless pleasure.

He drew her up and out of the chair, held her close. "Never that," he said, his lips at her temple now.

"Nathan."

His hands were drawing her sweater upward, making warm, soothing circles on the small of her back. "I want you," he said.

144

Mallory shivered as both his index fingers found their way beneath the waistband of her jeans and circled her to meet boldly at the snap in front. It gave way, and so did the zipper.

Mallory gasped as he drew her jeans down over her hips, her thighs, her ankles. "Nathan," she protested, even as she stepped out of the jeans, "This is the dining room!"

He was kneeling before her now, and his hands were idly stroking her ankles, first one, and then the other. "How appropriate," he said.

In the morning, Mallory awakened to find that the snow had stopped. Humming, pleased that she had for once woken up before Nathan, she scrambled out of bed and made her way into the master bath. There, in the massive sunken tub, she took a long, luxurious bath.

She was about to get out of the tub again when she noticed the froth of pink chiffon hanging, half-hidden, from a peg on the inside of the open door.

Do not jump to conclusions, Mallory, she thought. Slowly, she rose from the tub, climbed out and wrapped herself in a thick, thirsty towel. Her feet seemed reluctant to obey her mind as she forced herself toward the door and the bit of pink fluff hanging so naturally upon it.

It's probably mine, she assured herself. *I probably left it here, like the swimming suit and the teddy and—*

She took the garment down from its peg carefully, frowned as she turned it in her hands. It was a nightgown, short and tiered with lace-trimmed ruffles, and Mallory had never seen it before in her life.

She swallowed the aching lump that had risen in her throat and read the tiny gold label tucked away in one seam of the gown. The words stitched there made Mallory's eyes widen, replaced her rage with embarrassment, and caused her to stomp one foot and bellow, "Nathan McKendrick!"

He appeared as though summoned from a genie's lamp, peering with comical caution around the framework of the door.

"This isn't one bit funny!" she cried, waving the gossamer pink gown at him. "How long did it take poor Mrs. Jeffries to stitch 'Trust me, Mallory' onto this label!"

Nathan's broad, bare shoulders moved in an idle shrug. "Not long—she's a whiz with a needle."

She was still waving the nightgown. "I thought this was—I thought—"

"For shame, Mrs. McKendrick."

"Rat!"

He laughed. "Put your clothes on before I ravage you. We're spending the day in Seattle."

Mallory flung the nightgown at him, embarrassment still coloring her cheeks and quickening her breath. She couldn't have spoken if it had meant her life.

Nathan dodged the assault of pink ruffles and swatted her playfully on the backside. "Where is your sense of humor, woman?"

Seething, Mallory swung one foot at him, trying to kick him in the shins. She missed, and her towel slipped unceremoniously to the floor, baring her to his delighted gaze. She bent to retrieve the towel, but he was too quick—he grabbed it and waved it as though it were a matador's cape.

"Toro!" he yelled.

Despite her fury and her embarrassment, an involuntary smile tugged at one corner of Mallory's mouth. She kicked at him again, somewhat half-heartedly this time, and, in an instant, he had dropped the towel and caught both her elbows in his hands, pulling her close to him.

She wriggled, trying to free herself, but the motion only increased her awareness of Nathan's hard, masculine frame. "I th—thought we were g—going to Seattle," she stammered.

He laughed gruffly and buried his face in her neck to nibble at the pulsing flesh there. The clean scent of his hair confused Mallory's senses, so that she no longer knew whether she wanted to be loved or left alone. "We are going to Seattle," he said. "Later."

They caught a midmorning ferry and enjoyed a certain amount of privacy, since the early rush was over. Mallory, publicly visible only on the soap opera, was not generally recognized anyway, but Nathan was known the world over, and keeping a low profile was not so easy for him. He managed it that day, for the most part, having dressed circumspectly in old jeans, a plaid flannel shirt and a denim jacket. Though there were the usual questioning stares, not one of the other passengers approached either him or Mallory.

"I think I'm losing my touch," he confided to Mallory, with a grin, clasping his gifted hands together on the snack-bar tabletop and leaning forward.

Mallory giggled. "Not likely, handsome." She stole a surreptitious glance at two teenage girls sitting in another part of the snack bar. Though they were trying to be subtle, their wide eyes kept straying to Nathan. "They can't be sure whether you're you or not. It would be humiliating, after all, to ask for your autograph and then find out that you're a crane operator from Bremerton."

Nathan laughed softly, and there was something wistful in the sound. "Sometimes I wish I could be."

Mallory had been stirring her diet soda with her straw, but the motion stopped at her husband's words. "Really? Why, Nathan?"

But he was looking away now, and that wistful note that had sounded in his laugh and in his voice had stilled and risen to haunt his eyes. He watched the gulls soaring alongside the ferry, just a few feet beyond the window, and the muscles beneath the shoulders of his worn denim jacket were oddly slack.

Saddened for a reason she could not have begun to explain, Mallory reached out to cover one of his hands with her own. "Nathan?"

He sighed and turned back to her. "What?" he asked.

"Why do you wish you could be a crane operator from Bremerton?" she insisted.

He sat back in the unaccommodating plastic chair, and his shoulders were taut again. "I guess because their lives seem so peaceful and ordered to me. They go to work in the morning, come home to cold beer and good sex and the evening news. Some little kid in flannel pajamas tries to run over their feet with a plastic motorcycle that has pedals and—"

Mallory chuckled, though unaccountable tears were smarting in her eyes. "Do you wish we had children, Nathan?"

He looked down quickly at the Styrofoam coffee cup. "Maybe," he muttered after a long, painful pause.

Mallory looked out at the blue-gray sky, the water, the tree-lined shore in the distance. Inadvertently, she'd touched on a subject she hadn't meant to broach —children. Her arms ached for a baby of her own, a baby of Nathan's, but there had never been any time in their hectic lives to seriously consider starting a family.

Too, thinking of babies made her think, inevitably, of Renee Parker. Much of her pain, she knew now, had originated not so much in the fact of Nathan's alleged betrayal, but in his having a child that would not be hers.

With as much subtlety as possible, Mallory took a paper napkin from the table and dried the tears that glistened in her eyelashes. She drew a deep breath and forced a shaky smile to her mouth. "How dare you imply that only crane operators have good sex?" she demanded. "Not an hour ago, Mr. International Rock Star, you were pretty happy yourself."

Nathan laughed and made a growling sound, low in his throat, and, after that, they didn't speak of children again, but of their plans for the day.

Mallory loved her husband and was happy in this new wealth of time and closeness they were sharing, but she sensed a certain distance between them, too. Renee Parker was like a specter in their midst, unseen but always there.

After leaving the ferry, the McKendricks drove to a place they both loved—Pike Place.

The Pike Place Market, with its vegetable stands and open fish markets and craft items of every sort, was a big tourist attraction during the summer, but, now, in winter, it was less crowded.

After leaving the car, Mallory and Nathan ventured inside the large, aging building that comprised much of the market. Here, exotic parrots squawked in their cages, striking up incoherent arguments with the occasional wino. Shopkeepers sold everything from antiques to scrimshaw, dolls to old movie magazines. One merchant dealt in colorful kites of every size and shape, while another sold specially tinted photographs that made the posers look like fugitives from the distant past.

Nathan paused in front of this shop, his hand warm and strong over Mallory's, and studied the sample photographs on display in the windows. The men in the pictures were dressed, like the women, in period costume—some resembled outlaws, some lawmen, some cavalry officers. The women could choose from such nineteenth century gems as long dresses with high Victorian collars and sweeping feathered-and-flowered hats, the delightfully skimpy garb of a dance-hall girl, or the calico-and-bonnet attire of a pioneer wife.

Nathan extended a crooked elbow in a gesture of

grand invitation, his eyes sparkling. "Shall we, Mrs. McKendrick?" he asked formally, the merest hint of a grin tugging at his lips.

Mallory took the offered arm with decorum. "Oh, let's do, Mr. McKendrick," she replied.

The coming minutes were a delight of laughter and confusion—the McKendricks inspected costume after costume, before reaching a mutual decision. In the end, the photographer posed them as a lawman and a dance-hall girl—Nathan sitting sternly at a round table, a straight shot of pseudowhiskey in the curve of his gun-hand, a remarkably authentic handlebar mustache stuck to his upper lip, a star-shaped badge gleaming on his rough tweed coat. He wore a round-brimmed hat that gave him a sort of menacing appeal, and his Colt .45 lay within easy reach on the tabletop.

Mallory, wearing a satiny merry-widow and fishnet stockings, was posed beside him, one shapely leg resting on the seat of a wooden chair. Her hair, pinned up for effect, was half-hidden by a saucy little hat constructed mainly of satin, feathers and loose morals.

Both the marshal and the soiled dove had a hard time keeping straight faces until after the picture had been taken.

Chapter 8

THE CRAZY, QUIET JOY OF THAT DAY NOTWITHSTANDING, Mallory was still not well, and, once in her regular clothes again, she felt oddly deflated. Since there would be a twenty-minute wait for the special photograph, she sank gratefully into a chair at one of the tables in the wide hallway outside the shop and sighed.

Nathan gave her a gentle, discerning look. "Getting tired?"

She nodded. "I'll be all right in a minute, though."

Still standing, Nathan reached out and touched her face tenderly. "I'll scare up some coffee, pumpkin. Rest."

Coffee was one of Mallory's favorite vices—Nathan often said that it ran in her veins instead of blood—and a cup of that bracing brew sounded very good to her just then. "You drive a hard bargain, fella. Don't forget the artificial sweetener."

He laughed and turned away and, in only a moment, he had disappeared into the shifting, scattered crowds.

Mallory sighed and laced her fingers together on the tabletop, watching with interest as a little blond boy came bounding out of the nearby kite shop, clutching a colorful bag and beaming. He turned to look back at someone behind him and blurted, "Let's get ice cream now, okay? Let's get ice cream!"

"No way, Jamie," a very familiar feminine voice argued. "It's winter and I'm cold and it's hot chocolate or nothing!"

Mallory's mouth dropped open when Diane Vincent stepped into view. She looked away quickly, hoping that the woman wouldn't notice her, but she soon learned that she'd been unsuccessful.

"Hello, Mallory."

Mallory forced herself to look up, even to smile. *Might as well make the best of it, McKendrick,* she thought. "Diane," she said in greeting.

"It's incredible the way we keep running into each other, isn't it?" Diane asked as Jamie drifted off to look at a display of space-war books in a nearby window. "Is Nathan with you?"

"Yes, as a matter of fact," Mallory replied. Now that the child, Jamie, was otherwise occupied, she saw no reason to be polite. "Did you want to see him?"

Diane bridled slightly, then recovered herself. She was casual elegance itself in her trim flannel slacks, turtleneck sweater and blazer. "It's nice to see that you're putting on such a brave front," she said, ignoring Mallory's question.

Mallory sat back in her chair, pretending to be relaxed, though inwardly she was seething. She let Diane's remark pass and glanced at Jamie, who was still admiring the book store display.

"He's my nephew," Diane offered, without apparent emotion. "When are you going back to the soap, Mallory?"

Mallory met Diane's gaze again, shrugged. "I'm in

no particular hurry. Right now, I'm more concerned with my marriage."

Diane's pastel blue eyes sparkled with refined malice. "Now there's a hopeless pursuit, if I've ever heard one."

Swallowing hard, Mallory clung to her tenuous composure with all her strength. She could have kicked herself for giving Diane the opening she just had. "Speaking of hopeless pursuits, have you found a new job yet?"

There was a short, chilling silence, and then Diane smiled and tossed her beautiful head. "Oh, I'm in no hurry. Nathan was quite—generous—when we were together. I've got plenty of money. And now, plenty to do."

Mallory arched one eyebrow. *I should get an Emmy for this*, she thought. *Here I am, so calm and collected, when I'd like nothing better than to tear out this witch's hair, hank by shimmering hank.* "I'll bite, Diane. Why do you have plenty to do?"

"I'm planning to write a book—with a little help from a friend."

"Splendid."

"It's all about my affair with Nathan."

Mallory smiled slowly, acidly. "Oh, a novel. I would have expected nonfiction."

A fetching pink color rose in Diane's cheeks to complement the soft blue of her eyes. "You are so very good at deluding yourself, Mallory. That's probably how you're handling the paternity scandal, isn't it?"

"That suit is a crock, Diane, and we both know it."

Diane shrugged, and her eyes shifted briefly to her nephew before coming back to Mallory's face. "Maybe it is—she's a kid, after all. But I'm not, Mallory, and I've spent more nights with Nathan than you have. What do you think we were doing in all those hotel suites, all over the world—learning the languages?"

"Save it for your book, Diane."

"What book?" demanded a third voice, and Mallory looked up to see Nathan standing just behind Diane, a cup of coffee in each hand.

Diane squared her shoulders and faced him with a bravery Mallory couldn't help admiring. She ran one smartly gloved hand over the breast pocket of Nathan's denim jacket in an intimate, unpracticed-looking gesture and smiled. "I'm telling all, sugarplum. You don't mind, do you?"

Nathan looked, for just a moment, as though he would like to pour the coffee he carried down the front of Diane's sweater. "Of course not," he said, after a second or two. "Just make sure you get releases from all those bellhops and stagehands. That should take months."

Patches of crimson appeared on Diane's glamorous cheekbones. "Bastard," she hissed.

Nathan lifted one of the Styrofoam coffee cups in an insolent toast. "At your service," he said.

Bested, though Mallory suspected the condition was only temporary, Diane whirled away, collected her startled nephew from in front of the book shop and disappeared.

Mallory's hand trembled a little as she reached out for the coffee Nathan offered before sitting down at the table with her.

"Are you okay?" he asked after a moment.

Unable to look at him, Mallory nodded. "Sometimes I think that woman follows me around, just waiting for a chance to get under my skin."

"I should have fired her a long time ago."

Before Mallory had to come up with a reply to that, the clerk in the antique-photo shop came out and indicated with a gesture that the picture was ready.

They were inside the Porsche and well away from the Pike Place Market before either of the McKendricks spoke.

"Mallory, I'm sorry."

Mallory stole a glance at her husband, saw that he was looking straight ahead at the traffic. "For what?"

Still, he did not look at her; she would have felt his gaze if he had. "About Diane—about the paternity suit. All of it."

Mallory swallowed hard and laced her fingers together in her lap. "Do you have some reason to be sorry about Diane?"

"Nothing like you're thinking. I've never touched her, Mallory."

Closing her eyes, Mallory let the back of her head rest against the rich suede car seat. She couldn't help remembering the way Diane had touched Nathan back at the market. There had been some truth in Diane's words, too—she *had* probably spent more time with Nathan than Mallory herself. Could he have been in constant and close proximity with such a stunningly beautiful woman and never taken the pleasures she had surely offered time and again?

Weary misery squeezed Mallory's heart like a strong hand. Now, with her self-confidence at an unusually low ebb, it was so easy to think the worst.

"Mallory?"

She opened her eyes, stiffened in the car seat. Nathan was turning into the circular driveway of their apartment complex, shifting down, drawing the Porsche to a smooth stop. She stared at him in question, but said nothing.

"I think you need to rest for a while," he informed her, not quite meeting her eyes. "I'll see you upstairs and run a few errands while you're sleeping."

"What errands?" she retorted, and the words were rife with suspicions she hadn't meant to reveal.

Nathan's hands tightened on the steering wheel for a moment, then relaxed. When he looked at her, his dark eyes were snapping with sardonic fury. "I thought I'd go out and buy off all my former mistresses," he said coldly, "lest they write books. After that, I'll probably trip at least one old lady and roll a wino or two."

"Very funny!" Mallory shot back in a scathing whisper, as a delighted George rushed toward the car.

"If you're so worried about what I'm doing, Mallory," Nathan bit out, "why don't you hire a detective to follow me around?"

"That would make it too hard to keep on kidding myself!"

Before Nathan could reply to that, the doorman had reached Mallory's side of the car and opened the door to help her out. Her husband remained behind the wheel, glaring straight ahead, and when Mallory and George were clear of the vehicle, he shifted it into gear again and sped away, tires screeching on the slushy asphalt.

George cleared his throat but was careful not to let on that he'd noticed the obvious rift between the McKendricks. Graciously, he escorted Mallory all the way to the penthouse and left her only when she was safely inside.

Once she was alone, Mallory allowed the tears she'd been holding back in the name of dignity to flow unhampered. Damn it, she'd fallen right into Diane's trap, had allowed the bitch to spoil an otherwise delightful day.

Not bothering to dry her face, Mallory shrugged out of her coat and tossed it toward the brass coat tree just to the side of the doors, missing it completely and not caring. She paused to glance at the stack of mail waiting on the hall table. Even through blurred eyes, she could see that most of it was addressed to Nathan.

Except for one plain postcard, postmarked Eagle Falls. Mallory dashed away her tears and read the neat, flowing handwriting on the back with a sort of calm desperation.

I've been trying to call you. You're never where you said you'd be. My boyfriend got a job in Alaska, on a fishing boat. Could you get me a ticket to watch your TV show in real life?

Renee

At the end of the scatter-brained missive was a carefully printed telephone number. Mallory went to the closest phone—the one in the living room—and punched out the digits. After four rings, a woman answered.

"Is Renee there, please?" Mallory asked.

"Who is this?" the other party countered with tart suspicion.

"Mallory McKendrick," was the dignified response. *It's a good thing she can't see my mascara-streaked face,* Mallory thought. "Please—it's important that Renee and I talk."

There was a sort of irritated awe in the woman's voice as she called out, "Renee! It's that singer's wife!"

Mallory closed her eyes. *That singer's wife.* Well, at least she hadn't called her "Tracy."

"Tracy?!" chirped Renee, a moment later.

"Renee, my name is Mallory."

"Whatever. I've been trying to get a hold of you."

A minor ache began to pound beneath the rounding of Mallory's skull. "What do you want, Renee— besides a pass to watch us tape the show?"

"Just that. A ticket."

"What makes you think I'd be inclined to do you any favors?" The question was spoken calmly, evenly. Mallory was proud of herself.

"I never saw a real TV show before!" Renee wailed.

Instantly, Mallory was out of patience. Her dignity deserted her, and so did her determination to be civil. "Now you listen to me, you vacuous little bimbo, and you listen well. My husband is a good man, a decent man, and you've hurt him very badly with your lies. Furthermore, I don't give a *damn* that you've never seen a taping. Don't call me, Renee, and don't write to me—not unless you're ready to tell the truth!"

Incredibly, Renee began to cry.

But Mallory was not inclined toward mercy. She hung up the phone with a crash and was rewarded by the sound of applause from behind her.

She whirled and blushed hotly to see Nathan standing in the doorway of the living room, watching her. "Thank you," he said evenly.

A sob, sudden and raw, tore itself from Mallory's throat. "Damn you!" she shrieked, half-hysterical. "Why do you have to be handsome and famous and—and—"

He approached her cautiously, as one might approach a harmless creature flailing in a trap. Without a word, he drew her close, held her, tangled one soothing hand in her hair.

After a time, her grief abated a little, and the wracking sobs that had been rising from the very core of her soul became sniffles. "Damn," she whispered raggedly, "oh, damn—damn—"

Just then, the phone rang again. The sound so startled Mallory that she stiffened in Nathan's arms and gasped.

"I'll get it," he said gently, pressing the still-shaken Mallory into a chair before grasping the receiver and snapping, "Hello?"

Mallory watched as one of his eyebrows arched.

"How in the hell did you get this number?" Nathan demanded. His eyes, dark and unreadable, turned to Mallory as he listened to the caller's response. "She did? All right, so talk—yeah?— Thank you, Renee."

Mallory felt the color drain from her tear-smudged face as she saw the cold, murderous anger in Nathan's eyes. He hung up the telephone with a crash and

158

started toward the door without so much as a backward glance.

"Nathan!" Mallory cried out, scrambling out of the chair. "Where—what—"

He paused but did not turn to face her. "Brad Ranner," he said, in low, frightening tones. "Brad Ranner paid Renee to name me as the father of her baby."

Mallory's knees felt as though they'd turned to sand. "My God," she breathed, stunned. "Why?"

"I'm about to find out," Nathan replied, biting off the words, moving again. A moment later, he was gone.

After only a short deliberation, Mallory lunged for the telephone. She talked to a receptionist, then a stagehand before reaching Brad himself. He sounded harried, and his greeting was crisp and impatient.

"This is Mallory."

There was a short silence while Brad absorbed that simple statement. Apparently he'd accepted the call without his usual demand to know who was on the line first. At last, he sighed, and Mallory could almost see him rubbing his eyes with a thumb and forefinger, his customary gesture of annoyance. "Ah—my prima donna."

Mallory's voice was unusually high, but carefully modulated otherwise. "This is important, Brad."

"I'm sure it is, princess. Tell me, have you come to your senses, or am I in line for another spate of moral outrage?"

"What you're in line for, my former friend," Mallory replied calmly, "is orthopedic surgery. Nathan just found out why Renee Parker named him as the father of her baby."

Brad swore, then recovered himself admirably. "Wonderful."

"Brad, how could you?"

He sighed. "It's a long, complicated story, Mallory—"

"I'll bet it is."

"There were good reasons for what I did!"

"All of them taxable and very handy when the bills fall due, no doubt. You thought I'd be more likely to stay on the show if my marriage broke up, didn't you? Well you can take your stupid soap opera, Brad Ranner, and you can—"

"Mallory, for God's sake—"

She drew a deep breath. "Tut-tut, Brad, no time to quibble. If Nathan gets past studio security, you may find yourself in demand for body-cast scenes."

"You're calling from the island, right?"

"You wish. I'm calling from the penthouse."

Brad swore again and hung up.

Mallory replaced her own receiver slowly, pondering. Nathan would be furious that she'd warned Brad, but it had been the only thing she could do, in good conscience. When his storming rage had subsided, he would understand.

What would happen before that was anybody's guess.

Resigned, Mallory turned to walk away from the phone, only to be stopped again by its ringing. She stared at it for a few moments, and then answered with a sharp greeting.

"There you are," Trish said. "You rat, what are you doing in the city? We were supposed to arrange the sale of your house today."

Mallory sighed, relieved. "So arrange it. I trust you."

"Mall, are you all right? You sound funny."

She carried the phone to the teakwood bar, set it down and began the one-handed preparation of a stiff drink. "I'm fine. Wonderful. You and Kate were right —Brad Ranner did put Renee up to suing Nathan."

Trish drew in her breath. "Wow! Does Nathan know that?"

"Know it? He's on his way to the studio as we speak."

"No doubt planning to tattoo the whole ugly story on Ranner's face," Trish supplied.

"I hope he doesn't."

"Why?"

"Because I want to."

"Well, Mall, at least you're off the hook. I mean, now you won't have to go back and finish out your contract. Nobody would blame you if you didn't, not after—"

"Wait a second. A contract is a contract. I mean to honor mine, Trish."

"What?"

Mallory took a sip of her ineptly made drink and grimaced, setting the glass aside. "You heard me."

"Nathan will have a *fit!*"

"No, he won't, Trish. This is business and the other thing is private and—"

"And why don't you try rowing with both oars in the water for once, Mallory? He's going to *hate* that guy for the rest of his life, and I can't say I blame him! Do you really think he's going to want you *working* with the creep?"

"He might be mad at first, but—"

"Mallory, he'll be furious."

"Then he'll just have to get over it. When I promise to do something, I do it."

Trish made a disgusted sound and hung up on Mallory without further ceremony.

Mallory shrugged, hung up the phone and wandered off toward the bathroom. What she needed now was a hot bath and a long nap, and if the telephone rang again, she would simply ignore it.

It was dark when she awakened, and her stomach let

her know how hungry she was. With a sigh, she crawled out of bed, wrapped herself in a short pink satin robe and wandered out into the darkened living room.

There was a light in the kitchen, and she paused outside the swinging door for a moment, gathering her courage. When she entered that spacious room, she found Nathan sitting at the table, his back to her. The muscles beneath his plaid flannel shirt were rigid.

"You warned him," he said, without turning around.

"Yes."

"Why?"

Mallory lingered in the doorway, not daring to approach her husband. "I had to, Nathan."

His powerful shoulders moved in a weary sigh, and at last he turned to face her. There was a beleaguered look in his eyes, and he was pale beneath his Australian suntan. "Right—I know you did. But I really wanted to tear him apart."

Mallory entered the kitchen, letting the door swing shut behind her. "I'm starved," she said, making her way to the refrigerator. "How about you? Did you eat?"

He laughed, but it was a rueful, tired sound, and it tore at Mallory's heart even as she ferreted cheddar cheese and an apple from the refrigerator. "I'm not sure of very many things right now, pumpkin, but I do know that if I tried to eat anything, the results would be disastrous."

Mallory took the cheese to the cutting board, sliced off a haphazard hunk, and rewrapped what was left. When she had put that away, she joined Nathan at the table and bit into the apple with a lusty crunch.

"When do you start rehearsals for the Seattle concert?" she asked, hooking her bare feet in a rung of her chair.

Nathan rolled his eyes. "Soon. I wanted some time

with you before we started, but between Diane and Renee and now Brad, things have gotten pretty complicated."

Mallory nibbled thoughtfully at her cheese. "I know," she mused. "Maybe it would be better if you just concentrated on the concert for a while. After all, I've got a few more shows to tape, and—"

He broke in sharply. "Hold it. What did you just say?"

"I said you should concentrate on your concert. You know, choose the songs, rehearse—"

"After that."

Cold dread niggled and twisted in the pit of Mallory's stomach. She knew what he meant, but she widened her eyes in deliberate innocence. "About taping the shows?"

"Bingo."

"I have to, Nathan—I have a contract."

"Break it."

"No! I agreed to appear in a certain number of shows, and that's what I'm going to do."

An ominous calm came over Nathan as he rose slowly to his feet. "I don't believe this. After what that bastard did to us, you're actually going to *work* with him?"

Mallory bit her lower lip. So Trish had been right—all hell was about to break loose. "I'm not doing it for him, Nathan," she said quietly. "I'm doing it for myself. I don't want to remember it as an unfinished job all my life."

"How about our marriage, Mallory? How do you want to remember that?"

Fury stung Mallory like a giant bee, and the venom sent her surging to her feet, her late-night snack forgotten. "Are you threatening me, Nathan McKendrick?"

His face, so beloved, so familiar, was suddenly the

face of an angry stranger. "Damn it, Mallory, haven't we both been through enough without this? My lawyers can break your contract."

"Don't you dare call them in!"

"Why are you being so damned stubborn? You've been an asset to that show, but it isn't going to fold without you. Why can't you just cut your losses and run?"

"Nathan, this is a point of honor. *You've* never broken a contract in your life—why do you expect me to do it?"

A muscle in his jawline tightened, and dark rage shifted in his eyes. "This is different."

"Is it? Why—because it involves my career, not yours?"

He turned away from her then in an obvious effort at self-control, and drew a deep, ragged breath. "If it's so important to you, Mallory, why are you quitting at all?"

"Because I have no desire to get naked in front of several million people, for one thing!" The words were spoken impulsively, and when Mallory saw the responding charge of unbridled fury move in her husband's broad shoulders, she regretted ever saying them.

He whirled to face her. *"What?"*

She lowered her eyes. There was no going back now; it was too late to hedge. "The show is going on a cable network," she said evenly, "and that means they'll have a lot more freedom. There will be some nude love scenes."

"Brad wanted you to do *nude love scenes?"*

"Will you relax, Nathan? I said no, and that's the end of it. I'm just going to fulfill my contract and leave the show."

Nathan was standing stock still. "Why, that—"

"Nathan."

His dark eyes were fierce on Mallory's face. "Call

Ranner right now, Mallory," he ordered. "Tell him you're not coming back, ever."

"No."

Nathan's rage, like lava inside a volcano, was a frightening thing to behold. After raking his wife with one scathing, menacing glare, he turned and stormed toward the door without so much as a backward glance.

Mallory bolted after him. "Nathan, wait! Where are you going?"

His retreating form was a moving shadow in the darkness of the enormous living room. "Out!" he shouted back.

A second later, the front door slammed behind him.

Mallory had trouble focusing on the morning paper, and finally she yawned and tossed it aside in defeat. She hadn't slept the night before; she'd been consumed by rage one minute and wracked by pain the next.

Nathan had never come to their bed at all, though she had heard him pass by in the wee hours of the morning on his way to one of the extra bedrooms. She considered all the places he might have been before that and flushed with helpless fury.

Just then, the kitchen door swung open and he walked in, looking surly and unshaven and rumpled. He was barefooted, though he had, at least, pulled on a pair of old jeans.

"Good morning," Mallory said stiffly, watching, with irritated fascination, the play of the muscles in his naked back as he opened the refrigerator door.

By way of an answer, he scowled at her and then turned back to his perusal of the refrigerator's rather meager contents. Finally, he extracted a quart of milk and set it down on the nearest counter with a thump.

Mallory watched with amusement as he plundered the cupboards, one by one, too stubborn to ask where to find the items he wanted. When he'd found cereal and a bowl, the ransacking began all over again.

"Top drawer beside the dishwasher," Mallory said.

He made a face at her, wrenched open the drawer and took out a spoon. Some of the milk slopped over the side of his cereal bowl as he set it down on the table.

"The rock star at home," Mallory observed wryly as he fell into a chair and ate a spoonful of cereal. "If only *People* magazine could see you now."

He grumbled something insensible.

But Mallory was in the mood to plague him. "I hope that milk isn't sour," she mused. "The housekeeper only buys it to put in her coffee."

Nathan glanced sharply at the milk carton and then went on eating. Just the slightest color rose in his face as he munched; she knew he'd been alarmed and then realized that he'd already tasted the milk and found it palatable. No doubt, he felt a little foolish.

Before Mallory could say anything else, the telephone rang. She went to the wall phone nearby and chimed a sweet hello into the receiver.

"Hi," Pat said in a breezy, yet conspiratorial voice. "I trust Nathan is home?"

"Yep," Mallory said, watching him out of the corner of her eye as he opened the milk carton and sniffed it questioningly. "And I must say, he's the first person I've ever known who didn't trust his own taste buds."

"I'll refrain from asking you to elaborate on that remark, Mall. Don't call him to the phone—I just wanted to tell you that he spent most of last night on my living room sofa."

"Ah," Mallory said. "I was wondering."

"I thought you might have been," Pat replied. "Just to keep the peace, I wanted you to know the straight scoop. He's mad at you, and he's just ornery enough to try and make you think he was in the middle of an orgy."

Mallory looked at her husband and, despite the rigors of the night just past and the painful battles of previous days, her eyes danced with mischief. "Why of *course*, Mr. Hefner," she gushed. "I'd *love* to be a centerfold! May? Certainly! I'll start undressing now!"

On the other end of the line, Pat laughed uproariously. Nathan shot out of his chair, realized that he'd been had, and sank, scowling, back into it.

"Give him hell, McKendrick," Pat said before she rang off.

Mallory hung up the phone, squared her shoulders and swallowed a giggle. "Where were you last night?" she demanded imperiously, fixing her husband with a steely glare.

Nathan slid his empty cereal bowl away and tried hard to look guilty. "Wouldn't you like to know, woman?"

Mallory took up her empty coffee cup and went to the electric percolator on the counter to refill it. With a dramatic toss of her head, she imparted, "Such is my fate—to share you with uncounted women."

He laughed, and the sound was warm and intimate and comfortable to hear. "This has gone far enough. I was tossing and turning on Pat's couch and you damned well know it—Miss May."

"I'm holding out for October," Mallory said airily, coming back to the table with her fresh coffee. "I've always wanted to pose nude with seventeen pumpkins and a scarecrow."

"Kinky," Nathan observed. "You're not going to break your contract with Brad, are you?"

Mallory sighed. No doubt, the light repartee was over and there would be another fight. "No," she said, bracing herself inwardly.

But a grin lifted one corner of Nathan's mouth, and he shook his head in bewildered amusement. "How the hell am I supposed to be a domineering husband if you won't ever give in?"

"I'm not being stubborn, Nathan," Mallory replied seriously. "It's a point of honor with me, that's all."

"Honor is wasted on the likes of Brad Ranner, but,

for the sake of my sanity, I'm not going to fight you. Which is not to say I wouldn't like to fight *him*."

Mallory shrugged. "Do to him what you will, O avenging master—just don't get yourself thrown into jail. I've had all the separations I need."

Nathan looked away, toward the coffeepot, which emitted an electronic chortle. "I went to his apartment last night, before calling on my sensible sister."

"And?"

"And his housekeeper told me he was in Mexico, taking a vacation."

Mallory laughed. "He's in hiding!"

"If he's smart, he'll *stay* in hiding."

"Why did you go to Pat's house last night, instead of to the island or somewhere else?"

Nathan grinned. "I knew she'd make me see reason. Since when did she stop being my sister and become yours? She called me an idiot!"

"If the sombrero fits, wear it, señor."

He grimaced. "Very funny. Open your bathrobe."

Mallory arched one eyebrow and brought a protective hand to clasp the robe shut at the neck. "I beg your pardon?"

"I want to see if you're centerfold material."

She stood up in mock outrage, bent on fleeing the scene to shower and dress. But Nathan caught her arm, without rising from his chair, and wrenched her onto his lap.

She struggled—albeit half-heartedly—but he subdued her easily and situated her so that she was astraddle his lap, facing him. Then, with an animal growl, he opened her robe.

Mallory gasped in pleasurable indignity as he caught both her wrists behind her, in one powerful hand, and pressed them against the small of her back, so that her full and pulsing breasts, now deliciously vulnerable, were thrust toward him.

She shivered as he bent his head to flick tauntingly at

one nipple with just the tip of his tongue. The rosebud morsel responded with a fetching pout.

"Yum," he said, and his breath was warm against the tingling flesh of Mallory's breast.

Mallory moaned, and when she spoke, her breath came in soft gasps. "Will—I—do?"

He went to the other nipple, brought it to the same peak as its counterpart. "You definitely will," he rasped. "But not as a centerfold."

Mallory squirmed slightly in pleasure as he teased the chosen nipple, causing it to throb. "Why not?" she whispered.

Nathan laughed and opened her robe further, though he still held her prisoner, assessing her with smoldering approval. With his free hand, he touched her stomach. "There would be a staple here," he said, sliding fiery fingertips across her abdomen to the other side. "And here."

"We can't—ooooh—have that—"

"Ummmmm," replied Nathan, in a greedy purr. And then he chuckled as Mallory arched her back and tilted her head back, offering herself freely.

Slowly, sensuously, he drank his fill of her, his warm mouth tugging at one breast and then at the other, until Mallory was frantic with the need to join with him, to soar with him, to cause him the same tender torment he was causing her.

But Nathan was in no hurry. He feasted upon her until she was certain she could bear no more, and then he lifted her, so that she was standing, and feasted again.

And as he savored her, Mallory trembled, and her passions built to new heights. Whimpering low in her throat, she arched herself toward him and tangled her fingers in his dark hair. Again and again, he brought her to the very precipice of total release, only to draw back again, and bare her aching secret, and stroke it to maddening need with the tip of one finger.

"What do you want, Mallory?" he teased in a gruff voice.

In halting words, she told him, and he moved to the floor, drawing her with him, but even then he would not grant her what she was willing to plead for. She knelt, and he slid beneath her, drawing her down onto the warm, consuming motions of his mouth.

Her knees were spread far apart and she was frantic and she writhed upon the long, tormenting strokes of his tongue. Savage release stiffened her entire body, and her cry of gratification echoed throughout the kitchen.

She moved to free herself, but he held her, helplessly impaled on the pleasure he offered. "No—," she whimpered, "oh, no, Nathan—not again—please—"

He lifted her slightly, only high enough to vow, "I'm not through with you yet, lady. Not by a long shot."

"N—Nathan—"

But he was again kissing her, nibbling her, tasting her. Fierce and jagged desire shot through her; she could not hope to escape him and even if she could have, she would not have tried. With a sound that was part sob and part croon, she leaned forward to take the only vengeance available.

He moved beneath her in frantic surrender as she repaid him, and as she soared skyward on the wings of a searing release, he followed. Their cries mingled, ragged and primitive, and became one sound.

And when it was over, they lay still, casualties of the same battle, unable to move for a very long time.

Finally, Nathan sat up beside a still-supine Mallory, and caressed the love-warmed, passion-heavy breast that welcomed him.

"Enough?" she managed in a labored whisper, not knowing what she wanted his answer to be.

He laughed hoarsely. "Dreamer. I could make love to you from now till the day I draw my first Social

Security check, lady, and it still wouldn't be enough. I want more of you—a lot more."

Mallory had finally caught her breath, and she laughed, too. "You are insatiable."

He released her breast to lay his palm on the kitchen floor. "And you are prone to waxy yellow build-up. Since that would be an ignoble fate, I think I'll carry you into the bedroom and have my way with you."

"Again?"

He chuckled. "Pumpkin, consider yourself laid."

With that, Nathan stood, pulled Mallory after him, and lifted her into his arms. "I love you so much," he said softly, and his mouth was gentle as it touched hers.

Mallory pushed at him, though she made no move to free herself from his embrace. "Listen, mister—I love you, too. But maybe I'm tired of always being the submissive partner. Maybe I'd like to be the leader for once."

"Lead on," he said gruffly.

And just moments later, in the quiet comfort of their bedroom, Nathan proved how strong he was, how secure in his own concept of himself. He was strong enough to be vulnerable, strong enough to submit.

Chapter 9

THE NEXT DAY WAS A MOMENTOUS ONE FOR THE McKendricks—Renee Parker withdrew her lawsuit without comment, and Mallory's house was officially up for sale. Too, rehearsals for the Seattle concert began in earnest. Nathan prepared for it with a renewed spirit, and the house at Angel Cove rang with laughter and music.

Determined not to be a wet blanket, Mallory watched and listened as the days passed, but she also called on the administrator of the local elementary school and offered her services as a substitute teacher, read a backlog of books that she hadn't had time for before, and spent happy hours visiting Trish and Kate.

After two weeks, she was fully recovered.

Of course, she was delighted when her doctor pronounced her well, but there was a tiny tremor in the pit of her stomach, too. She had almost a month left to run on her contract with Brad, and she still meant to honor it, even though she dreaded every line and scene.

Tanned and probably well aware that Nathan was occupied in another part of the villa on Angel Cove, Brad Ranner appeared within an hour of Mallory's return from Seattle and her doctor's office, a new script under his arm.

Mallory met him in the main entry hall, her eyes on the script. "The death scene, I presume?"

Brad grinned. "Nothing so predictable, sweetheart. Tracy Ballard is going to be arrested for shoplifting and see the error of her ways. In the end, she'll be flying off to serve with the Peace Corps, thus atoning for her many sins."

In spite of everything, Mallory laughed. "Whatever else that storyline is, it can't be called 'predictable.' By the way, how are you accounting for Tracy's absence now?"

Brad passed Mallory and walked, with studied casualness, into the large, empty living room. There, he put the script on a coffee table and sat down on the sofa. "She's being held captive in the attic of an old church by her lover's crazed ex-wife."

Mallory shook her head in amused amazement and moved to the butler's cart, where Mrs. Jeffries had left a pot of hot coffee only minutes before. "Coffee?"

Brad cast a nervous look around the room and nodded. "Enough bravado. Is Nathan around?"

Mallory took china cups from the cart and filled them with the fresh, steaming coffee. "Nathan is busy in the studio, Brad—they're rehearsing for the Seattle concert."

"Good," Brad sighed in blatant relief. "Mallory, I—"

She stopped him with an icy look. "I think it would be better if we pretended all that stuff didn't happen, don't you?"

Brad was flushed. "No, I don't," he answered hotly. "Mallory, there are things I have to explain."

Mallory sighed and dropped into Nathan's favorite

chair, her eyes fixed on her coffee cup. "None of it will make a difference, Brad."

"It might. Mallory, the paternity suit was Diane's idea—I'm sick and tired of being the heavy in this melodrama."

Mallory rolled her sea green eyes. "That doesn't surprise me, Brad—both Nathan and I suspected Diane. But it doesn't excuse what you did either. You had to have set this thing rolling long before we had that row about my contract and the cable offer."

Brad spoke gently. "I did. It was a rotten and devious thing to do, I know—"

"You can say that again. Why *did* you do it, Brad?"

He looked away. "Because I love you, Mallory. I have since the day you walked into the studio and read for Tracy Ballard's role. I thought you were single, until the people in public relations clued me in." Brad returned distracted blue eyes to Mallory's face, and the high color of embarrassment burned in his cheeks. "When I found out you were Nathan McKendrick's wife, I considered jumping off the Space Needle. As time went by, I could see that you were ultraunhappy, so—"

"So you decided to sandbag my marriage."

Shame was clear in Brad's eyes. "Something like that. God, Mallory, I'm sorry. I was into the thing before I really thought—"

Either Brad Ranner was genuinely remorseful, or he was working on the wrong side of the cameras. In any case, Mallory had difficulty sustaining grudges, and she saw no point in hating Brad when the time they had to work together would be so short. "Forget it," she said in businesslike tones. And then she reached out for the script.

After that, the conversation centered on the neat disposal of Tracy Ballard. Though Mallory's contract still had more than thirty days to run, her commitment would be completed in only ten. She knew that this was a conciliatory gesture on Brad's part, and she was grateful.

When Brad was ready to leave, she walked him out to his car, chatting companionably. She was unprepared for the swift, brotherly kiss he planted on her cheek before sliding behind the wheel.

"Watch out for Diane, okay?" he said gently. "I may have seen the light, but she's into vengeance in a big way."

Mallory folded her arms and shook her head. "Surely even Diane must have given up by now."

"Don't count on it. I heard she was planning to make an offer on that house you're selling."

Openmouthed, Mallory stared at Brad, unable to speak. Dear Lord, surely Trish wouldn't sell her house to Diane Vincent! The moment she could, she would call and make certain.

Brad lifted one eyebrow. "Stay on your toes, baby doll. Even if she can't buy that particular house, she could find another to rent or something."

Glumly, Mallory nodded. At that time of year, there were empty houses aplenty on the island. She swallowed and changed the subject. "What about the cable deal, Brad?" she asked, stepping back as he started the engine of his white Corvette. "Did it go through?"

Brad shook his head ruefully. "Not yet. You're not that easy to replace, button. And let's face it, Seattle isn't exactly rife with accomplished actresses."

"It shouldn't be so difficult," Mallory argued. "Mine was only a minor role."

He shrugged. "Maybe I'm waiting for another Mallory."

She looked away, uncomfortable, anxious to get Trish on the telephone. "I'm sorry, Brad."

"Don't be. See you Monday, my love—and thanks."

Mallory arched an eyebrow. "For what?"

"For not throwing that contract in my face," he answered, shifting the car into reverse. His lips moved slightly, miming a kiss, and then he was backing out of the driveway, onto the main road.

Mallory waved, then hurried back into the house and made a dive for the hall telephone. She punched out Trish's number and tapped one foot impatiently while she waited.

"Good morning!" Trish sang after at least five rings.

"Don't sell my house to Diane Vincent!" Mallory blurted without so much as a hello to precede her words.

Trish laughed. "Mallory, I presume? She asked me and I told her we wanted a cool million, since you were semifamous and all. I do have a good offer from a young couple in Seattle, Mall—he works at Boeing and she's a painter—"

"Take it."

"Don't you want to know how much?"

"I don't care how much."

"I see. Well, they want those trees cut down first— the ones at the edge of the driveway. Afraid they'll fall through the roof next time we get one of our bridge-breaking windstorms."

Mallory sighed. She'd loved those trees, resisted every effort Nathan made to persuade her to have them chopped down. "Okay. The trees go. Can you arrange it, Trish, or shall I?"

"I'll do it, you pay the bill. Hey, why don't you come over here and have lunch with me?"

"The big real estate magnate has time for lunch with a neighbor?" Mallory teased.

Trish laughed. "The magnate in question is wearing an old bathrobe and cleaning out her fridge. It's a horror. I don't mind when food starts growing fur, but when it tries to learn the language, I draw the line."

Mallory rolled her eyes. "You actually expect me to

eat at your house when you've just made a remark like that? Come over here—the housekeeper made enough tuna salad to feed an army."

"Knowing you, you probably need to get out of there for a while," Trish retorted. "I suppose the band is there?"

"Along with wives, girlfriends, and the occasional impressed relative. Let's strike a compromise and meet at the Bayview for clam strips and french fries."

"You have a deal, McKendrick," Trish replied. "Meet you there in half an hour."

Trish was waiting when Mallory reached the Bayview Clam Bar, the only restaurant on the island. She looked patently terrific in a soft blue cashmere suit.

"Glad you didn't wear your bathrobe," Mallory observed dryly, taking her place at their favorite table.

Trish laughed and preened just a little. "Don't I look great? Thanks to you and the couple from Seattle, I can afford this getup!"

Mallory set her purse aside and folded her arms comfortably on the table edge. "You really like selling, don't you, Trish? Have you got any other clients besides me?"

Trish was beaming. "Do I. Mall, I think I've sold that old farmhouse on Blackberry Lane—the one with the ghost. I showed it to a doctor from Renton, and he loved it!"

A waitress came, bringing waterglasses and taking their orders, and wandered off again. "I hope you charged extra for the ghost. That's a definite plus, in my book."

Trish laughed, but there was something unsettling behind the merriment in her blue eyes. "Mall—"

"What?"

"After I talked to you, Herb called me from the office. He—he—well—"

Mallory was annoyed. "He what?"

"He wanted to know where the keys were for those new duplexes over on the Cove. His exact words were, 'a knockout blonde from Seattle wants to rent two bedrooms and a view.'"

Mallory frowned. "It might not be Diane, Trish," she said, somewhat irritably. "Surely she isn't the only 'knockout blonde' in Seattle."

"It's her, all right. Herb said she was driving a red MG roadster."

Mallory closed her eyes for a moment. If Diane rented one of the duplex units in question, she would be living just beyond Nathan's property line. In fact, she would be the McKendricks' nearest neighbor. "Damn," she muttered.

Trish was obviously torn. "I could ask Herb not to rent one to her, but he'll get a commission and he has a family and all—"

"No. Business is business. Maybe she won't stay long." When Mallory opened her eyes, she saw that Trish looked doubtful. As doubtful as Mallory felt.

"That bimbo," Trish declared. "I wonder what she hopes to accomplish."

Mallory didn't wonder, she knew. But she felt no compunction to burden Trish with her suspicions, so she deliberately shifted the conversation onto another course. Throughout the remainder of the luncheon, the two women debated the existence of the ghost on Blackberry Lane.

Reaching the house on Angel Cove again, Mallory found that the rehearsal was still going on. Staunchly she gathered up the script that Brad had brought by earlier and, since the weather was springlike, ventured outside to study it. She was sitting on a fallen log, facing the Cove and within sight of the villa, when she sensed that she wasn't alone and looked up from the meaty lines she'd been trying to memorize.

Nathan was standing before her, his back to the sun-shimmered, blue and silver Cove, looking undeniably handsome even in old jeans and a battered blue windbreaker. "Hi," he said softly.

Mallory swallowed and, even though it was the last thing she'd wanted to do, stole one wary look at the duplexes just down the beach. There was a rented trailer backed up to the front door of one, and Diane's bright blond head gleamed in the sun as she supervised the unloading of the vehicle. "Hi," she replied distractedly.

Nathan had followed her gaze, she saw a moment later, and the muscles in his jawline were bunched with annoyance. He muttered a swearword and started toward the scene, but Mallory leaped up from her perch on the log and caught his arm.

"Nathan, no," she said quickly, a plea in her voice. "There's nothing we can do."

He threw a menacing look in Mallory's direction, but he stopped. "That—"

"Nathan, we have to ignore her. Don't you see? If you go storming over there and make a scene, you'll be doing just what she wants you to!"

His broad shoulders moved in an irritated sigh, and she heard a raspy breath enter his lungs and come out again. "Damn it, I knew I should have bought that property when it was for sale."

Mallory smiled, albeit shakily. "You can't buy the whole world, you know. And if those duplexes hadn't been built, she would just have found some other way to get to us."

Nathan sighed again and touched an index finger to the tip of her nose. "You know something, lady? You're not only beautiful, but smart."

Mallory executed a sweeping bow and dropped the script into the soft, pungent carpet of pine needles cushioning the ground. Nathan's eyes fell to the familiar logo on its cover, and Mallory almost expected the thing to ignite under the fierce heat of his gaze.

"He was here," Nathan said in a rasp.

Mallory swallowed hard and nodded. "It's only ten days' work, Nathan."

Nathan's throat constricted, and he tilted his head back to glower up at the sky. "Starting when?"

"Monday. Nathan, don't worry, okay? He was contrite—he apologized—"

Nathan's gaze, when it came to Mallory's face, was scathing. "Sure he was. And you, of course, were forgiving."

"Nathan, I have to work with the man. I couldn't very well stir up a battle!"

"You don't have to work with the man, as you put it. Christ, Mallory, between Ranner and Diane, haven't we had enough trouble? Why do you insist on setting us up for more?"

"We've been all through this, Nathan. I gave my word, remember?"

Nathan muttered something and whirled away, and this time his attention was focused on Mt. Rainier, towering in the distance. "I need you here."

"You don't, and you know it. I've got to be in Seattle on Monday, Nathan, and that's all there is to it."

He sighed, and his shoulders moved in exaggerated annoyance. "You know, Mallory, sometimes it seems that I'm doing all the compromising here. I'm giving up concert tours—television specials—recording dates. Can't you give up ten days of acting?"

The disparaging note he gave that last word was not lost on Mallory. She stiffened, then bent to retrieve the script. "Okay," she said coldly. "You give up the concert in Seattle, and I'll quit right now."

He turned to face her, stunned. "That concert has been promoted, Mallory—the tickets are already sold out and I've signed contracts!"

Mallory grinned and held up one index finger. "Contracts. The magic word. Yours, then, are binding, but mine aren't?"

"Damn it!" Nathan spat, and then, without another word, he turned and stormed back down the wooded path toward the villa.

Though she wanted to follow after her husband and double up her fists and beat on his impervious back in frustration, Mallory was determined to be professional to the end. With great effort, she sat down on the log again, opened the script and went back to learning her lines.

The boathouse was dark, and Nathan didn't bother to turn on the light. Even though it had been hours since the latest confrontation with Mallory, he was still smarting from it. The shabby structure where the previous owner of the villa had stored fishing gear was the only place on the island where he could be reasonably sure of a few minutes' privacy.

Even after years of disuse, the place still smelled of oil and bait and kelp. There was no sound, other than the distant complaint of a ferry horn and the rhythmic lapping of the water beneath the filthy wooden floor. Nathan muttered an ugly word and felt better for it.

He sat down on the floor, wrapping his arms around his knees, and sighed. Just when he had thought he and Mallory were really linking up, really communicating, everything had gone to hell again.

Why did he have to corner her like that, when he knew the one thing she absolutely couldn't deal with was being ordered around? Why was he making such a big thing out of ten lousy days' work?

The answer to that question wasn't easy to face. Nathan knew it all too well, whether he permitted himself to confront the issue or not. He was jealous of Brad Ranner.

Just then, the door of the boathouse creaked open, admitting a shaft of weak, dust-flecked light. Without thinking, Nathan cursed softly and betrayed himself, and the beam of the flashlight swung immediately in his direction.

"Leave me alone," he growled, turning his head.

The intruder was undaunted, drawing nearer. After a second or so, Diane Vincent knelt beside him, impulsively tangling gentle fingers in his hair.

"You look rotten, babe," she commiserated.

Nathan deflected her hand roughly. "Go away, damn it."

It was as though he hadn't spoken. Diane's fingers found their way into his hair again, offering a treacherous comfort. She turned off the flashlight, and it rattled on the dusty board floor as she set it aside.

"I can make it all better," she crooned, and the exotic, specially blended scent of her perfume whispered against Nathan's raw senses like a caress.

For one insane moment, he wanted her. He even drew her close, and his lips brushed against hers in the darkness, seeking, not caring who she was.

Mallory. The name rang through him like the toll of some infinite bell. He thrust Diane aside harshly and sprang to his feet.

Diane spoke with disdain. "Still the faithful husband. Oh, Nate, baby, you *are* a fool."

Nathan wanted to leave the boathouse, but for the moment, he couldn't seem to mobilize the muscles in his legs. "Shut up," he snapped. "Just shut up and get the hell out of here."

Diane had never been easily intimidated. "Do you really think your gamine girl has been saving her sweet favors just for you?" she challenged in a silken voice.

Nathan closed his eyes and his midsection tightened into a steel knot. He tried to speak and failed.

In an instant, Diane was close to him again, pressing her thighs against his, moving her hands in circles on his chest. He pushed her away again in a furious need to be free of her.

It was then that the overhead light came on, glaring, blinding Nathan for a fraction of a second. When his vision cleared, he swore again.

Mallory was standing in the doorway, Cinnamon's leash dangling from one hand, her face chalk-white, her green eyes emerald with pain. She took in Diane's triumphant grin, muttered something unintelligible and turned to flee.

Nathan bolted after her, shouted her name. But she kept right on running.

It was dark, and the wharf was treacherous with its coiled ropes and mooring rings, so Mallory dared not run her fastest, even though her heart urged her to keep pace with its frantic, stricken beat. As she scrambled up the slight, rocky hillside above the wharf, she knew that Nathan was gaining on her, felt his approach in every one of her screaming senses.

At the base of the lawn fronting his gigantic house, he caught her, and his hands were inescapable as they grasped her shoulders, harsh with controlled desperation as they turned her to face him.

"Mallory."

She looked up at him in the moonlight, too broken to struggle. His face was in shadows. "Damn you," she whispered in a ragged, tortured voice. "Damn you, you lying, cheating—"

Mallory could feel his pain as well as her own—it was a fathomless chasm between them, pushing them apart rather than drawing them closer.

"Stop it," he demanded.

Mallory was gasping now, trying to close her mind to what she had seen in the boathouse just moments before. They'd been alone there, Nathan and Diane, in the darkness—

Nathan's hands moved from her shoulders to her upper arms, and his voice was a gruff plea. "Mallory, listen to me."

Mallory's black, pounding rage made her need to kick and scream, but she couldn't move. It was as though someone had coated her entire body in plaster. She gave a small, strangled cry.

"Mallory, it wasn't—I didn't—"

At last, Mallory found her voice. "Don't say it, Nathan," she warned. "Don't give me that trite old line about how it wasn't what it looked like. It was *exactly* what it looked like, and we both know it."

A harsh sigh tore itself from his throat. "Everything I say right now will be a cliché, won't it?" he asked with raw, dismal resignation. "Mallory, I wasn't going to make love to Diane."

Mallory trembled, remembering a certain look in Diane's eyes. "You kissed her," she said, whirling in his grasp.

But he would not release her, and his grip was fierce as he wrenched her back. "You're not going anywhere until we settle this, lady. If I have to drag Diane over here by the hair, you're going to hear the truth!"

"The truth was all too apparent in the boathouse, Nathan!"

He shook her hard. "Damn it, Mallory, this is all a mistake!"

"You can say that again, handsome. I guess it's been that from the first—our marriage, I mean."

"What?"

"I want a divorce, Nathan."

He released her so swiftly that she nearly fell into the wet grass that had so recently been buried in snow. "No way!" he snapped.

Mallory turned and scrambled across the lawn, too stricken to consider dignity now. Nathan kept pace easily, and at the base of the porch, she faced him again. "Why fight it, Nathan?" she asked in a contemptuous, pain-laced whisper. "Now you won't have to lie and meet in boathouses."

Nathan didn't make a sound, and yet it was as though he had shouted. The night air seemed to reverberate with his rage and his frustration.

Mallory hurried across the porch toward the garage. For once, a bad habit stood her in good stead—her keys were in the ignition of the car.

She drove carefully out of the driveway, knowing that Nathan would pursue her if she didn't, and a few minutes later, let herself into the house that had been home all her life. The house that would soon belong, no doubt, to happy strangers.

Inside, she locked the doors and then sank down into a chair at the kitchen table, not bothering to turn on a light. Only then could she release the terrible, scalding sobs. They racked her, leaving her exhausted and mute when they finally abated.

Never had Mallory endured a longer night.

Though she took a long, hot bath and swallowed a sleeping pill, rest eluded her. She tried reading and couldn't retain so much as a sentence. Music was out of the question—she dared not turn on the radio for fear of hearing Nathan's latest hit, and the stereo might as well have been a thousand miles from the bed.

Again and again, Mallory relived the disaster in the boathouse, and the resultant agony was beyond anything she had ever experienced before.

In a far corner of her mind, a small voice pleaded a reasonable, rational case, but Mallory could not or would not listen. She couldn't afford to delude herself; she'd done enough of that.

With the gray, stormy dawn came more snow. Dispiritedly, Mallory packed a few clothes, called Trish to let her know that she was leaving Cinnamon behind in her care.

"What's going on, Mall?" Trish demanded, sensing that something was terribly wrong even though her friend was doing her level best to hide it.

Mallory sighed. "If I talk about it, I'll start blubbering. How about if I call you from the city, tomorrow or the next day?"

"Mall—"

"Please, Trish. I can't."

"Okay, okay. But what about the house? Is it still for sale, or what?"

"It's for sale. I—I'll have somebody come and p—pack up my things if that c—couple wants to buy it—"

"Don't worry about that," Trish admonished in a gentle voice. "Mall, honey, are you sure you want to sell the place? Don't go ahead with it if—"

"I'm sure, Trish. Really."

"You'll call tomorrow or the next day?"

"I promise."

"Take care, love."

Mallory couldn't say any more. Trusting Trish to understand, she hung up, left the house and drove to the island's small ferry terminal.

Diane's beautiful face was tear swollen, and her meticulously applied mascara made inky streaks down her cheeks. Her knuckles were white where they gripped the edge of her sofa.

Nathan, leaning back against the mantel of the fireplace that graced her small living room, felt no pity, no inclination toward mercy. He'd already shouted at Diane, and now he didn't trust himself to speak again; he wanted only to leave.

Diane swallowed convulsively. "I'll go to her, Nathan. I'll explain."

He made no effort to quell the cold hatred he knew was glittering in his eyes. "It's probably too late for that," he said in clipped tones as he made his way through the maze of half-packed boxes littering Diane's floor.

She caught at his arm as he passed. Her voice was small and peevish, and it chafed Nathan's already ragged nerves. "I'm sorry."

He wrenched open her front door. "Oh, thank you," he retorted sardonically. "I'll remember that when I crawl out of the courtroom, suddenly single."

Diane sniffled, lifted her chin in a theatrical gesture of martyrly acceptance. "Blame me if it makes you feel better, Nate, but it isn't all my fault and you know it. Your marriage was a shambles long before we met in the boathouse."

Nathan laughed, and it was a hoarse, cruel sound. "Before we *met?* You followed me!"

Diane's face seemed to crumble. "So I did. But you're a big boy, McKendrick, and you weren't forced into that kiss."

Nathan watched her for another moment, wondering idly if the show she was putting on might be based in real emotions. In the final analysis, he didn't care, one way or the other. He turned and strode away, leaving Diane's front door gaping open behind him.

He walked fast, with his head down, and nearly collided with Jeff Kingston, his drummer, on the wooded path leading back to his own house.

Jeff was the only member of the band who had been with Nathan from the first. Because of that, there was a special empathy between the two men. "Hey, Nate— hold it. What's going on around here?"

Nathan stopped, braced himself against a tree with one hand and drew a deep breath. With his eyes carefully trained on the water, barely visible through the thickening curtain of snow, he told Jeff what had happened in the boathouse the night before. His tones were grim and concise.

When he'd finished, Jeff muttered a colorful word. "We're talking dumb moves here, Nate."

Nathan nodded distractedly.

"Have you called Mallory?"

Nathan shook his head. "She wouldn't talk to me if I did."

"Then go and see her."

Nathan turned his back to Jeff and ran one finger along the rough, cool bark of the tree he leaned against. "That wouldn't help either. I've lost her."

"There has got to be some way—"

Nathan turned suddenly. "What do I say to her, Jeff? That Diane has been throwing herself at me for six years and that I was confused and mad as hell and before I thought about what I was doing I kissed her?"

"Is that the truth?"

"Yes!"

"Then tell her that. Mallory is a class act, Nathan, and she loves you. She'll understand."

"I don't think so. Jeff, she's been through so much—the paternity thing, now this—"

Jeff sighed wearily. "Okay. Let her go, man. Ranner and about ten million other guys will appreciate the gesture, but it sure as hell won't do you any good, or Mallory either."

"What the hell are you saying?"

Jeff shrugged. "If you don't want her, step out of the way. She won't be lonely long."

"God, you're a big help!" Nathan roared, gesturing wildly with his arms. "I can't stand the thought of anybody else touching her, and you know it!"

Jeff's expression was somewhere between a smile and a smirk. "Then why don't you get your act together?"

"I thought it was," Nathan replied with less spirit. "I really thought it was."

"Why? Damn it, Nate, the rest of us have seen this coming since before the Australian tour. Mallory looks like a lost kid half the time, and you're always on edge."

"Doesn't it bother you that you're going to be out of

work? That we're not going to be doing concerts after Seattle?"

"Sure, it bothers me, but I think it bothers you more. You don't want to quit the circuit, do you, Nate? The bottom line is, you just don't want to quit."

Nathan sighed and started walking toward the house again, his hands wedged into the pockets of his jeans. He could feel snow melting on his neck, but he didn't care. "No, I don't want to quit. But I didn't want to lose Mallory either."

"Suppose you have lost her. What would you do?"

"Book more concerts. And I have, Jeff—this time, I *have* lost her."

"Maybe, and maybe not. If I were you, I guess I wouldn't even try to sort all this out until the concert is over and Mallory's off that soap opera. Then, old friend, take your wife away somewhere, alone, and work this out, one way or the other."

"It's hopeless," Nathan said in despair. "There are two ladies in my life—music and Mallory—and one of them has to go."

Sunday was a crummy day for Mallory, from start to finish. She stumbled through it blindly, ignoring both the telephone and the doorbell, knowing instinctively that none of the callers or visitors would be Nathan. She tried repeatedly to study the script Brad had brought to her, but the lines ascribed to her character made even less sense than they normally did. At the rate she was going, she thought dismally, she was going to have to ad lib every scene.

At dinner time, she made a quick search of the cupboards and was not really surprised to find them bare. The refrigerator contained only what remained of Nathan's carton of milk, and hot tears smarted in Mallory's eyes as she remembered how close she'd felt to him that day, how she'd soared in his arms.

Glumly, Mallory took the carton from the refrigerator shelf and tossed it into the trash compactor. Despite her jangled nerves and her heartache, she was hungry, and yet she certainly didn't feel like venturing out to a restaurant or even a grocery store.

After some moments of deliberation, she finally called her favorite Chinese restaurant and ordered a meal. She would shower and wrap up in a cozy bathrobe and, by the time her supper arrived, maybe she'd feel better. Maybe she'd even be able to learn her lines.

Her shower taken, her old, red corduroy bathrobe soft against her skin, Mallory was brushing her hair dry when the doorbell rang. "Dinner," she said with forced cheer as she pulled open the door.

"You shouldn't do that," Pat said, arching one eyebrow. "For all you knew, you could have been opening the door to a rapist or even a vacuum cleaner salesman."

"Horrors," Mallory replied, eyeing the cartons of Chinese food sheltered in Pat's capable arms. "Since when do you deliver for Chow May's?"

"Since I bribed the kid in the elevator. Mall, damn it, how come you aren't answering your phone or your door?"

"Maybe because I want to be alone," Mallory said archly, reaching for the cartons.

Pat withheld them and stepped past her sister-in-law to enter the penthouse. "Not so fast, hungry person. I charge one eggroll and two fortune cookies for my delivery services."

Mallory sighed and followed after Pat as she walked resolutely through the hallway to the living room. She put the cartons down on the coffee table and turned to glare at her brother's wife.

"What are you trying to do, Mall—scare all your friends and relations to death? I've been here twice and called four times, and I've been getting calls from Trish and Kate all day."

Stubbornly, Mallory folded her arms. "I don't feel guilty, if that's what you want from me."

"Far be it from me to inspire guilt," Pat retorted smoothly. "I mean, just because I thought you jumped out of a window and Trish thought you slit your wrists—"

"What was Kate's guess?" Mallory broke in irritably.

"She was going for the head in the oven tactic. You and Nathan are on the outs again, aren't you?"

"Permanently," Mallory said, opening the sweet and sour pork and dipping in with a finger. "And don't try to talk me out of it."

Pat's bright blue eyes were flashing. "I wouldn't think of it," she said, taking an eggroll from one of the cartons. "You're both idiots, as far as I'm concerned, and I wash my hands of you."

Mallory made a face and then wandered off toward the kitchen for plates, knives and forks. And even though she and Pat didn't exchange a civil word while they were eating, she was still glad of the company.

Chapter 10

Monday morning was a disaster.

Mallory arrived at the studio half an hour late, and all the makeup in the world wouldn't have disguised the pallor in her cheeks and the quiet torment in her eyes. To make matters worse, the set was crowded. Several fans had been admitted, and there were reporters and photographers from one of the magazines specializing in the doings of soap opera performers. Mallory's lines sounded wooden when she delivered them, and she couldn't remember her cues.

Finally, Brad shouted an order to the cameramen, and everyone took a badly needed break. His grasp was hard on Mallory's arm as he dragged her off the set, through a maze of cameras, light stands and thick electrical cables snaking along the floor.

"Damn it, Mallory," he hissed, glaring at her. "Is this your idea of revenge, or what? If you're trying to sandbag the whole production, you're succeeding!"

Mallory wanted nothing so much as to get the taping

right and be done with television forever, and her zombielike behavior was anything but deliberate. Tears of frustration smarted in her eyes, and her lower lip trembled. But she couldn't manage a word.

Brad's tension seemed to ease; his bright blue eyes searched her face and then he sighed and raised tender hands to her cheeks. "What is it, button? What's happened?"

Even if she'd had a voice, Mallory would have been too proud to explain. She swallowed and shook her head in a reflexive gesture of helplessness.

It was clear in an instant, however, that Brad had read much of the situation in her eloquent eyes. "Nathan," he said with angry acceptance.

Mallory hadn't meant to cry, but, suddenly, she was doing just that. A terrible sob tore itself from her throat, and Brad drew her into his arms in a brotherly embrace. He was whispering gentle, innocuous words of comfort when his arms suddenly went rigid.

"Oh, Lord," he groaned.

Mallory's spine stiffened; without turning around, she knew that Nathan was in the studio, that he was striding toward her, that when she faced him, his expression would be murderous.

A throbbing silence descended, stilling even the jovial conversations of the light crew, the other actors and actresses, the writers and the camera people. When Mallory forced herself to turn from Brad to Nathan, she focused not on her husband's face, but on the reporters and photographers so obviously anxious to record whatever drama that might be offered.

"Call Security," Brad muttered to a gaping script girl.

Nathan laughed low in his throat, and it was a brutal, terrifying sound. "That won't be necessary," he said. "I promise to behave myself."

Mallory felt no fear—not for herself, at least. She peered in Nathan's direction, but his face was hidden in shadows, just as it had been during their last argument that night on the island. There was really no need to see his features; all his disdain had been evident in his voice.

"What do you want?" she demanded after a long, uncomfortable silence.

Nathan's powerful shoulders moved in a deceptively casual shrug. "A few minutes alone with my wife, if that can be arranged."

Pride made Mallory square her shoulders and stand tall. "Fine," she said stiffly. "We can talk in my dressing room."

Brad cleared his throat. "Mallory, I don't think—"

She cut him off politely. "It's all right, Brad—really."

Nathan offered his arm in a suave parody of good manners, and Mallory took it. The walk to the dressing room she shared with two other actresses was the longest of her life.

Nathan looked wan when she turned to face him after closing the dressing room door. His thick, dark hair was rumpled, and, as he folded his arms across his chest and leaned back against the wall a shadow writhed in the depths of his eyes.

Mallory took in the blunt masculinity of his form with a dispatch that was entirely false. In truth, the corded muscles of his blue-jeaned thighs had a very disturbing effect on her determination never to surrender to him again. Beneath the expensive cream-colored sweater, his broad shoulders moved in another shrug.

"Aren't you going to compliment me on my self-restraint, Mallory?" he asked, his eyes raking over the revealing pink satin robe she'd worn in the last scene. "I didn't even comment on your—costume."

Mallory lifted her chin. "I trust you aren't here to demonstrate your boundless nobility."

There was a change in his face; the deadly white line

edging his lips and his jawline faded, and there was a soft look in his eyes. "I love you, Mallory."

She would have found a bitter, scathing invective easier to deal with than this simple lie. "Don't."

"Don't love you, or don't talk about it?"

Mallory bit her lower lip and refused to look at him, to speak, to react.

"It's true, you know. I've loved you since the day I met you." His voice was even, reasonable—so damned reasonable! "Mallory, that incident in the boathouse was a misunderstanding. It was innocent, like that hug you were just exchanging with Brad."

"*Innocent?*" Mallory whispered. "You *kissed* her, Nathan. You admitted that yourself! And even if you hadn't admitted it—"

"You would have known," he finished smoothly. "Mallory, I guess I did kiss her, if you can call it that—it was really more of a touch." He paused, drew a deep breath and flung his arms out in a gesture of frustration. "I needed somebody—anybody. And Diane was there."

Mallory was trying hard to hate him, but her love was so fathomless that it threatened all her thinking processes, all her desperate resignation. "In that case," she replied coldly, "I shudder to think what would have happened if I hadn't intruded."

Nathan's fingers drummed on the sweatered expanse of his upper arm, but that was the only outward indication of his impatience. "I think you know what would have happened, Mallory, whether you'll let yourself accept it or not. When I realized what I was doing, what I was throwing away, I backed off."

Mallory's resolve was wavering fast; she wasn't even sure it mattered whether or not he was lying. "What else could you have done, Nathan? Carried on as if your wife hadn't just walked in?"

A muscle flexed in his jaw and relaxed again. "Listen

to your heart, Mallory. Forget all the garbage that's been programmed into you and listen to your instincts. Damn it, you *know* I'm telling the truth."

Mallory turned away, ostensibly to rearrange the jumble of creams and lotions and powders on her dressing table. In actuality, she was fighting tears and a growing need to believe him. "Please go," she said calmly. "Right now."

He said nothing, nor did he move. Mallory lifted her eyes, horrified to see that he'd been watching her reflection in the mirror, reading her real feelings in the tortured planes of her face.

In a fluid motion, Nathan crossed the small room and turned her to face him, trapping her against the vanity table with the hard pressure of his steellike thighs, his stomach, his chest. The sound he made, deep in his throat, was somewhere between a moan and a growl.

And then he kissed her.

Mallory struggled at first, but then her body betrayed her pride, offering its own surrender. She opened her mouth to the plundering invasion of his tongue, then responded with her own. His right hand moved up her rib cage to cup her breast through the thin pink fabric of the robe. Even as that same hand strayed beneath the robe and the lacy camisole under it to claim the hard-peaked breast hidden there, Nathan did not break the shattering kiss.

Stormy winds of passion howled through Mallory's troubled spirit. Gasping, she tore her lips from his and buried her face in the soft, fragrant knit of his sweater.

He lifted her chin with a rough sort of gentleness. The knowledge that he could play her body in the same accomplished way he played countless musical instruments burned in his eyes, a savage, infuriating flame, and he made no move to free the imprisoned breast.

Sweet anguish affected every fiber of Mallory's being; the core of her womanhood was already preparing to receive him. Desire made her conscious of little other than the hardness of his need pressing against her.

And yet, somehow, she found the strength within herself to thrust him away. "No," she said in a shaky voice. *"No."*

He shrugged, bent his head and nuzzled the satiny flesh on her neck briefly. Then he went to the door.

"You know where to find me," he said in a low, flat voice.

The insulted rage that seized Mallory in that moment was more than equal to the passion of seconds before. She snatched up a jar of cleansing cream and sent it whistling past his arrogant head, and flinched as it shattered against the door. Unruffled, Nathan turned the doorknob and assessed his wife with paradoxically tormented and amused eyes. He recited his phone number in matter-of-fact tones and walked out.

Mallory stood, hands clenched at her sides, trembling with impotent fury. "Damn you, Nathan McKendrick!" she screamed after him. *"Damn* you!"

It was then that a photographer appeared in the doorway and brazenly snapped Mallory's picture. Blinded by the flash and by renewed outrage, she screamed again and flung a hairbrush at the stranger.

She had no idea what she would have done after that, if Brad Ranner hadn't intervened just then. The possibilities didn't bear even the briefest consideration.

With admirable composure and aplomb, Brad cleared the set entirely, except for the necessary members of the cast and crew, and recruited two older actresses to put Mallory back together again.

Though she longed to sink into a screaming, mindless fit of hysteria, Mallory's anger sustained her. She would *not* give in; her self-respect was at stake.

All the rest of that day, Mallory got her lines right, and she gave the best performance of her short, crazy career.

Hours later, at home in the plush, lonely penthouse,

she stripped off her clothes and stepped under a steamy shower, scrubbing her flesh with fierce motions, letting the hot, hot water soak her hair and stream down her face. Telling herself not to think about Nathan McKendrick was like playing the childhood game of telling herself not to think about blue elephants. His image raged in her mind and spirit like a brush fire.

When she could bear it no longer, she screamed in wordless fury, doubled her fists, and hammered wildly, senselessly, at the shower's tiled walls.

Eventually the hot water soothed her. She stepped out of the shower stall, dried herself methodically with a waiting towel, then slipped into a cozy terrycloth robe and pink floppy scuffs. When she'd brushed and blow-dried her hair, Mallory walked aimlessly out into the living room. There, at the imposing teakwood bar, she mixed herself an unusually strong drink.

The aching tension in her shoulders and the nape of her neck eased a little as the bourbon burned her veins. But it did nothing for the frantic tremor in the pit of her stomach or the desolation in her heart.

She set the drink down with a forceful thud when the doorbell rang.

Stiffening her spine, Mallory ignored the incessant ringing until it stopped. Then, with resolve, she found the script for the next day's taping and began learning her lines and cues. She stayed up very late that night, working. When she knew her lines cold, she stumbled off to bed and fell, mercifully, into a dreamless and untroubled sleep.

She awakened to a stream of sunlight radiating from the huge skylight overhead and a spasm of incredible nausea. One hand clamped over her mouth, she scurried into the bathroom. After that, breakfast was out of the question; she couldn't even face coffee, and on the set she turned away in horror from the goopy doughnuts offered by the head writer.

"Are you feeling all right?" Brad asked idly, when

she paled at the sight of the fast-food breakfast he was consuming.

"Flu, I guess," she said lamely, falling into a canvas chair and averting her eyes. But the scent of the scrambled eggs sandwiched between the slices of Brad's half-eaten English muffin suddenly sent her bounding across the cluttered studio and into the women's room.

She was just in time.

Never one to stand on custom, Brad was waiting when Mallory stumbled out of the stall and approached one of several porcelain sinks. He watched her in silence, his arms folded, until she'd recovered and begun drying her face with a rough brown paper-towel.

"We can do your scenes tomorrow," he offered quietly.

Mallory shook her head. The color was coming back into her face, and she felt infinitely better. "I'm fine, Brad."

"Slightly pregnant, perhaps."

Mallory was stunned, and she gripped the edge of the sink for support. *Pregnant?* The word seemed to echo in the room.

She counted calmly, realized that she hadn't had a period since before Nathan left for Australia. "Oh, God," she whispered. *"Oh,* my God—"

"Uh-huh," Brad said, with crisp detachment. And then he considerately left the women's room.

Mallory tightened her grasp on the sink to keep her knees from giving way. Her emotions spun inside her, hopelessly tangled. She wanted the baby desperately—there was no question of that. But why couldn't it have been conceived when she still had a solid marriage?

She drew a deep, restorative breath. "Hold on, McKendrick," she ordered herself. "Maybe you're not pregnant. Maybe it was something you ate—"

And maybe it was that passionate farewell before Nathan flew off to Sydney, taunted a voice deep in Mallory's whirling mind.

She remembered, with both remorse and a sweet stirring in her middle. In early November, despite the forbidding weather, she and Nathan had spent a delicious, bittersweet weekend on his boat, exploring Puget Sound. Late that Sunday afternoon, probably dreading their impending separation, they'd argued.

And Nathan had flung Mallory's new packet of birth control pills overboard.

The action seemed significant in retrospect, as Mallory stood, stricken, in the studio restroom, trying to get a grip on herself. At the time, however, it had been nothing more than a gesture of anger.

Nathan had been trying to tell her, even then, that he wanted a child. Now that she was about to give him one, it was probably too late. Biting her lower lip, Mallory lowered her head and cried.

The rest of the day was ruined, for all intents and purposes, though she somehow got through it. She got no sleep at all that night—she spent it pacing, torn between calling Nathan and keeping her suspicions to herself.

In the end, she chose the latter course. After all, the pregnancy hadn't actually been confirmed, and the whole thing could be a mistake. She'd been to her doctor's office very recently, and it seemed to her that if she'd been pregnant, Dr. Sarah would have noticed it.

Noticed? She laughed ruefully as she refilled her coffee cup in the huge, gleaming penthouse kitchen. There had been no pelvic examination or lab tests, and pregnancy wasn't something people *noticed,* like a new blazer or a different haircut. Not in the early stages, at least.

With Brad's expansive blessing, Mallory drove to her doctor's office first thing in the morning. Her stomach was still quivering from another bout of raging nausea when she was squired into an examining room and told to undress.

Mallory obeyed, eyeing the examining table and its metal stirrups with dread. *Woman, the indignities you are heir to,* she thought wryly as she took off her black flannel slacks, her blue silk shirt, her lacy panties and bra.

She was wearing the obligatory scratchy white cotton gown when the doctor entered, smiling her most engaging smile. "Good morning, Mallory."

"Sarah," Mallory returned cordially, with a slight nod of her head.

"What's the trouble?"

Mallory grinned humorlessly. "I think I may have picked up a slight case of pregnancy."

"I see." The doctor frowned and ran one hand through her already tousled gray hair. "Correct me if I'm wrong, but it seems to me that you've wanted a child for a long time."

Mallory lowered her head, pressing back the tears that burned behind her eyes. "I do—very much," she said.

"But?"

"Nathan and I are separated."

The physician permitted herself a sympathetic sigh. "Serious?"

"I asked him for a divorce."

Sarah Lester went to the shiny metal sink and began washing her hands. "Perhaps you can still work things out. In any case, Mallory, women everywhere are raising children on their own."

Mallory said nothing. She submitted to the examination, knowing all the while what the diagnosis would be, mourning the fact that Nathan wasn't pacing the outer office like a standard expectant father.

"Well," Sarah said, as she scrubbed her hands again and Mallory sat up. "We'll run the usual tests, but that's a formality. You've got a passenger, all right."

Mallory couldn't help feeling joyous, even though

nothing else in her life was going right. She fairly floated back to the studio, mentally sorting through the prospective names she'd horded over the years.

The cast and crew were on a break when Mallory reached the set, but Brad was waiting at her dressing room door. The sight of him reminded her that her marriage was in ruins and sent her spirits plummeting.

"Well?" he asked gently.

"August," Mallory said in a tight voice.

Brad planted a brief kiss on her forehead. "Congratulations, love," he said.

Mallory lifted her chin, forcing herself not to cry. "Thanks," she said woodenly, turning to open the door. She was already late, and she still had makeup and a costume to deal with.

But Brad caught her arm and made her face him again. "Why don't you call Nathan?" he asked softly.

Mallory shook her head. "I can't, Brad."

"Why not? It's his kid, too—he has a right to know about this, Mallory."

"Since when are you so concerned with Nathan's rights?"

Brad laughed wryly. "I'm not. I think he's an obnoxious, arrogant bastard, but the fact remains that he fathered that child."

Mallory pressed her lips together and thought for a moment before she spoke again. "I don't suppose it's any big secret that Nathan and I are separated, Brad," she said evenly. "And it's probably equally obvious that I love him. If we can work things out, I want it to be because it's right for us to be together, not because he feels paternal responsibility."

"Responsibility?" Brad shot back. "Do you think that's all he'd feel? Listen, Mallory, I don't like the guy and he sure doesn't like me, but I do know him well enough to be sure he cares about you."

Mallory was not seeing Brad's face, or the studio

behind him. She was seeing Diane and Nathan alone, in that darkened island boathouse. "Maybe."

Brad grasped her shoulders in a sudden and rather desperate grip and shook her slightly. "Damn it, I love you too much to see you eaten up inside like this! I'm sorry—God, *so* sorry—that I let Diane talk me into that paternity suit scam. But Mallory, that's all it was—a scam!"

"That isn't the problem, Brad."

"Then what is, pray tell?"

"Diane."

Brad did not release her shoulders, and he tilted his head back, with a sigh of frustration, to study the dark, high ceiling of the warehouse-turned-studio. "I suppose you found them together somewhere," he said, his voice filled with affectionate scorn.

Surprised, Mallory nodded.

His fierce blue eyes turned to look at her face. "Mallory, what did I warn you about, that day I came to the island? Didn't I tell you that Diane might try to do something to hurt you and Nathan both?"

Again, Mallory nodded, her eyes widening.

Brad swore in irritation. "Sure as I'm standing here, she set him up."

Mallory swallowed—*talk about wishful thinking!* And yet, the fact that Brad would offer that as a possibility, feeling the way he did about Nathan, gave the idea undeniable weight. "He kissed her," she said, though she hadn't intended to reveal that humiliating tidbit of information.

Brad was clearly annoyed, clearly torn. "Somebody tell me why I'm defending Nathan McKendrick. Am I losing my mind, or what? Mallory, maybe she got to him for a second—God knows she's been working on it long enough. What is one stupid kiss against a happy life together?"

Before Mallory had to answer, the other members of

the cast were straggling back, their break over. Gratefully, she escaped Brad and hurried in to change clothes and have her makeup done.

Again, as she had the day before, Mallory turned in an excellent performance. Somehow, she was able to shift her churning, confused emotions to another level of consciousness and concentrate on Tracy Ballard's outrageous pursuits.

For the first time, as Mallory left the studio at seven that night, she thought that she might miss performing —at least in one respect. It was certainly easier, and much less painful, to be Tracy Ballard than Mallory McKendrick.

The night air was brisk, though the snow was gone. Slush, muddy and slick, filled the parking lot, and Mallory made her way carefully toward her car. She was brought up short by the fact that Nathan's silver Porsche was parked beside her own sporty Mazda.

For a moment, Mallory considered rushing back inside the studio to hide. Before she could decide, one way or the other, however, Nathan was out of his car and striding toward her.

The lights rimming the parking lot didn't illuminate his face, but she could see that he was wearing tailored slacks, an Irish cableknit sweater and his favorite brown suede jacket. Without a word, he caught her arm in a gentle grasp at the elbow, and ushered her to his car. She was too overwhelmed to react until she was already seated inside the plush leather confines of the Porsche.

"Nathan—what?—" she stammered stupidly, unable to read his expression in the shadowed profile of his face as he slipped behind the wheel and slammed his car door.

"Dinner," he said shortly, without looking at her.

"Now just a minute, you!"

Nathan shifted the Porsche into reverse with a smooth, practiced motion of his right hand, and the slush beneath the tires made a grinding sound as he backed the powerful car out of the parking space. "I've got an idea," he said, with gruff mockery grating in his voice. "Just for once, let's not argue. If that means saying nothing at all, so be it."

The spicy scent of his cologne was doing disturbing things to Mallory's carefully maintained defenses, and she could sense the hard strength of his body even though they weren't touching.

"Okay," she agreed.

They drove in silence for some minutes before Nathan slipped a cassette tape into the slot on the dashboard and Willie Nelson's voice filled the car. Mallory couldn't help smiling at the realization that Nathan never, but never, listened to his own recordings. And even though rock was his career, he enjoyed everything from Indian music and jungle drumming to the classics.

When both sides of Willie's tape had been played and they were still driving, Mallory shot an anxious glance in her husband's direction. "Where are we going?" she ventured. *Oh, and by the way, I'm pregnant.*

They'd left the heart of Seattle far behind by then, and joined the swift traffic on the freeway going south. "To dinner," Nathan answered irritably.

"Where?" Mallory snapped back. "In Wenatchee?"

Nathan tossed her a scathing look. "Peace— remember?"

Mallory sighed and bit her lower lip.

The restaurant Nathan had chosen was small and secluded and overlooked the dark waters of the Sound. Mallory could hear the unmistakable creak of a wooden wharf as they entered the tastefully rustic establishment.

Nathan spoke to the hostess who greeted them in a terse undertone.

"This way," the woman replied, proceeding across a carpeted, dimly lit and totally empty dining room.

"Where is everybody?" Mallory dared to ask as Nathan put one imperious hand on the small of her back and propelled her along.

"This is a private party," Nathan replied in a biting monotone.

"How private?" Mallory wanted to know, her eyes wide with mingled amazement and alarm.

"Very private. You and I add up to everyone."

"That's what you think," Mallory argued, only to regret her impulsive words instantly.

Nathan's gaze pierced her, impaling her for one shattering moment. "I'll thank you to explain that remark," he said in a low, even voice, standing stock-still in the middle of that elegant and deserted dining room.

Mallory felt betraying color rise in her face, and her answer came out in an unconvincing jumble. "I merely meant that—I mean—surely there will be other customers—"

A muscle in Nathan's jaw flexed, and an ominous white line edged his taut lips. "Not good enough."

Mallory closed her eyes. "Nathan—"

He took her arm again, roughly, and led her to the table selected for them. Then, impatient, he fairly thrust Mallory into her chair.

"Brad called me," he said bluntly, midway through the first course.

Mallory stared at him, a forkful of shrimp cocktail poised halfway between the glistening crystal dish and her open mouth.

Without waiting for her to speak, Nathan went on, his voice chafing Mallory's heart. "I can't tell you," he drawled in sardonic tones, "how I appreciate hearing news like that from Brad Ranner. Thank you so much."

"I'll kill him!" Mallory muttered, dazed.

There was violence in the forced stillness of Nathan's hands, in the crackling electricity of his ebony gaze.

"You weren't going to tell me," he accused with quiet fury. "My God, Mallory, did you think you could hide the baby from me forever?"

Tears of pain and outrage stung Mallory's eyes and brimmed in her lashes. "Of course not!" she cried, leaning forward and slamming down her fork.

"When?" he demanded. "When will I be a father, Mallory? That is, if you consider it any of my business."

Mallory's throat ached savagely, and for a moment, no words would pass it. When they did, they were interspersed with little soblike catches. "August—the b—baby will be born in August. The t—timing is great, isn't it?"

With a harsh motion of his arm, Nathan slid his untouched shrimp cocktail summarily aside. His dark eyes were snapping, piercing Mallory's spirit like lethal swords. "Why weren't you going to tell me?"

She uttered the first retort that came to mind. "Because I thought you'd drag me back to the island!"

"Would that be so terrible? I know you're not crazy about me, but you've always liked the island!"

"We've got so many problems, Nathan! And a baby is the world's *worst* reason for two people to stay married!"

"Not to me, it isn't!" he snapped. Suddenly, his powerful hands closed over Mallory's wrists in an inescapable grip. "Listen to me, Mallory, and listen well. That child is as much mine as yours, and I *will not* be one of those fathers who conducts tours of Disneyland every summer and visits on alternating Sundays!"

Mallory swallowed hard but said nothing. She merely stared at her husband, wide-eyed and stricken by the force of his determination.

"Finish out your contract—whatever. But then you're coming back to the island—specifically to Angel Cove."

"I am, am I? You can't force me to live with you!"

He smiled, but there was no humor in the expression. His eyes, scorching Mallory only moments before, were now chilling. "Don't make me prove that you're wrong, sweetness. You don't have to sleep with me or even pretend that you're any kind of wife—but you *will* live under my roof!"

Mallory was fairly blinded with shock and fury. "Who do you think you are?" she challenged, keeping her voice down only by monumental effort.

His eyes slid with dark contempt to her breasts and then to her stomach; it was as though he were looking right through the table, right through her clothes. "I'm that baby's father," he answered, and the conversation was clearly over.

Mallory did eat her dinner, but she tasted none of the skillfully prepared food. She could think of nothing but the bitter, ruthless stranger seated across from her. He was, she knew, completely serious; he meant to drag her to his island house, if it came to that, and he would not let her leave with his child, be it born or unborn.

It was all so high-handed! Apparently, Nathan thought he could control independent human beings as easily as he hired restaurants and chartered airplanes.

The journey back to Seattle was made in numbing silence.

But when Nathan drew the Porsche to a stop in front of the apartment building and blithely tossed his car keys to the doorman, Mallory was furious enough to fight. She stiffened in the car seat and refused to get out, even after Nathan opened the door and the cool night wind rushed in to chill her.

He smiled savagely. "Think of your dignity, Mrs. McKendrick. Your *image*, if you will. How is it going to look if I throw you over one shoulder and carry you inside?"

With a small exclamation of frustration, Mallory got out of the car. In the elevator, she fixed her husband with a look as scathing and fierce as his own. "If you think we're going to live together, to sleep together, after all that's happened—"

Nathan touched her nose lightly. "I won't attack you, love, so don't worry." He shrugged in a manner that made Mallory dizzy with anger. "But, then, I probably won't have to, will I?"

Soundly, with all the force of her fury and her pain, Mallory slapped him. "I despise you!" she hissed.

"I know," he said.

Inside the richly furnished penthouse, Nathan gravitated immediately to the bar. Ignoring him as best she could, Mallory marched into the master bedroom, carefully locked the door behind her, and began tearing off her clothes. Naked and trembling with rage, she strode into the imposing bathroom and wrenched on the shower spigots.

When she returned to the bedroom, a full half an hour later, wearing only an oversized T-shirt of Nathan's, she found him stretched languidly out on the bed, pretending to read a news magazine.

Her throat closed, and something treacherous rippled through her stomach. "How did you get in here?"

Nathan smiled winningly, as though they'd never argued, as though an impassable barrier hadn't been erected between them. "I used the key," he said.

"Now you listen to me, Nathan McKendrick—"

But Nathan wasn't listening. He rolled easily off the bed, onto his feet, and pulled the soft cableknit sweater up over his head. After tossing that aside, he began undoing his belt, then the zipper on his slacks.

Finally, stark naked, he feigned an expansive yawn.

Mallory was gaping at him, as stricken by the bronzed, sculpted perfection of his masculine form as she had been the first night they were ever together. After a few moments, however, she regained her equilibrium and fled through the open door and into the living room. From there she rushed on to the kitchen.

She was perched on the cool, glistening yellow Formica of the counter, despondently munching on a chocolate sandwich cookie, when Nathan walked into the room. He hadn't bothered with a bathrobe, and Mallory averted her eyes stubbornly as he leaned back against the opposite counter and folded his muscular arms across his chest.

That, no doubt, was why she was so unprepared for his approach.

Facing her, Nathan placed the palms of his hands on the tender flesh between her knees.

Though the motion stirred treacherous sensations in Mallory, and she knew that her face had pinkened, she lifted her chin and summarily took another bite of her cookie.

Nathan laughed and shook his head. When he pushed her knees further apart, it became much more difficult to sustain her indifference.

She groaned involuntarily as he caressed the secret of her womanhood, cried out as he went on to claim a fiery preliminary possession.

"You and I should never talk, Mallory," he said in a hoarse, hypnotic whisper. "The minute we stop making love, it's war."

Mallory was writhing slightly, hating him for what he was doing and not wanting him ever to stop. "Damn—you—"

The thrust of his marauding fingers made her gasp; she was barely conscious of being lowered onto the counter, stripped of the T-shirt. She cried out in sweet misery as he nibbled endlessly at her tightening nipple.

His voice was a ragged, strangely vulnerable rasp. "You are so—soft—so warm—so sweet—"

Mallory was grasping at his bare muscle-corded shoulders now, wanting him, needing him. "Nathan," she pleaded. "Oh, Nathan, please—"

He chuckled hoarsely. "On a kitchen counter? Woman, thy name is wanton."

Mallory trembled, frantic and furious and dazed with passion. "You didn't mind the floor," she argued in a choked whisper.

He laughed and lifted her gently into his arms, then carried her back through the penthouse to the bedroom. There, they made sweet, fierce, sensuous love.

When, at last, Nathan slept, Mallory watched him for a long time as she lay on her side in the big, tousled bed, one cheek propped in her hand. If she lived to be a thousand, she thought ruefully, she would never fully understand this man.

At the restaurant and then in the elevator, he had been hard and recalcitrant—almost cruel. And yet, as a lover, he was unfailingly gentle. Tenderness aside, Mallory knew that he would not change his mind. No matter how unpleasant their marriage might become, he would not release her from it easily.

Her feelings about this were mixed; on the one hand, she found the prospect of being near her husband, whatever his past sins, very appealing. On the other, however, she was insulted by his imperious attitude. No matter what, it was wrong for one person to control another in that way, to dictate where someone would live and with whom.

Sleep eluded Mallory, and she finally got up to read over her lines for the next day. It proved a difficult task, since her thoughts kept sneaking back to Nathan, alternately tender and furious.

Chapter 11

IN THE MORNING, NATHAN WAS UP AND DRESSED AND already charming the housekeeper when Mallory ambled sleepily into the kitchen and helped herself to a cup of coffee. Nathan immediately exchanged the mug of steaming brew for a glass of orange juice, and while the housekeeper was amused, Mallory wasn't. She glared at him in surly challenge.

Paper bags rustled crisply as the housekeeper began unpacking all the groceries she'd apparently brought to work with her, and Nathan folded his arms across the front of his green velour shirt and grinned. "From now on, you're off caffeine," he said.

Mallory scowled, but since her concern for the child growing inside her was as great as Nathan's, she cast one baleful look at the forbidden coffee and drank her orange juice without protest.

The huge and ghastly breakfast Nathan and the housekeeper eventually assembled was another matter, though—Mallory's stomach was threatening mayhem.

She managed one piece of toast, but no power on earth could have coerced her to eat more.

When Nathan sat down across from her, prepared to consume two eggs, hash brown potatoes and link sausage, she leaped to her feet and fled inelegantly to the nearest bathroom. Nathan followed, refusing to respect her privacy.

"Go away!" she gasped in wretched desperation.

But he wouldn't. He held her hair and was ready with a cool washcloth when the violent spate of sickness finally ended.

"See?" he drawled companionably. "You need me."

Mallory glared at him. "If it weren't for you, fella, I wouldn't *have* this problem!"

He laughed and then shrugged. "I am a man of many talents, pumpkin."

Mallory couldn't help grinning. His talents were undeniable. "You're not going to follow me around with a washcloth all day, are you?"

"Certainly not," he answered, his dark eyes bright with tender amusement. "But tonight is another matter. I've got rehearsals today, but I'll pick you up at the studio when you're through."

True to his word, he was there at the appointed time.

That day set the pattern for those to follow; each day, while Mallory was taping the show, Nathan went to a rented hall to rehearse with the band. They spent their evenings together in unaccustomed solitude, listening to music, watching television, making love. There was a tenuous sort of peace between them, but, in the last analysis, the only deep communications they shared were expressed by their bodies.

Mallory was reluctant to rock the proverbial boat by bringing up sensitive issues, such as Diane Vincent or Nathan's unreasonable decree that she would live with him at Angel Cove. As attractive as the idea was, it was *still* unreasonable, and she sensed that he felt the same way.

213

Mallory's commitment to the soap was completed the day before Nathan's concert, and there was a huge party that evening, given by Brad Ranner, to bid her farewell. It seemed that everyone Mallory had ever even met was invited to that party, with the notable exception of Diane Vincent. The banquet room of the posh hotel where it was held was packed to the rafters.

Secretly, Mallory dreaded the fuss of it all, but she was determined to play this final role well. She wore a simple white silk caftan, bordered with glistening silver stitching, a sumptuous blue fox jacket and a slightly shaky smile.

"Star treatment," Trish Demming whispered in awe, looking appreciatively at the great crystal chandeliers and the embossed silk on the walls, her hand linked comfortably to the crook of Alex's arm. "Wow, Mall, I'm impressed."

Kate Sheridan's assessment of the affair was typically acerbic. "Don't let her stay in this madhouse very long," she ordered Nathan in a stage whisper. "She's about to drop as it is."

"I'll hold up," Mallory said, but her tone lacked conviction.

Nathan grinned, making no comment. He was a breathtaking sight in his tailored black tuxedo, which he hated, and impeccable white silk shirt.

Trish drew Mallory aside briefly to tell her that her things had been packed and removed from the little house on the island, and that the trees along the driveway had been cut down without incident. The Johnsons would be moving in any day. Mallory felt sad and slightly bereft. Cutting herself off from that part of her past was the wise thing to do, and she knew it. But that didn't make the parting any less painful.

The rest of the evening dragged on, seeming endless to Mallory. First, a dinner worthy of a Roman banquet was served, and she couldn't choke down so much as a bite. Following that, Brad made a flowery speech that brought stains of embarrassment surging into her cheeks.

Throughout that first segment of the night, Nathan sustained Mallory with well-timed touches, comical looks of wonder when the praise grew to ridiculous proportions and an occasional wink. "Give 'em hell, McKendrick," he whispered, when it became clear that Brad expected her to join him at the podium and speak.

Embarrassed almost beyond speech (somehow, this was so different from performing in front of cameras) Mallory made her way to Brad's side, graciously accepted an engraved plaque and an innocuous kiss on the cheek, and managed a few faltering words of gratitude and farewell. Returning to her seat beside Nathan was a vast relief, and she tossed a slightly frantic look in his direction as he stood and drew out her chair for her in a quiet display of chivalry.

He bent to brush his lips provocatively against her earlobe. "Pardon me, lady," he whispered, "but you wouldn't happen to have a chocolate cookie, would you?"

Mallory laughed, glad of the fact that the lights had been lowered, thus hiding her blush.

No protest was forthcoming when Nathan insisted that they leave the party early; from the looks of things, it was going to continue until all hours. And, as the Porsche navigated the dark, rain-slickened streets, Mallory was grateful to be on her way home.

Home. A corner of Mallory's mouth lifted in a reflective smile. Home had always been the island, but now it was wherever Nathan happened to be at the moment.

"What are you smiling about?" he asked, looking away from the road for only a moment.

"Nothing," Mallory lied. "So tomorrow is the big concert. What happens after that?"

"We go into seclusion for the promised year," Nathan answered without meeting her eyes again. "Mallory—"

Their constant lovemaking had lent the relationship an intimacy it had never had before, in spite of the odd distances that often intruded, and Mallory reached out, without thinking, to lay one hand on the muscular length of his thigh. "What?"

"I'm sorry for telling you that you had to live on the island with me, whether you wanted to or not. I know that wasn't right." He paused, shifting the car into a low gear to make a stop at a traffic light, and turned to look at her. "I was desperate."

Mallory's heart climbed into her throat. "Desperate?" she whispered.

"Losing you and that baby doesn't bear considering, Mallory. I know we've got a long way to go before we get this marriage back on its feet, but please—don't leave me."

Hot tears glistened, scalding, in Mallory's eyes. Never in the six years she'd been married to Nathan had she seen him reveal so much open vulnerability. "The other night you said we should never talk, just make love. Why is it that we fight the way we do, Nathan?"

The traffic light changed to green, and the car was moving again. Nathan appeared to be concentrating on the road, but a muscle flexed and unflexed at the base of his jawline. "I don't know. Maybe we'd better start by finding that out, Mrs. McKendrick."

At the apartment complex, Nathan surrendered the silver Porsche to the night doorman and ushered Mallory quickly across the elegant lobby and into an elevator. During the swift, silent ride to the penthouse, he studied the changing numbers over the doors with solemn interest.

After their showers, taken separately for once, they made love in the bed beneath the magical, ever-changing view presented by the skylight. Both reached shattering levels of fulfillment, and yet there was a hollow quality to their joining, a sense of never really touching.

Knowing that Nathan was still awake, and brooding, Mallory laid a cautious hand on the mat of dark hair covering his hard chest. "What is it?" she asked softly.

There was a long, discomforting silence before he answered, not with a statement, but with a question. "Did you really want to quit the show, Mallory?"

She raised herself onto one elbow, her free hand still moving on Nathan's chest. "Yes," she replied in complete honesty.

Even though it was dark, she could feel his ebony gaze touching her, searching her face. "I've hated the whole thing from the first," he said in a low voice, and the words had the tone of a reluctant confession. "All the same, if I forced you to give up something you really wanted—"

Mallory had a dreadful, inexplicable feeling. It was almost as though they were survivors of some horrible shipwreck, clinging to the flimsy debris of some hopelessly mangled vessel foundering in deep and threatening waters. "You didn't," she said quickly, but she knew, even as she leaned over to kiss him, even as her lips brushed his, that he wasn't convinced.

It was a very long time before Mallory slept, and the meter of Nathan's breathing revealed that he was awake, too. Underneath all her happiness about the baby and her freedom from the grueling hours on the set and the new closeness she and Nathan seemed to be establishing, was a layer of solid pain. Nathan might really love her, as he claimed. On the other hand, he was a gifted performer and it would be easy for him to pretend such feelings.

Mallory sighed and turned away from him, afraid that he would somehow sense the tears that were gathering on her cheeks. He wanted the child growing within her, and, remembering that intimate scene she'd stumbled upon in the island boathouse, Mallory had a suspicion that he was merely accepting her as a necessary part of the bargain.

When sunlight streamed through the huge window in the roof, Mallory awakened to find herself alone in the spacious bed and numb with a cold that bore no relation at all to the temperature of the room. Thanks to a medication Dr. Lester had given her, which she swallowed before even getting out of bed, Mallory did not suffer her usual bout of violent illness. That was a mercy, she reflected, since she already felt sick on some fundamental, half-discerned level.

She was startled when Pat appeared in the bedroom doorway, a fetching blonde, her slender frame regal even in blue jeans, a T-shirt and a pink hooded running jacket. Roger's diamond engagement ring flashed, like silver fire, on her left hand.

"Hi, there, pregnant person!" she chimed in greeting.

Mallory burst into tears.

Pat approached slowly. "Wow. What did I say?"

Mallory sniffled and dashed away the evidence of her doubts and fears. "Nothing," she reassured her sister-in-law quickly. "You know how it is—my hormones are suffering from the Cement-Mixer Syndrome."

Pat laughed, looked vastly relieved and sat down on the end of the bed, her hands balled in the pockets of her jacket. "Nathan is walking the customary two feet off the ground," she commented. But then there was an almost imperceptible change in her startlingly pretty face. "So why does this place have all the ambiance of a battlefield?"

Mallory sank back on her pillows and studied the skylight. It was still beaded with dew, and tiny rainbows framed each droplet. When she said nothing, Pat continued bravely.

"Something is amiss here. You and Nathan are living

together again—you're expecting a baby—but something is definitely wrong. And don't try to throw me off the track, sister dear, because I'm wise to all your routines."

Mallory summoned all she'd learned in her year as an actress and fixed a bright smile on her face. It ached, trembling as though it might fall away to lie among the hundreds of miniature rainbows reflected from the skylight onto the white satin comforter on the bed. "Both Nathan and I are still a little raw from all the troubles we've had lately, Pat—that's all."

"Sure," Pat said with angry skepticism.

Mallory had let slip the disaster in the boathouse to Brad, but she had no intention of dropping it on Nathan's sister. The burden would be both unnecessary and unfair. "Your brother has already left for one last rehearsal, I take it?" she hedged.

"You know Nathan. If it isn't right, fight."

Mallory sighed, nodded. Nathan could probably have given a dazzling performance with no rehearsal at all. But he was, where his music was concerned, a raging perfectionist. She certainly didn't envy the band the demanding day and night ahead. "How were the ticket sales?"

Pat shrugged. "What tickets? They've been gone since Day One. Mallory, you are going, aren't you? To the concert, I mean?"

Mallory's eyes shot back to Pat's face. "Why wouldn't I?"

"Nathan said you might be—well—busy."

Busy? On the night of what could be his last concert ever? It was inconceivable, and Mallory was stung to think that he would doubt her that way. The hurt gave her words a biting edge. "Gee, it *is* my bowling night," she said sardonically. "But the league will surely forgive me if I don't show up."

"Mallory—"

But Mallory knotted her fists and pounded them down on the bedding in furious frustration. "Damn that man! What kind of wife does he think I am?"

"Oh, Mallory, shut up!" Pat snapped, neatly stemming the flow of her sister-in-law's diatribe. "It's no big deal and I'm sorry I said anything!"

Mallory flung back the covers and swung herself to a sitting position on the edge of the bed. "That *rat!*"

Pat was instantly on her feet, her face flushed with responding anger. "Mallory, it's too damned easy to make you mad, you know that? Is temperament a fringe benefit from the soap, or did you have it all along?"

Ignoring Pat, Mallory stormed into the bathroom to fill the intimidating tile bathtub that always reminded her of a small swimming pool. When she returned, a half hour later, she was chagrined to find that Pat was gone.

Now you've done it, McKendrick, she berated herself as she slathered cream cheese onto a sliced bagel with fierce, jerky motions. *Pat's always there for you, and you repay her with your best bitch act!*

After choking down most of the bagel, Mallory exchanged her flannel robe for jeans, a cotton blouse and her gray rabbit bomber jacket. She hadn't intended to intrude on the final rehearsals, but now she would have to; Pat would almost certainly be there, and Mallory wanted to extend an immediate apology.

Probably because they were Seattlites, the guards already posted at the Kingdome entrance Mallory selected recognized her and allowed her inside unchallenged. She made her way quickly into the auditorium itself and was instantly transfixed by the swelling, poetic tide of the ballad Nathan was singing. When the song was over, she walked down a wide aisle, her hands in her coat pockets, toward the small group of people sitting in the first row of seats. Nathan, busy conferring with the drummer and the lead guitar player, did not notice her approach.

Her guess had been correct—Pat was there, along with several other women, her sneakered feet propped unceremoniously on the edge of her seat. Mallory touched her shoulder tentatively. "Pat?"

Pat stood up and turned to face her brother's wife with shy eyes. "Hi, Mall."

"I'm so sorry!" Mallory blurted, tears brimming in her lower lashes, her chin trembling.

"Me, too!" Pat cried, flinging her arms around Mallory, in spite of the seat back rising between them.

"This is all very touching," Nathan drawled irritably, into his microphone, "but we're trying to work here."

Mallory grimaced, but Pat turned and put out her tongue with all the impudent aplomb reserved for a younger sister.

Some of the tension left Nathan's face, and he laughed. At his cue, the band and members of the sound crew dared to laugh, too.

"So *that's* how you handle the dreaded Nathan McKendrick!" Mallory grinned, watching her sister-in-law with bright eyes.

"An occasional kick in the shins works, too," Pat confided in a loud whisper.

Mallory chuckled and again touched Pat's shoulder. "I'm getting out of here. Kicked shins or none, he'll be a beast all day. Am I forgiven?"

Pat's eyes glistened. "If you'll forgive me, too."

"Done," Mallory said softly, and then she turned to leave.

Just as Mallory left the main part of the auditorium, Diane Vincent stepped into view, her face a study in sadness and resignation. She tossed her head toward the swinging doors, beyond which the band was already playing again.

"I hope you're happy now, Mallory," she said.

Mallory lifted her chin. "What's that supposed to mean?"

"You've clipped his wings," Diane replied with an eloquent little shrug. "He'll rot on that damned island of yours. But it all went your way, didn't it?"

Mallory started to reply, and then stopped herself. Diane might be Nathan's favorite playmate, but she, herself, owed the woman nothing—not explanations, not reassurances.

"You're ruining his life, Mallory."

Mallory moved to leave, but Diane cut her off in one agile step. Something soft and broken haunted her bewitching powder blue eyes.

"At least I loved him enough to let him be himself," she went on when Mallory didn't speak. "For God's sake, Mallory, Nathan *needs* his music!"

"You're certainly an expert on what he needs, aren't you, Diane?" Mallory retorted finally, in acid tones.

A responding smirk shimmered in Diane's eyes and danced briefly on her lips. "You really didn't think you were woman enough for a dynamic, vital man like that, did you?"

Mallory had had the same thought herself, many times, but she was damned if she would let Diane Vincent see that. Green eyes shooting fire, she leveled a savage retort at her beautiful enemy. "Ever notice that while men like Nathan fool around with your type, Diane, they marry mine?"

The shot was a direct hit: Diane wilted visibly, and a look of pain trembled briefly in her eyes. Mallory wasn't the least bit proud of herself as she walked briskly away.

She spent the next few hours browsing in the baby departments of Seattle's finest stores, but the activity lacked the quiet glow Mallory had anticipated. The encounter with Diane had cast a shadow over her day, if not ruined it entirely.

Her heart, looking forward to the peace and pine-scented sanity of the island where she and Nathan would, at last, be alone, Mallory finally hailed a cab and went back to the penthouse. There, the part-time housekeeper, Mrs. Callahan, was marauding through the spacious rooms with her vacuum cleaner, singing Nathan's latest hit in a loud, exuberant and off-key soprano.

Mallory crept past her, unseen, to the bedroom. She locked the doors and huddled on the bed for half an hour, like a hunted creature with no place to hide. She was tormented by images of Diane and Nathan making love in posh hotel rooms, on Australian beaches kissed with moonlight, in auditorium dressing rooms—images that would no doubt be deftly described, for all the world to read, in Diane's forthcoming book.

Mallory closed her eyes and rocked back and forth in helpless hatred. How would she bear seeing that book on display everywhere? How would she stand knowing that Diane lived so near the villa on Angel Cove?

When it was time to eat supper, Mallory had no appetite. Instead of consuming the meal Mrs. Callahan had left for her, she dressed for the concert, selecting jeans, a woolly gray sweater and a colorful lightweight poncho. Her mood was dark indeed by the time she met Trish and Kate and Pat at an agreed place and entered the Kingdome with them.

The crowds were so thick backstage that Mallory despaired of catching so much as a glimpse of Nathan before taking a seat in the third row with her friends. She didn't know whether to be disappointed or relieved. But, suddenly, despite the crush of people, Nathan was there, looking magnificent, as always, in his simple black tailored slacks and gleaming white silk shirt. Mallory suppressed a wifely urge to button the shirt, which was gaping provocatively to his muscled, ebony-matted midriff.

"Hi," she said shyly as Kate and Pat exchanged conspiratorial looks and slipped away to find Trish again.

Nathan laid his gifted hands on Mallory's shoulders and his smile warmed his dark eyes and softened his lips. "You came," he said in a gentle, surprised voice.

Mallory bridled a little, hurt. "Nathan, why wouldn't I?"

He shrugged slightly, but a shadow of pain moved in the depths of his eyes. "I guess I thought you would be anxious to get back to the island."

Mallory barely stopped herself from flinching, and Diane's bitter words echoed in her mind. *He'll rot on that damned island of yours—he needs his music—*

"Not so anxious that I'd miss something this important, Nathan," she said in a voice tight with doubt. She stood on tiptoe to kiss him lightly. "Break a leg, babe."

He smiled and raised both hands to the dark softness of her hair. "Everything is going to work out," he said gruffly. "I promise."

Mallory longed for that same certainty the way a drowning swimmer longs for a life preserver, but she knew better than to let wild wishes overwhelm her reason. Outside, the enthusiasm of the crowd was rising to a deafening roar. They were claiming him now, those thousands of faceless women, and Mallory felt a wrench at giving Nathan up to them, even temporarily. Silently, she touched his lips with an index finger, turned and walked away.

"The natives are getting restless," Trish observed dryly as Mallory sank into her seat on the aisle. "What's he doing back there?"

Mallory shrugged and looked around at the surrounding concert-goers with a tremor of alarm. Their mood was petulant—almost hostile—and some of them were crying.

They don't want Nathan to retire, even for a year, she thought, and, at that moment, nothing in the world could have made her admit that she was his primary reason for turning his back on them.

The stage went dark, and suddenly the auditorium was throbbing with an almost tangible expectancy. When the lights came up again, Nathan was there and the crowd seemed to call to him in one discordant voice. With lithe motions of his powerful arms, he reached out for the microphone, pretending a slight difficulty with the trailing black cord. When he held the small electronic marvel in both hands, he muttered, "Hi, group," in a rumbling, sensuous voice. "Fancy meeting you here."

The audience went wild—shouting, applauding, stomping their feet.

Nathan lowered his dark, magnificent head, and waited, the very picture of patience. When the thunderous welcome ebbed a little, a female voice from several rows behind Mallory pleaded plaintively, "Nathan, don't go!"

"I'll be back, baby," he promised, and, as another wave of screaming madness swept through the crowd, Mallory felt a small spike of jealousy puncture her heart. It was beginning then, this strange, spiritual lovemaking between Nathan and the adoring horde.

When Nathan slid into a gruff, sensual ballad, Mallory felt like flotsam adrift on a sea of communal grief. She was grateful for the darkness that lent her what would seem to be a very timely anonymity, and she wasn't surprised when Kate nudged her during a brief lull between songs, and whispered, "Maybe you should have stayed backstage, Mallory."

Mallory was glad to have someone so sensible confirm her own sense that the mood of this multitude of fans was unfavorable toward her. But she brought herself up short. In the press conferences preceding the concert, Nathan had not given any specific reason for his unexpected sabbatical. It wasn't as though someone had circulated fliers imprinted with Mallory's face and the words, GET THIS WOMAN, SHE MADE HIM QUIT!

Despite this logic, the mood of that audience was the mood of a spurned and vengeful lover. Mallory slid down in her seat, dreading the time when the concert would end and the auditorium lights would come up, revealing her in all her guilt to the furious masses.

Three songs later, Mallory's worst suspicions were confirmed when the woman in front of her whispered to her companion that Nathan's defection could be laid at the feet of his "bitchy wife." She'd read it in one of the supermarket scandal sheets and regarded it as gospel.

The atmosphere seemed to pulse more dangerously with every song after that—finally, it was so tangible, this rising fury, that Nathan raised both his arms in the air, perspiration glistening on his face, to stop the music mid-beat. To the accompaniment of a petulant rumble from the crowd, he strode to the side of the instrument-cluttered stage and spoke inaudibly to someone just out of sight. In a moment, however, he was back, speaking soothing words, moving easily into another song.

The horde was calming down a little when two security guards came and quietly collected Mallory from her seat to usher her out through the nearest exit. In the glaring light of the empty passageway, the hum of the crowd was muted, though it was still as frightening as the swarming sound of enraged bees.

Standing there, between the two middle-aged men appointed as her protectors, Mallory marveled at the change in the mob's mood. It was almost as though Nathan's fans knew that she had been removed.

One of the security guards took her arm gently. "Mrs. McKendrick, we have orders to take you home immediately. I'm sorry."

A shaft of terrible disappointment impaled Mallory. "Couldn't I just wait backstage?" she asked, stricken.

"I'm sorry," the man repeated, and he had the good

grace to sound as though he meant it. "Mr. Mc-Kendrick wants you off the premises as soon as possible, and I can't say I blame him."

Mallory stiffened for a moment, but then she knew that there was no use in arguing. Rather than defy Nathan, these men would probably remove her forcibly. As they discreetly squired her outside to a waiting limousine, she resented Nathan's fans as never before.

Back at the penthouse, Mallory took off the casual clothes she'd worn to the concert and slipped into a sleek white cashmere jumpsuit. With quick, angry motions of her hands, she brushed her hair up and pinned it into the Gibson Girl style Nathan liked. Maybe that faceless horde had won by sheer number, but that was the battle, not the war. No one would stop her from attending the party that would follow the concert, from taking her rightful place at Nathan's side—no one.

At eleven-fifteen, the concert ended; Mallory saw the headlights of thousands of cars leaving the Kingdome in splendid, jewellike tangles.

The sudden, shrill ring of the telephone made her start. But, after a moment of recovery, she pounced on it. Nathan's voice was hoarse with exhaustion and worry. "Are you all right?" he demanded without preamble.

"Yes," Mallory managed after an awkward moment. "Nathan, just tell me where to meet you, and—"

"No."

Disappointed fury jolted Mallory. "What?"

"Stay exactly where you are, Mallory," he bit out in tones that brooked no argument. "I'll be home as soon as I possibly can."

Before she could object, he summarily hung up.

Frustrated, hurt and outraged, Mallory had no choice but to obey his dictate. The party could be held in any one of a hundred places; searching would be fruitless. She paced for a time and then, in desperation, strode into the study and snapped on the seldom-used television set.

The late news was on, and the entertainment commentator couldn't say enough about the performance of Seattle's own Nathan McKendrick. Alone, Mallory sputtered out a commentary of her own, and it was not so flattering as that of the man on television.

There were a few feet of footage showing the high points of the concert itself, and then a shot of a harried, annoyed Nathan striding into the wings from the stage, his eyes flashing, his face glistening with the exertion of more than two hours on stage.

"Enough already!" Mallory shouted at the flickering screen. "Can't you talk about a war or something?"

And as if to spite her, there was Nathan on the screen again, now showered and clad in a navy blue blazer, dress shirt and slacks. At his shoulder bobbed the glistening, proud blond head of Diane Vincent. Weak with shock, Mallory reached out, snapped the set off and sank dispiritedly onto the study sofa, too stricken to cry or shout or even move.

It was three o'clock in the morning when Mallory felt the bed shift slightly under Nathan's weight. He sighed and fell into an instant, fathomless sleep.

"Not tonight, Diane," he muttered.

Nathan awakened late the next morning. Even so, he was fully conscious for several seconds before he dared to open his eyes. When he did, he was met with a fierce sea-green gaze and an intangible, bone-numbing chill. Mallory was beside him in bed, but she might as well have been ten thousand miles away. Everything about her relayed the message: Don't talk, don't touch.

She had definitely seen last night's newscast.

Nathan swore and reached out for her, intending to explain that Diane, with her usual audacity, had purposely fallen into step beside him and smiled into the camera, that he'd gotten rid of her in a hurry. But Mallory drew back ferociously, her eyes wild.

"Babe," he began awkwardly. "Listen—"

She slapped him.

The blow stung fiercely, but Nathan did not flinch, did not look away. He caught Mallory's wrists in his hands and pressed them down, over her head. "About the newscast," he said evenly. "Diane didn't go to the party with me, Mallory. She simply chose an inopportune time to walk beside me."

Mallory's splendid oval chin lifted defiantly, and she glared up at him in sheer hatred. "I realize that," she said in acid tones.

"Then why the assault and battery?" Nathan demanded, watching her closely, still holding her prisoner.

"I don't want to talk about it!"

Nathan swore in frustration and released her. *"Mallory."*

"Drop dead, you bastard!"

He reached out again, this time to grasp her upper arm, hard, although he was, as always, careful not to hurt her. Even now, the savage desire for her was stirring in his loins, but he suppressed it even as he pinned her beneath him. "Start talking, lady. Right now."

She struggled and squirmed, clearly furious, and the motion intensified the desire Nathan was trying to ignore. "Leave—me—alone!" she sputtered.

Frightened, Nathan bore down on her harder. "Mallory, for God's sake, talk to me!"

"You liar—you *cheat*—" she mourned, and tears seeped through her thick, tightly clenched eyelashes. The sight wounded Nathan, transformed the need to possess into an equal or greater need to comfort and protect.

"How did I lie?" he asked with gentle reason. "Or cheat?"

She was turning her head from side to side, and sobs escaped her throat in soft, breathless gasps. Nathan remembered the precious child within her and eased the pressure he'd been exerting with his body.

"Please, Mallory," he pleaded, in a raw voice. "Please tell me what's wrong."

She cried out like something wounded and shoved at him with her small, frantic, furious hands. But he would not be moved. Not until he knew.

"I hate you, Nathan—dear God, how I hate you—"

Nathan's raw throat constricted, and he closed his eyes momentarily against the fierce sincerity in her voice, in her face. "Please," he said again, and if that constituted begging, he didn't care.

Mallory was watching him when he opened his eyes again. "You act so innocent!" she hissed in a sharp undertone.

Defeated for the moment, Nathan released her and rolled away. "I *am* innocent," he answered dejectedly.

"Liar!" she choked. "You talk in your sleep, Nathan!"

Nathan sighed, sat up, his back to Mallory, and braced his head in his hands. "What, pray tell, did I say?"

There was a brief, awful silence. " 'Not tonight, Diane,' " she finally replied, her pain blunt and savage and hopeless in her voice.

He turned back to look at her. "You're getting pretty desperate for something to hate me for, aren't you, Mallory?"

She would not meet his eyes or answer, and, in that moment, Nathan knew that there was no hope of convincing her that the remark, made in his *sleep* for God's sake, had meant nothing. He had never slept with Diane, never actually even considered it.

Slowly, he rose to his feet and walked into the bathroom, where he wrenched on the shower spigots and stepped under the hot, piercing spray. He would lose her now, lose the baby. Bracing himself with both hands against the tiled wall of the shower stall, Nathan McKendrick lowered his head and cried.

The coming week was a wretched one for Mallory. Without her role in the soap opera, she had no reason to stay in Seattle. And yet she had no island house to flee to either, for it was the Johnsons' house now, and not her own. She could not go there to hide and cry and be close to things and memories from another, less complicated time in her life. Besides, Nathan lived on the island and she didn't think she could bear to encounter him after the way she'd made such a fool of herself and driven him away.

Day by day she fought down her senseless, fathomless love for him, and day by day it grew, like a flower forcing its way up through asphalt.

"I want to hate you," she said aloud one grim winter afternoon to the photograph taken at Pike Place Market that day, the one that portrayed Nathan as a marshal and Mallory as a dance hall girl. "Why?"

In her mind, she heard his voice. *You're getting pretty desperate for something to hate me for, aren't you, Mallory?*

"Yes," she said aloud, putting the framed photograph back onto the study's fireplace mantel and taking up another, one that showed her mother and father standing on the deck of their boat, displaying huge, freshly caught salmon and enormous grins.

She was angry with them, these cherished people in the photograph. How dare they die and leave her, when she'd loved them without reservation?

The question made Mallory draw in a sharp breath. She'd been deliberately sandbagging her own marriage, for weeks and months and years because she was afraid, afraid that if she loved Nathan completely, he would die.

In a flurry to reach him, she grabbed her purse and coat and fled the penthouse without looking back.

Chapter 12

THE VILLA OVERLOOKING ANGEL COVE WAS ALMOST AS imposing in the darkness as it was in the light of day. Mallory's heart caught in her throat at the sight of it, just as it had when she had first seen the place during childhood explorations of the island. It had been a place of wonder and mystery then, standing empty for so many years, and Trish and Mallory had worked up any number of fascinating fantasies concerning its past. Then, seeking refuge from the insane pace of his lifestyle, the famous Nathan McKendrick had bought the property and brought in an army of carpenters and decorators to refurbish it.

Mallory had met Nathan that summer at an island picnic and fallen in love with a soul-jarring thump that still vibrated within her whenever she even glanced at Nathan. Before winter, they had been married.

Now, standing forlornly on the sweeping front porch, Mallory wedged her hands into the pockets of her coat and swallowed hard, trying to work up the courage to knock. Oh, it would be so easy just to dash back to her car and drive away—

But no. She was through running.

Suddenly, one of the heavy front doors opened with a soft creak, and Mallory could feel Nathan's dark gaze upon her, even though her own eyes were clenched tightly shut in preparation for harsh rejection.

But the rejection didn't come. "Open your eyes, Mallory," Nathan ordered, not unkindly, but not warmly either.

She obeyed but could only stare at him.

"It always helps if you knock," Nathan commented, taking her arm in a gentle grip and drawing her into the dimly lit entry hall with its black and white marble floor and tastefully papered walls.

She looked up at him and her throat constricted painfully, but she still could not manage so much as an offhand "hello."

Nathan clearly suffered from no such problem, but he wasn't inclined to make things easier for her, it seemed. He simply watched Mallory, his arms folded across his chest.

Mallory bit her lip. *Get on with it, say something!* she told herself.

"Is my dog here?" she choked out after several torturous seconds.

A tender smirk curved one side of Nathan's mouth upward. "Is that why you're here, Mrs. McKendrick? You're looking for your dog?"

Mallory squeezed her eyes shut for a second, and then opened them again. "If you're trying to make this difficult, it's certainly working."

He laughed and took her hand in a warm grasp. "I'm sorry," he said, leading her along the darkened hallway and into the brightly lit kitchen at the back of the house. There the fickle Cinnamon was gnawing at an enormous soupbone.

Nathan gestured grandly toward the beast. "Your dog, madame."

"That animal has no scruples!" Mallory complained, only half in jest.

"None," Nathan agreed in a low tone that seemed to reach inside Mallory and caress her weary heart.

Mallory turned to face her husband squarely and lifted her chin. "I love you very much, Nathan McKendrick," she announced in an unsteady voice.

Deftly, Nathan reached out and drew her close. The pale blue cashmere of his sweater made her nose itch.

With one finger, he caught the underside of her chin and lifted it so that she was looking at him again. She saw the words in his dark eyes even before he voiced them. "And I love you."

Compelled by forces older than creation, Mallory pressed close to him, comforted by the hard strength of his body, but disturbed by it, too.

Nathan moaned low in his throat. "Talk about no scruples. Lady, do you know what it does to me when you hold me like this?"

Mallory knew that her eyes were bright with mischief. "I have an idea," she confessed.

He tilted his head to one side and studied her with cautious, weary eyes. "Far be it from me to rock a very promising boat, sweet thing, but if you came over here to do me some kind of retaliatory number, I'll tell you right now that I can't handle it."

Mallory frowned. "Number? Nathan, what are you talking about?"

"This. It's going to wipe me out if we spend the night loving and then you leave again."

She lifted a gentle finger to softly trace the outline of his lips. "You really think I like to hurt you!" she accused.

Nathan shrugged, an action that belied the fierce and sudden pain darkening his eyes. "Nobody does it quite

235

like you, lover. If revenge is what you want, kindly get it through your lawyers."

Mallory drew back at the sharp impact of his words; if he'd slapped her, he couldn't have caused her more anguish. "My lawyers?" she echoed. "Nathan, what—"

His embrace tightened, and it was no longer tender. "Listen to me," he said in harsh, measured tones. "I love you. I need you. But I'm through playing stupid games, Mallory—either you're my wife and you live with me and share my bed, or you're just somebody I used to know. The choice is yours. If you decide to stay, remember this—I've never made love to Diane— I've never been unfaithful to you at all—and I don't intend to be tortured for some imagined transgression from now till the crack of doom. Do we understand each other?"

Mallory's lips moved, but not a sound came out of her mouth.

Nathan's hands were moving in sensuous, compelling circles on the small of her back. "Go or stay, babe," he went on, "but if you walk out of here tonight, don't ever come back."

The hardness of his words chafed Mallory's proud spirit, but she knew he was right. A final decision had to be made and then abided by. Her voice trembled when she spoke.

"Aren't you being just a bit arbitrary, Mr. McKendrick?"

Nathan sighed, and his hands moved down to cup her firm, rounded bottom and draw her closer still. "Ummm," he said, closing his eyes for a moment. "Stop stalling, woman. Do I take you back to Seattle, or do I just take you?"

Mallory's cheeks brightened to a deep pink. The hard evidence of his desire for her was pressed against her abdomen, making it difficult indeed to think clearly. "This is coercion," she accused in a whisper.

Nathan's lips coursed warmly over her temple to nuzzle the soft, vulnerable place beneath her ear. "I didn't say I was going to fight fair," he reminded her, his voice gruff with need.

Mallory trembled; in truth, her decision had been made before he had opened the front door, before she'd left Seattle. What was the use in pretending, playing childish games? She swallowed hard.

"If you don't mind," she said softly, "I'll stay."

Trish and Mallory watched with comically serious faces as Pat modeled one of several wedding gowns she was considering.

"Too many ruffles," Mallory commented.

"Too few," Trish countered.

Pat paused, a vision bathed in spring sunlight, to glare at the spectators lounging on the living room sofa. "You two are no help at all!"

Mallory and Trish exchanged a look and then burst into a simultaneous fit of giggles.

Mallory, her stomach well rounded with the cherished weight of her child, Nathan's child, sat cross-legged, like a small, plump Indian. Beaming, she reinspected Pat's beautiful gown. "You look lovely. Yes, indeed, I think that is *definitely* The Dress."

"Me, too," Trish admitted. "Of course, I looked much better in mine, you know. Some of us just have better bodies than others."

Mallory and Pat both laughed, and Mallory glanced eloquently down at the dome of her stomach. Though it was only April, she was big enough that she couldn't join in the good-natured teasing by claiming any superiority for her own figure. "No comment from this quarter!"

"I should say not, fatso," Pat answered.

Trish rolled her eyes and sighed theatrically. "And it's April, for heaven's sake. By August, they're going to be transporting El Tubbo here with a block and tackle!"

Mallory gave her friend a good-natured shove and pretended to pout. "Nathan thinks I'm beautiful!"

"What does he know?" Trish countered.

Pat laughed. "Maybe we should ask Weight Watchers to send over their emergency squad."

Eyes twinkling, Mallory shot to her feet in dramatic indignation and summoned up her most imperious glare. "When are you two going to let up on the fat jokes?" she cried. "You'll destroy my ego!"

Pat lifted her chin and grinned. "If you run out of ego, sis, just borrow some from Nathan—he has plenty. As for the fat jokes, we'll let up when you can see your feet again, McKendrick. You remember—those things south of your knees?"

Mallory laughed and the child moved within her and she thought, in that moment, that she had never been happier in all her life.

Pat and Trish exchanged a look and giggled. A moment later, Pat was off to an upstairs bedroom to change out of the wedding gown and back into jeans.

Trish patted Mallory's hand with affection. "All jokes aside, old friend, you look wonderful. I know it's corny, but you actually *glow.*"

"Thanks," Mallory replied, sitting down on the sofa again and resting her hands lightly on the protrusion beneath her blouse.

Trish frowned, looking briefly in the direction of the distant room where Nathan was locked away. "What's that man of yours up to these days? Rumor has it that you clubbed him over the head with a package of frozen shrimp and stuffed the body under the cellar stairs."

Mallory smiled at Trish's remark and turned the simple wedding band on her finger, so that it caught the invading spring sunshine and transformed it to golden fire. "He has been something of a hermit lately, hasn't he?" She lowered her voice to a whisper, unable, in her pride, to keep the secret to herself. "Trish, he's writing a soundtrack for a movie, and it's wonderful."

Trish made a funny face. "What else would it dare be but wonderful? But what about you, Mall? Do you miss all that glamor?"

Decisively Mallory shook her head. "I taught the fourth grade yesterday," she confided, beaming at the memory. "The regular teacher was sick and they called me. It was so much fun, Trish!"

Trish grinned. "You are easily entertained, my friend. Since when is a raging horde of preadolescents considered *fun?*"

"Trish, they're darling," Mallory protested as the residual joy of the experience came back to her, full force. "It was show-and-tell day, and this one little boy brought a sandwich bag full of hermit crabs—"

Trish was shaking her head slowly in amused, affectionate wonder. "You are something else, McKendrick," she broke in. "My God, you don't even miss the soap one little bit, do you?"

"It wasn't the way selling real estate is for you, Trish—I never enjoyed it. I never got excited about it, like I do about teaching."

Just then Pat returned, clad in battered blue jeans and an old sweatshirt, her potential wedding dress in a box under her arm. "Could I catch that ride back to the ferry terminal now, Mall?"

Trish rose quickly from her seat on the sofa. "I'll take you over. I'm late for the office, anyway."

"Great," Pat answered, the prospect of another evening with Roger shining clear in her eyes. Quickly, she bent and planted a kiss on Mallory's forehead. "See you around, sis. And don't let that brother of mine write himself into collapse, okay?"

It was May, and the weather was glorious. Sitting at the very end of the boat dock in front of the villa, her feet dangling between water and wharf, Mallory reveled in the singular splendor of Puget Sound. The clear sky cast its cobalt blue reflection onto the receiving waters, and the Olympic Mountains were like snow-clad giants in the tree-lined distance, their peaks craggy and traced with jagged purple streaks. And everywhere, gulls sang their contentious songs, swooping and circling against the pearlescent sky.

Mallory laid gentle hands on the folds of her well-filled madras maternity blouse and smiled to know that her baby would grow up in this marvelous place. She glanced toward the duplex where Diane had lived until a month or so before, when she'd suddenly given up her writing aspirations and gone off to do press work for a punk rock group.

"Is this a private daydream, or can anybody join in?" Nathan asked softly from just behind her.

Mallory hadn't heard his approach. She turned to look up at him; he was framed in a dazzling, silver aura of sunlight.

When she said nothing, Nathan sat down beside her, Indian-style, on the creaking, spray-dampened wooden wharf. He sighed, shoved his hands into the pockets of his worn blue running jacket and turned his dark eyes to the panorama of trees, sky, sea and mountains.

"If you could paint a picture of God's soul," he said quietly, "it would probably look just like this."

Mallory nodded, loving the man beside her even more than she had before he spoke. "How's the movie score going?" she asked, sliding her arm through the crook of his and resting her cheek against the warm rounding of his strong shoulder.

Nathan laughed wearily. "Who can work in that place? Every time I try to set a note to paper, some caterer shows up, flanked by two legions of florists."

Mallory smiled and kissed his rough, fragrant cheek warmly. "I'm glad the wedding is tomorrow," she confided. "Pat is hysterical."

Nathan grinned and draped an arm around Mallory's

ample waist, drawing her close. *"Pat* is hysterical?" he teased. *"I'm* hysterical. What if I blow my lines?"

Mallory laughed. "All you have to do is walk your sister to the front of the church and say 'I do' when the minister asks—"

"Who giveth this woman in marriage?" Nathan boomed, in a comically ponderous, clerical voice.

"Right. Considering that you've dazzled the crowned heads of Europe with command performances, you shouldn't have all that much trouble with two words."

Nathan's eyes were suddenly serious, almost brooding. They rose to a distance well beyond Mallory's reach. "Do you think Pat will be happy?" he asked.

Mallory gave him an affectionate shove. "Stop worrying. Pat isn't some besotted teenager, you know—she's a grown woman, perfectly capable of recognizing the right man for her."

He brought his gaze back from the unreachable hinterlands to sweep Mallory's face with tenderness and hope. "How about you, Mrs. McKendrick? Are you happy? Did you choose the right man?"

Mallory pretended to search the shoreline behind them. "Sure did. He's around here somewhere—"

Nathan caught her chin in his hand. "Mallory, I'm serious," he said, and the anxiety in his features bore witness to his words.

Something ached in Mallory's throat. "I've never been happier," she vowed. And it was true—she hadn't thought it possible to feel the wondrous things she felt, not only during their now-cautious lovemaking, but at mundane times, too, like when they walked the island's beaches or ate breakfast on the sun porch or watched the old movies they both loved.

He bent his head to brush her lips tenderly with his own. "You weren't always happy, were you?" he asked.

Mallory sighed and searched the sun-dappled waters dancing before them. "No. I remember thinking, one winter day, that we were like snowflakes on the sea, you and I. Our love was so beautiful, so special, but, like the snowflakes, when it touched something bigger, it dissolved."

Poetry was an integral part of Nathan's nature, and he smiled, somewhat sadly, at the imagery in her statement. "Snowflakes on the sea," he repeated thoughtfully, his eyes locked now with hers. "Did it ever occur to you that that snow didn't really cease to exist at all? Mallory, it became a permanent part of that 'something bigger'—a part of something eternal and elemental and very, very beautiful."

A smile trembled on Mallory's lips, and sudden tears made the whole world sparkle before her like a moving gem. "I love you," she said.

Nathan bounded to his feet and drew his wife with him, pretending that the task was monumental. And Mallory's laughter rang out over the whispering salt waters like the toll of a crystal bell.

Mallory stood on tiptoe in the pastor's study, trying to straighten Nathan's tie. Beyond, in the main part of the small, historical building, the voices of guests and a few intrepid reporters hummed in expectation.

"Stop wiggling!" Mallory scolded, as Nathan fidgeted before her, impatient with the doing and redoing of his tie. "It's Roger's job to be nervous, not yours."

He glared at her enormous flower-bedecked picture hat. "Does that thing have a sprinkler system?" he scowled.

Mallory laughed and then pirouetted to show off the rest of the outfit—a flowing pink organdy dress, strappy shoes and a bouquet of mountain violets.

Nathan was still uncomfortable. "Everything has to be right," he grumbled. "What if—"

Mallory caught his face in both hands. "Nathan, relax. Just *relax!*"

He laughed suddenly and shook his head. "I can't."

With a sigh, Mallory gave his tie one final rearrangement. "Think of it as a performance," she suggested.

Just then the door leading into the main sanctuary opened with a creak, and Roger came in, flanked by the pastor. The groom shot a terrified look in Nathan's direction and swallowed hard.

Seeing his own discomfort mirrored in Roger's face seemed to ease Nathan. Mallory felt his broad shoulders relax under her hands, and saw a sudden mischief dance in his eyes.

"Don't you dare tease that poor man!" she whispered tersely, giving her husband a slight shake.

Nathan smiled down at her wickedly. "Would I do a thing like that?"

"Absolutely," Mallory replied.

The pastor, himself an aged and revered institution on the island (he'd married Mallory and Nathan, too, in that same small church) cleared his throat in an eloquent signal that the time was nigh.

"Be nice!" Mallory admonished her husband in a fierce whisper before leaving the room to join Pat in the tiny adjoining social hall.

At the sight of her sister-in-law, Mallory drew in a sharp breath and fought back tears of admiration and love. The other bridesmaids quietly slipped out, to wait in the sunny churchyard.

"Oh, Pat, you look wonderful!"

The tiny pearls stitched to Pat's gown and veil caught rays of stray sunshine from the fanlight window high on the wall behind her and transformed them to tiny rainbows. Even their splendor could not compete with the happy glow of the bride's face or the shine in her eyes. "Mall," she choked softly, "oh, Mallory, I'm scared!"

Mallory embraced this woman who seemed as much her own sister as Nathan's. "Take a deep breath," she ordered with mock sternness.

Pat complied, but her blue eyes looked enormous

243

and a visible shudder ran through her slender lace-and-tulle clad figure. "What if I faint? Mallory, what if I can't remember what to say?"

Mallory chuckled. "You're as bad as Nathan. You're not going to faint, Pat, and you know your vows inside and out."

Pat shivered. "We shouldn't have written them ourselves!" she cried in a small rush of last-minute panic. "We should have let Pastor Holloway read from his book! Then it would only have been a matter of repeating what he said—"

"Patricia!"

Pat closed her eyes tight and swayed a little inside Mallory's hug, but then she opened them again and smiled. The first strains of the elderly church organ wafted into the little, sunlit room.

"Mall—we're on!"

Mallory laughed. "Knock 'em dead, McKendrick," she said softly, and then she led her trembling sister-in-law outside into the fragrant spring day and around to the front doors of the church. There, she surrendered Pat to Nathan.

Being the matron of honor, Mallory walked proudly down the sun-and-stained-glass patterned aisle, on the arm of Roger's best man. She thought what a picture she must present, with her flowered hat, flowing dress and bulging stomach, and bit her lip to keep from giggling. Out of the corner of her eye, she could see the occasional reporter scribbling on a notepad, but there were no bursts of blinding light from flash cameras—Nathan and Pastor Holloway had seen to that personally.

At the orchid-strewn altar, Mallory and the best man parted ways, both turning, as Roger did, to watch Pat's magnificent entrance.

Mallory's heart ached in her throat as Pat and Nathan proceeded slowly toward the front of the church—his face with a touching, concentrating grimace, hers hidden beneath the glistening white net of her flowing veil. When Nathan's sleeve brushed Mallory's, she looked up at him and winked discreetly, in silent reassurance. He grinned in response.

"Who giveth this woman in marriage?" Pastor Holloway demanded, raising his bushy white eyebrows and bending forward slightly to stare at Nathan expectantly.

Nathan drew a deep breath, and his arm slipped casually around Mallory's waist. "We do," he said in a clear voice, and, at the pastor's crisp nod, he withdrew to take his place in a front pew.

Mallory was still grinning at the way Nathan had included her in that important moment when the minister began to speak. "Dearly beloved, we are gathered here—"

The house and garden at Angel Cove were positively overflowing with wedding guests and those who had been invited to the reception. Mallory's feet were throbbing, and she was beginning to feel cornered and slightly frantic when Nathan suddenly appeared beside her and took her arm. He ushered her into the outer hallway with dignity, but, there, he swept her suddenly up into his arms. "I think you've had all the celebration you can take in one day," he announced in a gruff yet tender voice.

Mallory started to protest that Pat would expect her to stay, but her husband's determined look silenced her. She was very tired, and she longed for a little quiet solitude, so she didn't challenge him.

Without drawing any apparent notice from the crowds gathered to wish Pat and Roger well, Nathan carried Mallory out the front door, down over the lawn and onto the wharf. When he finally set her down, it was on the deck of his impressive cabin cruiser, the *Sky Dancer*.

"What—" she muttered, looking around in amazement.

Nathan grinned and deftly freed the cruiser from its mooring. "We're escaping," he said.

And only minutes later the boat was cutting majestically through the Sound, casting wakes of diamond and sapphire behind her. Mallory sat patiently in the seat beside Nathan's, filled with a sort of amused wonder.

At last, the *Sky Dancer*'s powerful engine died, and they dropped anchor in a secluded cove they had visited many times before. Gently, Nathan gripped Mallory's arm and led her below into the vessel's well-appointed cabin.

It was even more well-appointed than usual, that day—the covers on the wide berthlike bed were turned back to reveal inviting pink satin sheets, and a pine-and-sea scented breeze billowed the new white eyelet curtains covering the portholes.

Nathan gestured grandly toward the bed. "Much as I'd like to undress you," he said with a speculative lift of one eyebrow, "I don't dare. I'll be back in five minutes, Mrs. McKendrick, and when I return, I expect to find you sleeping." With that, he turned and left the cabin.

Feeling lushly loved and shamefully pampered, Mallory removed the dress she'd worn in the wedding, along with her fussy picture hat and the dainty shoes that had been cutting into her swollen feet without mercy. Her tired flesh hungering for the restful, cool smoothness of those satin sheets, she took off her underthings, too, and crawled into bed with a sigh of fathomless contentment.

Nathan returned, as promised, in five minutes, and he frowned sternly when he saw that Mallory wasn't sleeping.

"My feet hurt," she complained.

He sat down on the end of the bed, still clad in the

elegant shirt and trousers he'd worn in Pat's wedding ceremony, and deftly brought both Mallory's feet onto his lap. When he began to massage them with strong, gentle hands, she sighed with sheer pleasure.

In spite of the cool breeze of the day, a powerful heat surged through Mallory's body as he caressed her toes, her heels, her aching arches.

"Make love to me, Nathan," she said in a sleepy, languid whisper.

"Wanton," he teased. "You're too tired and too pregnant."

"Too *fat,* you mean," she pouted.

With a sudden motion and a comically evil laugh, Nathan was standing beside the bed, leering. "Too fat, is it?" he boomed, and then he flung back the covers, baring her pear-shaped form, and knelt to kiss her satiny knees tantalizingly, first one, and then the other.

Mallory moaned, lulled by soft, insistent passion, by the delicate scent of the summery breeze from outside, by the caress of the smooth sheets and the gentle rocking of the boat itself.

Nathan's lips travelled up one thigh to the small mountain that was her stomach, scaling it with a series of soul-jarring, butterfly kisses.

"Nathan—"

His hands stroked her stomach gently, possessively. "No," he said.

"You made me want you," Mallory argued. "How do you expect me to sleep now, you brute?"

Nathan laughed gruffly, but one of his hands was already caressing the silken vee between her thighs. "Too much lovemaking is bad when you're so tired."

Mallory tilted her head back, wordless with weary need, and, of their own accord, her hips rose and fell in rhythm with the motion of his hand.

Nathan swore hoarsely and, with gentle fingers, bared the pulsing bud hidden from all eyes but his.

247

Mallory cried out and entwined her fingers in the richness of his hair as he pleasured her.

August. Nathan could hardly believe that so much time had passed so quickly.

He stared at the squalling infant beyond the thick glass barrier, searching the tiny, crumpled face for some subtle resemblance to himself or Mallory. As far as he could tell, the kid looked like Don Rickles.

"Well?" Mallory prodded from her wheelchair beside him. "What's the verdict?"

Nathan smiled at his wife, at the returning light in her fatigue-smudged eyes. Delivering their baby had been difficult for her, and Dr. Lester had recommended rather forcefully that they forget having more.

Mallory had taken that decision hard, though with typical courage, and there were now faint traces of color in her pallid cheeks and a quickening flickered within her spirit that Nathan could feel in his own.

"Who does Baby McKendrick look like?" Mallory pressed, looking up at him, a mischievous twitch pulling at the corner of her mouth.

"What kind of name is 'Baby McKendrick'?" he stalled.

"Nathan."

He turned to study the child again, ponderously and at great length.

Persistent to the end, Mallory tugged at the sleeve of his corduroy suit jacket. "Say it. Your daughter is a dead ringer for Ike Eisenhower."

Nathan laughed uproariously, but when he looked at Mallory's face, her eyes were serious again, and wretched. He ached inside, all his amusement vanishing like vapor. He squatted beside the wheelchair to cup her trembling chin in one hand. "Come on," he teased hoarsely. "She'll grow out of it."

Mallory sniffled miserably. "There won't be any more babies," she reminded him in broken tones.

Nathan released her chin to smooth back a tendril of her taffy-colored hair. "What are you, woman—greedy? We've got Ike!"

Mallory's smile was like the first glimmer of light in a dark sky, shimmering and brave and full of hope. "And each other."

He kissed her briefly, tenderly. "And each other," he confirmed.

Mallory stood in the sound booth, Brittany perched on her hip, and watched the darkened stage below with as much anticipation as any of the other thousands of fans packing the Kingdome that rainy February night. When the stagelights were turned up to reveal Nathan, the auditorium rocked with a roaring, pounding welcome.

Looking splendid in his flashy red shirt and tailored black slacks, he raised both his arms in response to their greeting and lowered his head slightly. The gesture was both triumphant and humble, and Mallory felt tears of pride and wonder burn in her eyes. Their carefully considered decision had been the right one; she knew it in that moment as never before. Nathan McKendrick was back where he belonged.

At his almost imperceptible signal, the regathered band, which had been rehearsing at Angel Cove for a full month, began a skillful introduction to Nathan's greatest hit of all time, a throaty, sensuous love song. He sat down casually, on a high stool, and reached for his guitar. When he began to sing, the crowd was finally silent.

Mallory swallowed hard. *He's mine,* she exalted silently. *He's mine.*

Brittany babbled happily and pointed toward the distant stage.

Mallory chuckled and then whispered, in order to avoid bothering the technicians working in the booth. "Yes, that's Daddy."

One of the sound men looked up at Mallory and grinned, shaking his head. "One song and he's got them on their knees," he marveled.

Mallory only nodded, since the man was wearing earphones and probably wouldn't hear anything she said anyway.

Nathan was clearly in command, clearly glad to be performing again. Throughout the long concert, he wove his singular spell. During the livelier numbers, the audience clapped and stomped and sang along, while the ballads stilled them to a silence Mallory wouldn't have believed possible.

By the end of the performance, Nathan's face shone with sweat, as did the ample, darkly matted portion of chest revealed by his half-open shirt. Once again, he had given everything, and the massive audience roared its appreciation.

When he sprinted offstage, they summoned him back. The adoring mob clapped and shouted and stomped their feet. As was his custom, Nathan did not reappear.

Mallory could envision him backstage, toweling his face, his neck, his chest, congratulating the band. She felt the distance between them keenly, but did not leave the sound booth. She had promised Nathan that she and Brittany would remain in that remote bastion until the crowds had dispersed and someone came for them. He had not forgotten the mood of the audience at the last concert, and he was taking no chances.

The friendly sound man removed his earphones and stood up. "Hi," he said, chucking Brittany's plump little chin. "That daddy of yours really brought down the house, didn't he?"

Brittany's Nathan-brown eyes widened, and her soft, dark hair tickled, fragrant, against Mallory's cheek. A moment later, she tossed back her head and began to scream.

"What did I say?" The sound man grinned, looking a bit abashed.

Mallory shook her head in reassurance and went to the back of the booth, where there was a narrow bench. From the looks of things, there were still a lot of people milling in the aisles below. It might be a while before they could leave.

Brittany was sound asleep when Pat and Roger and two security men came to claim them. They rode to the penthouse in a limousine, Pat protectively holding the sleeping baby, Mallory anxious to change clothes and rejoin Nathan.

The two security guards were waiting discreetly in the lobby when Mallory hurried out of the elevator again, feeling beautiful in her slinky powder-blue dress, strappy shoes and silver fox jacket. By their own choice, Pat and Roger had stayed behind in the penthouse to look after Brittany.

Her escorts delivered her to the door of the private hotel suite where the party was to be held and left her only when Nathan pushed his way through the crowd of promoters, musicians and press people, grinned, and held out his hand.

Mallory McKendrick's heart sang a sweet song of its own as she hurried toward him.

If you enjoyed this book…

Thrill to 4 more
Silhouette Intimate Moments
novels (a $9.00 value)—
ABSOLUTELY FREE!

If you want more passionate sensual romance, then Silhouette Intimate Moments novels are for you!

In every 256-page book, you'll find romance that's electrifying…involving…and intense. And now, these larger-than-life romances can come into your home every month!

4 FREE books as your introduction.

Act now and we'll send you four thrilling Silhouette Intimate Moments novels. They're our gift to introduce you to our convenient home subscription service. Every month, we'll send you four new Silhouette Intimate Moments books. Look them over for 15 days. If you keep them, pay just $9.00 for all four. Or return them at no charge.

We'll mail your books to you *as soon as they are published.* Plus, with every shipment, you'll receive the Silhouette Books Newsletter absolutely free. *And Silhouette Intimate Moments is delivered free.*

Mail the coupon today and start receiving Silhouette Intimate Moments. Romance novels for women…not girls.

Silhouette Intimate Moments

Silhouette
Intimate Moments

more romance, more excitement

--- **$2.25 each** ---

Silhouette
Intimate 💑 Moments

more romance, more excitement

Silhouette Intimate Moments

Coming Next Month

Silver Zephyr by Maura Seger

Allegra's life was all business but in her heart she dreamed of one special man. Simon York was a man committed to a secret mission, but when they met aboard the great zeppelin Silver Zephyr, together they discovered a magical world where all their dreams would come true.

A Breed Apart by Monica Barrie

To fulfill a dream Deena would risk all to buy Vindicator—but she didn't count on Trent Chandlor's desire to own the champion colt himself. Trent wanted to be Deena's partner on the racetrack *and* in love, but was it for money or for their hearts that they'd be gambling?

Bedouin Bride by Barbara Faith

Katherine Bishop felt as if she were living a novel when Rashid Ben Hasir kidnapped her and carried her off into the desert. They were two worlds on a collision course, yet their hearts beat as one when they clashed on the shifting sands beneath the star-filled sky.

Reasonable Doubts by Brooke Hastings

Laura Silver was determined to best Gregory Steiger—the son of the man who had destroyed her happiness—and finally lay the ghosts of her past to rest. But Gregory swore to show Laura the truth about herself, and in his arms she found a heaven that she'd ceased to dream of.